THE
TROUBLE
WITH
LAZY
ETHEL

The Trouble With

LAZY ETHEL

Ernest K. Gann

WILLIAM SLOANE ASSOCIATES, NEW YORK, 1958

c. 2

HR

THE
TROUBLE
WITH
LAZY
ETHEL

1

On the first day the freighter anchored just outside the narrow channel which led into the lagoon. In the morning the people of the construction company unloaded enough amphibious equipment so that the dynamiting and pile-driving could proceed. A new wharf was completed before darkness, and moving in cautiously, the freighter became a temporary part of Nikki atoll. Then there was night.

On the second day the cargo booms worked with monotonous regularity depositing all manner of equipment upon the new wharf. There were set down tractors, earth-moving machines, diesel generators, pumps, fuel tanks, pipes of many sizes, and great clanging squares of corrugated steel. There were sacks of cement, racks of lumber, stacks of wallboard, toilets and stoves, huge spools of wire, boxes of nuts, bolts, screws, tools, barrels of tar and nails, steel girders with numbers painted on each end, cases of crockery, valves, medicines, candy bars, mattresses, and bedsprings.

Upon all this the natives of Nikki gazed in awe. They stood patiently in the blinding sun on the opposite side of the channel. They kept their backs to their own village and were silent. They stood so until it was night again.

On the third day one hundred and thirty-seven skilled men, most of them stripped to the waist, dispersed among the coconut palms which from the opposite side of the channel seemed to grow out of the freighter. And all of this third day the equipment roared and snorted and screeched at the bidding of these men. By nightfall a principal street had been crushed into the coral, four auxiliary streets traversed it at right angles, three miles of drainage ditches had been dug, stakes covered with hieroglyphics had been methodically set out along the streets, and one mile of heavy pipe had been laid.

On the fourth day, while the grunting earth-movers leveled an airstrip and transported the fill to obliterate a swamp, the carpenters, fitters, joiners, plumbers, sheet-metal men, masons, roofers, electricians, and crane operators moved across the staked area beyond the freighter. Before the trade wind subsided in the late afternoon they had erected thirteen structures of wood, steel, and wire screen. Each was almost exactly like the other.

Upon all this the natives gazed in amazement, for they had barely time to split the husk of a coconut and drink of its milk before another building met their eyes.

On the fifth day eleven additional buildings were completed, as was the airstrip. A seventy-foot control tower was bolted together and the radio equipment installed.

The pumping station was set in operation and seventy-six toilet bowls flushed at the press of a handle. The diesel stove was installed in the mess hall. Four radioteletype machines were placed in the small prefabricated building which would serve as the communications center, but there was as yet no electricity to operate them. The foundation boss said he wanted to let the cement set another day before he subjected it to the vibrations of the main generator.

The natives on the opposite side of the channel were unaware of this minor delay. Now surfeited with miracles, they found it a relief to study the swift six-knot current as the ocean spewed through the channel toward the vast lagoon.

On the sixth day there was less noise from the settlement area as most of the workmen were engaged within the buildings. Minor frustrations caused a certain amount of cursing and some laughter, which echoed clearly between the empty buildings and could sometimes even be heard by the natives on the opposite side of the channel. Yet by noon the main generator was started and there were lights in the buildings and on the airstrip and on the new wharf—a development which left the natives aghast, since the sun was bright. The refrigerators which were just behind the mess hall were started, and so was the water evaporation plant. The X-ray equipment in the hospital was tested and approved. Radioteletype communication was established with the control island of Tuamani, which was three hundred miles to the northeast. The lathes in the machine shop and the power saws in the carpenter shop were pronounced ready for such efforts as the future might require. Thirty-eight small iceboxes scattered throughout the settlement began making ice cubes. Eight Coca-Cola vending machines were filled and began to vibrate slightly with the life of their compressors. The line of six automatic washing machines in the laundry churned their water with busy efficiency, although they were empty of apparel.

A crew of three men passed from building to building in a jeep. They nailed stenciled signs over the doors of certain buildings—PHOTO LAB—WEATHER—SERVICE PERSONNEL—HOSPITAL—COMMUNICATIONS—SCHOOL. In time they paused before a building set apart from the rest. They took a moment to admire its favored location, which was between the sea and a row of coconut palms; then they nailed a more carefully lettered sign over the door—HERBERT ZEBULON PIKE. Along the bottom of the sign in much smaller letters were these symbols: Brig. Gen. U.S.A. Ret.

And again there was night. One of the last men to leave the settlement tested the electric barber-shop clippers on his sideburns.

At the end of the sixth day the ship employed the swift current in the channel to swing out from the wharf and at once proceeded to sea. She did not bother to blow her whistle.

The natives watched her mast lights mingle with the stars and were lost in wonder. This night in their two churches they sang the familiar hymns without enthusiasm. Both the Mormon elders in their church and the Catholic priest in his church had difficulty in capturing their attention. There was so much else to think about—on the other side of the channel.

On the seventh day, just as the bells of both churches proclaimed the Sabbath, a second vessel crept slowly toward the newly created wharf. It was smaller than the first and her decks were lined with passengers.

Herbert Zebulon Pike stood on the bridge wing behind the Captain and watched the approach to Nikki through a pair of massive binoculars. And he said to himself, It is good. He breathed deeply of the fresh morning air, and he thought that he would feel even better if there had been time to take his morning calisthenics. But there wasn't time, dammit! Innumerable problems had assailed him since before dawn. He had twice cut himself during the process of shaving in his cabin. Five teeth were missing from his comb, and for a man of sixty who still had use for a comb and liked to see each hair aligned with mathematical precision, this was enough to merit some comment upon the dubious qualities of plastic and why the hell didn't they still make steel combs like they did during World War One?

It was just then that his wife, Sue-Anne, rose up in her bunk and threw a slipper at him. The slipper had a heel and the hit was direct and the back of his neck was still sore from the impact.

She said in a voice that must have been heard all over the ship or at least in the adjacent cabins, "For criminy sakes, Zebulon! Will you stop splashin' around like a water buffalo and yellin' like you been wounded? You goin' to make every morning of my life just as downright miserable as you can? It's not even light yet and you have to be milling around and primping as if you was agoing to stand dress parade! Well, you ain't, honey. No more parades of any kind for you, so forget about them. Nobody's going to salute you 'cause from now on you're just plain Mister Pike and you better get used to it! So stop thrashin' around like a battery of horse-drawn and leave me get some sleep before I have to look at your silly island!"

Of course Sue-Anne was still a little confused from her

energetic celebration of the last night aboard. It was also true that her speech contained certain elements of fact which her husband preferred to ignore. Pike had completed his toilet in such silence as he could manage, put on fresh khakis, and made his way to the dining saloon where he hastily swallowed a glass of tomato juice and a cup of Sanka. Customarily this would have rendered him capable of facing the day, but past experience had never prepared him for the problems which arose even before he had time for what he affectionately referred to as his "morning's morning." Albright, who was his aide and who would have appeared quite at home in a brokerage house, began the day by asking, "What about personnel gear, General? Do you want that unloaded before the dry stores or the other way around?"

"I suppose our people will be happier if they get their own stuff ashore first. I want to start our people off smiling."

Regardless of his past command, Pike had always referred to his soldiers as "our people" and he saw no reason to change now.

"If we do that the stores may not get up to the mess in time for dinner. The kids are bound to be pretty excited and tired and will probably set up an awful howl."

"Unload the stores first then."

"What about all that movie equipment in number three hold? Do you want it ashore so we can have a movie tonight, or can it wait?"

Pike's eyes lit up, for if he had one passion in life, it was the movies. He identified himself with every male star since the silent days, he read the credit titles, and when he could do so without being observed, he read the fan magazines. He particularly liked war movies, perhaps because he had never seen actual combat.

"We ought to have a movie tonight if we can," he said as if he really didn't care. "Starts things off right. Builds morale."

"General, what about the natives on Nikki? I suggest we establish some kind of a policy now before we get there and while everybody is together in one place. It might avoid trouble later on. You could use the ship's loud-speaker system and tell them right after breakfast."

"Good idea. Set it up with the Captain. And, incidentally, I think you better call me Governor instead of General. It sounds better under the circumstances, and I've observed that civilians are touchy about such things. Same thing as when I was in the Army. Never used the Herbert part of my name. Sounded better."

"Right, sir."

By the time the sun rose the ship hummed with activity. And Zebulon Pike found all of it bothersome and confusing. Things were vastly different than he had imagined they would be. Why, sir, on a troopship everything ran like clockwork. This, he thought, as he searched his memory for an exact military simile, was more like the Italian mess at Caporetto. Well, sir, things would fall into line soon enough. Human beings, in or out of uniform, required and were most content with a firm leader.

Later, on the bridge, Pike stepped smartly to the microphone which the Captain held out to him. Those passengers who bothered to make their way to the well deck forward looked up to see a husky man with thick gray hair and deeply tanned face. His eyes were small and set too close together, perhaps, but there was certainly no suggestion of weakness about his mouth or lack of determination in his chin. He held his shoulders well back, so much so that the buttons on his shirt seemed in immediate peril of popping their moorings. The hand which seized the microphone was large and square. Before he spoke he smiled benignly down upon the small cluster of people. Then he covered the microphone with his hand and asked the Captain where everybody was.

"Most of them are still eating breakfast or getting packed. Go right ahead, General, the system goes all through the ship. They'll hear you wherever they are, whether they want to or not."

A flash frown passed across Pike's face. Ah, the Navy, he thought. You could spot a Navy man whether he stood on the bridge of a battleship in full uniform or chose to disguise himself as a merchant skipper. The pompous bastards were all alike. Utterly spoiled ice-cream eaters.

Pike caressed his West Point ring. His confident smile returned and in a carefully modulated voice, with, he thought, just the proper hint of authority, he began to speak.

"Ladies and gentlemen. May I have your attention, please? This is your Governor speaking . . . and the children, of course, too . . . we mustn't forget the little ones. Perhaps I should say citizens of Nikki, for that is what you will be for the next year. . . ."

He paused to let his opening take effect and pretended to clear his throat. Then suddenly an approach occurred to him which he fondled mentally for such a long time that several of the men on the foredeck sat down, lit cigarettes, and gazed off toward the horizon. Pike ignored them. Patton must have felt the same before the Bulge, he decided. Or Eisenhower before Omaha Beach.

He began again, more slowly, and his smile vanished as quickly as it had come.

"I am not Moses leading you to the promised land. But there, just on the horizon, is your new home. Nikki atoll. It is sixteen miles in diameter and the highest land on it is one hundred and fifty feet. It's a long way from anywhere. . . . About all we can say about it is it's in the Pacific Ocean. . . . Ho, ho!"

Pike waited for a responding laugh. There was none.

"There is a lagoon inside that coral reef where we're going to live. . . . I don't mean we're going to live in the lagoon. . . . It's just there, that's all. Anyway, it's a big lagoon, more than ten miles wide from one end to the other . . . and I understand the fishing is pretty good. Unfortunately, there isn't much more to do on Nikki except work. . . . Which is what we came for. There's good quarters for all, plenty of food, water, plumbing, recreation facilities, and even a movie. The Atlas Construction people do things right, and who couldn't if they had a couple of million dollars to throw around. Ho . . . Ho!"

Pike had once read that Teddy Roosevelt had inspired his Rough Riders with a boisterous laugh and he thought that his own must be very akin to it. This time Pike detected a faint titter among his audience, and he saw with satisfaction that several additional men and women had found their way to the foredeck.

"Maybe I'm not Moses, but you are all chosen people . . . chosen by the Commission because of your various skills . . . and believe me we have everything from bankers and bakers to astronomers. All kinds of talent and brains in this outfit! Let me briefly restate our mission . . . the reason we are here . . . the reason the A.E.C. pays us to be here. I have been authorized at this time to inform you of certain additional details because now we are all officially a part of Operation Zeus. On or about February tenth of next year a thermonuclear explosion will take place to the north of us. This will not be a little fire-

cracker like past bombs, but an explosion of such proportions not even the big brains know what the effect will be."

Pike quickly held up his hand. It was almost a gesture of benediction.

"Now, tut, tut . . . you mothers. And all the rest of you. We have nothing to worry about on Nikki. No one really has except the enemies of our country. The actual explosion will be a very long ways from here. Our job is to serve as an auxiliary base to the island of Tuamani. As you all know, most of the project will be directed from Tuamani and I should say we're pretty lucky to be out here more or less on our own. Our job is to get ready for what happens later this year because Operation Zeus will spread over several thousand miles, and it takes a lot of doing the ordinary person just never thinks about. And maybe that's a good thing . . . if he's a taxpayer. Ho. . . . Ho!"

On this Pike obtained a very recognizable laugh, but it was spoiled for him almost instantly. He became aware that his wife had somehow found her way to the bridge. She leaned against the pilothouse, lit a cigarette, and blew the smoke toward him. The wind whipped the smoke away, but her eyes and the hopeless way she shook her head caused him to cover the microphone.

She said, "Go on, blowhard. Don't let me stop you."

Pike smiled sheepishly at the Captain and set his jaw. He brought his hands together and his West Point class ring scraped along the microphone. It made a hideous scratching noise out of all proportion to his movement. His face reddened and his voice boomed unnaturally as he spoke again.

"Our mission here is to supply and service such auxiliary guard ships, research ships and project aircraft as may come to Nikki. In addition we will house and service a complement of scientists and foreign observers. Now there's just one thing more . . ."

Herbert Zebulon Pike's wife said, "Thank God for that!"

"Just this. Nikki atoll has been leased from the French government under certain conditions. The main condition was this, and I don't want you to forget it. The natives will be left strictly alone. They have been living here a long time and we're not supposed to louse them up. They aren't cannibals and they don't wear grass skirts. So you younger fellows just forget what may come to your minds. They're all Mormons or Catholics anyway and they don't smoke or drink. Their village is separated from us by a deep-water channel and I'm told that anyone who tries to swim that pass is just about committing suicide. The current runs six knots through here . . . so I say to you again, just forget about it. Let the natives go their way and we'll go ours. Okay? So much for that. . . ."

Pike's wife said, "That's what *you* think."

"A few last details. We should dock in about thirty minutes. Go ashore as soon as you wish. My aide, Mr. Albright, will be standing at the bottom of the gangplank. He will give you the quarters assignments . . . and I want to ask you bachelors to let the married men and their families get set up first. . . . They've got kids and all. Which reminds me that Miss Summer, our schoolteacher, rings the ol' bell at eight tomorrow morning . . . so at least the kids will be off to a flying start. Readin' and writin' and 'rithmetic . . ."

Pike almost sang his last words; then his manner changed abruptly and his voice became husky with emotion.

"We have a big job to do, my friends. Operation Zeus

will be a monument in the history of mankind. It is a new shield for democracy. Good luck to you."

Pike waved his hand and lowered the microphone. His wife said, "What's the trouble, honey? You run out of wind?"

When Pike disappeared from the bridge rail, most of the people on the deck split into groups of three and four and watched the black line of Nikki atoll on the horizon. They saw it first as two islands. The more knowing explained that the illusion was caused by the channel which cut through to the lagoon. In a few minutes they were able to distinguish individual palms and on one side of the channel a splatter of faded red roofs among the trees. Someone pointed out a red church spire, and listening, they could hear a bell tolling.

One man ignored the approaching land. He was slim and very tall. He was not handsome; in fact he had often been told that he bore a remarkable resemblance to the young Abe Lincoln. While the similarity was lessened by his short-cut hair, there remained a certain quiet dignity which successfully preserved the illusion. Now he appeared entirely absorbed in the sky. He stood with his hands in his pockets and studied the quickly changing cloud formations, and on his face there lingered a smile of appreciation, as if he alone shared a secret with the variety of cumulus and cumulo-nimbus and the wisps of cirrus far above them. After a while he took a short pipe from his shirt pocket and sucked on it thoughtfully. Since he stood as far apart from the others as the foredeck would permit, his reverie was undisturbed until the ship slowed to approach the wharf. Then Albright, the Governor's aide, came to him.

"You're Adam Smith, aren't you?"

"What?"

Albright's diction was not easy to follow. His voice was peculiarly resonant and he puckered his lips into a small rosette as he spoke. And so the effect was a mixture of a lisp and also that of a man who had just severely burned his tongue. He spoke so rapidly there was almost no separation between his words and thus his question emerged as a fuzzy outburst deep within his throat. He waited with one eyebrow cocked expectantly. He stood with his feet placed closely together, holding a snap board and wavering slightly, which was intended to suggest jauntiness but instead created the impression he was in danger of losing his balance.

"I said you're Adam Smith."

"Well, yes . . . I am."

"Right. I'm Albright, the Governor's aide."

"Pleased to meet you, Mr. Albright."

Adam automatically extended his hand. He withdrew it when he saw that Albright had not the slightest intention of clasping it.

"Right. The Governor would like to know if it will rain tonight."

Adam smiled and shook his head in disbelief. Finally he said, "Well now . . . I just couldn't say one way or . . ."

"You're our weather chap, aren't you?"

"Well . . . yeah. But, golly . . . I'm not a fortune-teller."

"The Governor is extremely anxious about the movies tonight. It's an open-air theater, you know, wooden benches, no roof . . . that sort of thing, and the Governor is most anxious that our first evening go off without a hitch."

"Well, golly! I just got here . . . I'm not even there

yet. I have no map and I don't know the local conditions and even if I did, forecasting weather is a complicated . . ."

"Look, old fellow. The Governor wants an answer. And in case you're not aware of it, Governor Pike does not like equivocations. Is it going to rain or is it not?"

Adam said slowly, "I just don't know."

"I can't tell him that. Come along. Give me some kind of an answer."

"All right. You tell the Governor that I don't think it's going to rain . . . but anybody who's going to the movies had better take their raincoats."

"I doubt if the Governor will appreciate that report."

"Well, it's the only one I have. By the way . . . You happen to know where I'll be living?"

Albright ruffled the papers on his snap board.

"Building C with the other bachelors. You chaps should have some jolly times in there."

"Thanks a lot."

"Right."

Albright turned on his heel and was gone as suddenly as he had appeared.

Now, with the ship barely moving toward the wharf, Adam looked away from the sky and found interest in the land. He saw that the shore shelved up from an outer reef in the manner of most coral atolls, and he saw how the channel split the land and led directly to a further expanse of water which would be the lagoon. He could not perceive any sign of land beyond the lagoon; in fact, it appeared as limitless as another sea. As the ship approached the wharf, he looked down at the water and watched a multitude of fishes moving effortlessly against the channel current, and he saw that the violent colors which he had admired in the sky were exactly duplicated in the clear depths.

He was surprised and unaccountably disappointed in the native village, now fully revealed behind the palms which stretched along the shore. It was much smaller and much neater than he had anticipated. It appeared deserted and only the occasional cry of a rooster gave any indication of life. Then he remembered it was Sunday morning.

Crossing to the opposite side of the deck he looked out upon the village created by the Atlas Construction Company. And he was neither disappointed nor pleased. It was exactly as he had thought it would be with the same old barracks-like buildings arranged according to a master plan that never varied. Heritage from the Second World War, he thought, and then he wondered how he had conceived the idea since he had been some five years too young to have any part of that war.

When the ship came to rest alongside the wharf, Adam went down to the cramped cabin he shared with two other men and picked up his suitcase and a duffel bag. Then he made his way to the deck again, excusing himself several times as he collided with other passengers, all of whom, he thought, appeared to be in a near panic to get ashore.

A Marine sergeant with whom Adam had struck up a nodding acquaintance during the two-day voyage down from Tuamani was trying to herd the women and children into some semblance of order. Adam knew that his name was Doolan, and now he appeared to be dangerously harassed. So when Doolan passed close to him, breathing short as if to contain his frustration, Adam smiled. Doolan accepted the smile as a signal of sympathy. He halted and mopped his dripping face. Scowling at the people milling around him, he said, "I'm a diamond-shaped son of a bitch. You'd think the Governor really was leading them to the promised land. We only got just so much transport and everybody wants to get settled down with their grandmaw's picture over the mantel in sixteen seconds!"

Sgt. Doolan passed on and Adam sat down on his duffel bag. The separate sounds of confusion about him melted into each other and became a monotonous hum. He had almost dozed off when he felt a small and very moist hand touch his own. Adam opened his eyes and saw a scrawny boy standing before him. The boy's eyes were filled with tears. He caught at his breath, but he made no audible sound.

"You see my mother, mister?"

"I'm not sure I know your mother."

"She's purty."

"Most mothers are. What's the matter? Lost her?"

The boy nodded his head.

"She'll turn up. They always do. What's your name?"

"Floyd Dunbar."

Adam held out his hand. Sitting on his duffel bag his head was just slightly above the boy's. The boy squeezed his hand more firmly and Adam managed to maintain his smile though he saw their clasp was sealed with the drippings of a candy bar. He said that his name was Adam.

"That's the name of the first man ever invented, ain't it?"

"That's right."

Adam got up from his duffel bag and, holding the boy's hand, he made his way through the crowd around the gangway entrance until they emerged upon the deck.

There were several women on the fringes of the crowd. None of them displayed the slightest interest in the boy. When they reached a free place along the rail, Adam hoisted him to his shoulder so he could look down upon the wharf. Below, Adam recognized Albright and saw that he was surrounded by a huddle of men and women.

"Any of those people belong to your family, Floyd?"

"Nope."

"Let's just wait here till they do show up."

"I have to go pee-pee."

"Right this minute?"

"Pretty soon."

Adam heard a woman's voice behind him call Floyd's name. He turned and was surprised to see that the woman was very young. She wore a simple cotton dress over a figure which already suggested dumpiness.

"Floyd! Where you been?"

"Just lookin' around at things. Me and Adam here."

Adam said, "Floyd and I have had a nice talk."

The woman shot him a harried look. She brushed aside a lock of blond hair which had fallen over one eye. As Adam set the boy down she took his hand.

"Thanks, mister. My husband had to go ashore right away and fix some piece of machinery that already busted down. He left me with all the baggage and the kids and all, and I got stuff stacked all over the boat. Just like pioneer times, ain't it? I feel like we should be riding in a covered wagon. Come see us when we get settled in. Our name's Dunbar."

"Sure."

They melted at once into the crowd at the gangway. Adam was about to return to the comfort of his duffel bag when Carlos Raveza joined him at the rail. Carlos was fat and just now he was very hot and his shirt was already sopping with moisture. He touched his wisp of mustache and belched. Adam had never known a man who belched so often. He thought that Carlos must look very much like a hippopotamus suffering from gastric distress.

Carlos said, "I think they keep us here all day, maybe, no?"

"Seems like there's some tie-up in transportation."

Carlos pushed his belly against the rail until it resembled a punctured tire. He shoved his battered straw hat defiantly over one eye and peered down at the wharf.

"That Mr. Albright. His English no comprendo."

"I had a little trouble myself. But then I think he must be an Easterner and they talk funny . . . or a lot of them do."

"He speaks in the manner of a Limey."

"I guess he's just trying to earn a living."

Carlos belched again and seemed enormously satisfied with his effort. Then suddenly a sadness came to his eyes.

"This place looks some little like Mexico. . . . Tampico, you would say. But, naturally, not so gay. In Tampico no person gets excited . . . ever. Positively never. It is, how you say, against the law."

"You mean against custom."

"However you desire it. *I* was born in Tampico."

Poking a fat finger into the upper roll of his belly, Carlos made the announcement as if it were an historic occasion. Then he added, "You can see by my teeth that I was born in Tampico."

"Your teeth?"

"In Tampico there is not one single dentist. It has something to do with the water."

Parting his lips, Carlos displayed his teeth. "Regard! Not so much as one single excavation!"

"They look pretty good."

"They are perfect! In the same way is my liver. Superb! I am sorry you cannot examine my kidneys also. Not so much as a stone. Not even a small pebble!" He made a pinching gesture with his fingers.

"You're lucky. Nothing like a healthy liver."

"In the same way are all of the parts of my body. Whores adore me. They say I am fantástico!"

"Congratulations."

"The secret is never to become excited. Life is like electricity. You must allow it to flow freely, and do not overload. If you do, you blow a fuse. It is as simple as that."

Carlos turned the palms of his hands upward and moved them apart slowly. Then he said, "I have turned my most excellent ear to the Governor and his speech. Simpático, señor . . . very simpático . . . and also full of horse manure."

"It struck me as sort of a pep talk."

"It commence with manure and end with manure. . . . Especially the part about chosen people. I observe only a collection of how you say—misfits and miswits—of which I am the most."

"I dunno. Most of them seem to be pretty nice people."

"To *you*, señor! Ah! But what do you know about these creatures in special? Have you inquired of yourself, for example . . . how in the world did I ever get the job as chief electrician?"

Adam laughed. "Why not? Aren't you a good electrician?"

"Christ no! If I knew my business I would not be here. Naturally I was not so honest when I made application.

Not so much as a single one of these people would be here if they could make a good living back in the United States. This includes Carlos Raveza."

"It just so happens that I can."

"Then may I ask just what the hell you are doing here, or did you commit rape or rob a bank or kick opium?"

Adam hesitated. Yes, why was he here on Nikki? Certainly not because he was interested in a nuclear explosion! Or even because of any special interest in the Pacific weather. He took a moment to search his mind for a logical reason and found none that would provide a satisfactory answer. Finally he said, "It beats me."

"Exactly! Now you have say a thing of intelligence. The Governor also say one thing of intelligence, but he forget the main thing. Yes, this must be a big affair . . . very grand, as who but men with very large brains could think up such a big firecracker and have the braveness to light the fuse? But the Governor forget to say that children should not play with dynamite."

"I guess the scientists know what they're doing."

"They do . . . but *we* don't. And we, my friend, happen to be you and I, the little brains in this big world. And it is the little brains not the big ones, who are really going to use this firecracker . . . which is why we will wake up some day and God or the devil will ask us how we got where we are and the only intelligent thing to say will be 'It beats me.' "

2

Trillions of organisms which united and perished together so that Nikki atoll might project above the surface of the sea were thus engaged for, some said, a thousand years. Others said five thousand years and others said five hundred years. It depended on who held forth upon its creation; whether it was Yip Kee, the young Chinese merchant; or Fat Sue, the old Chinese merchant; or André, the Mormon elder; or Father Louis, the Catholic priest. Or you might listen to the soft explanation of Tanni, the native chief who had little respect for the theory of coral organisms; or his wife Lua, who had even less; or M. DeLage, who ran the post office and the atoll's feeble wireless that was supposed to maintain contact with the outside world. M. DeLage, who had found his way to Nikki all the way from Lyons via America and consequently knew a great many things, said that Nikki was only partially built by coral polyps and offered as proof the fifty-meter hill which rose on the southerly side of the formation. No other atoll in the whole Pacific had such a hill. Therefore, according to M. DeLage, some volcanic disturbance must have been involved at the birth of Nikki. DeLage proposed that Nikki was a poor relative of Tuamani which had heaved itself frothing toward the sky and left a jagged pyramid which could be seen for a hundred miles. Tuamani was brooding and cloud-covered and thick with jungle. Even in the finest weather its appearance was as savage as the fierce people who once dwelt in its valleys and dined upon each other as often as possible.

Life had always been more tranquil on Nikki atoll, and some gave credit to the easy topography. Nikki was shaped like a flat doughnut. The organisms apparently had become exhausted from their efforts just before they completed the gigantic circle and so failed to meet by a few hundred yards. Some of the older inhabitants who kept faith with the ancient beliefs maintained that a hungry sea monster took a bite out of the atoll and thus formed the pass which led into the lagoon. They said, "Ahwei! You can see it yourself!"

Even the climate on Nikki was different from Tuamani. Except for a month of almost continuous rain during December it was relatively dry and the nearly constant trade winds gave an illusion of vigor to the air. Storms were rare and there had not been a hurricane for a very long time. There were relatively few flies. No one had ever seen a snake. The fish were abundant, mostly non-poisonous, and co-operative. The coconut palms were healthy and bore well enough so that the gathering and drying of copra had long been the chief source of income for the inhabitants. A second source was found in the lagoon, where the clear bottom provided enough mother-of-pearl shell to keep the divers busy three months of every year. This was just enough to pay off their debts at the two Chinese stores. Many things ran in pairs on Nikki, and now there were two settlements.

Certain unpleasantnesses prevented Nikki from becoming a paradise. The rat population was large and bold. There were countless land crabs for which no one had ever been able to discover the slightest use. There were sharks in the lagoon, most of which were considered harmless, but those which lurked in and about the channel were known to be extremely antagonistic. And so the native divers avoided the channel, and even when the sharks showed an interest in their work in the lagoon, they climbed aboard their outriggers and moved to another area. There were a few cases of elephantiasis on Nikki, but these were regarded as a part of life and those who suffered from it flatly refused to go to the clinic in Tahiti. And there had always been the "No-nu" fish which concealed itself in the sand along the inner and outer reefs.

This fish terrified the natives. For the No-nu was cleverly camouflaged and almost invisible. Its venom apparatus was efficient and complicated; the dorsal, anal, and ventral spines containing poison sacs fed from the glands through lateral grooves. If a man was so unfortunate as to step on one he instantly discovered true agony. It was so that a No-nu's spine contained such vicious poison that the victim was invariably driven mad with pain and, frothing at the mouth, usually welcomed death within a few hours.

Thus the combination of evils and blessings on Nikki atoll was reflected in the temperaments of the people,

31

who had dwelt there long before the first missionaries arrived to confuse them. Because of their isolation they were healthier than most Polynesians. Impetigo, yaws, pneumonia, and malaria were nonexistent. They were also more industrious. Poverty was unknown and so was crime. Authority was vested in the chief, who was elected every six years, and the candidate was invariably chosen for his wisdom, gentility, and good nature.

Three days after the ship had disembarked her passengers, Tanni, the Chief of Nikki, stood on the opposite side of the channel and waited for an approaching motor launch. He was dressed in his best for the occasion: white shirt with tails hanging out, and immaculately laundered shorts. He wore his wrist watch although it had not functioned for some time. Beside him stood Terry Mack, who was a Melanesian instead of a Polynesian and was therefore hirsute and was therefore constantly in need of a shave. Terry Mack was a Cook Islander who had wandered as far as Nikki looking for a place to settle down. He was very small and blind in one eye. He was not regarded as a first citizen of Nikki, but since he hailed from British-mandated territory he did speak English, which accounted for his present position of honor. The entire population of Nikki village including several squalling babies was dispersed loosely behind the pair.

When the motor launch bounced against the old wharf, Herbert Zebulon Pike was the first occupant to step ashore. He was followed by five men, all of them unnaturally solemn, for Pike had said, "All right now, gentlemen. Let's watch our behavior. This is important. We must get off on the right foot with the locals. I've always found getting on with the locals of the utmost value in any operation."

All of the men with the exception of Sgt. Doolan, who had been warned to leave his side arms in his quarters, made a clumsy departure from the launch. Albright's sun helmet fell forward and temporarily blinded him when he reached out for the wharf. Dr. Case, to whom Pike had said, "You just might have a look at the medical situation over there . . . probably find all kinds of weird diseases . . . our own protection, you know," became so entranced with the fishes beneath the wharf he almost fell between the pilings and the launch. Capt. Michaud, the handsome French observer assigned to Operation Zeus, was equally taken with a group of maidens behind the Chief and missed his footing twice. However, one of the many press relations men assigned to Zeus required Doolan's assistance in leaving the launch. He had already discovered that he was the one man on Nikki whom Pike feared, and consequently he could get as drunk as he pleased any time he felt like it. He finally staggered into the informal line which had formed behind Pike.

Pike covered the distance which separated him from the Chief in three forceful strides. There was a faint click from the vicinity of his heels as he came to a halt. His hand started involuntarily toward his right eye as if he would salute and then shot forward. And for a moment he seemed at loss for a greeting. Finally he said, "How do you do, sir."

Tanni took his hand most gently in the Polynesian fashion, which was far more of a caress than a contest of strength. Pike managed to conceal his displeasure.

"Pike's the name. I bring you greetings from your new neighbors across the channel."

It was an opening Pike had rehearsed several times in the privacy of his bathroom. Now, he thought, it sounded just right for the occasion and he was pleased until he realized that Tanni had not understood a word.

The Chief turned to Terry Mack and they conversed quietly in Tahitian. Finally Terry Mack focused his good eye on Pike and said, "The Chief thanks you jolly much, m'lad. 'E sez 'e's glad to see you lookin' so fat."

Pike instantly sucked in his stomach. His lips worked impatiently as Terry Mack continued.

"The Chief sez 'e 'opes you and all yer people are 'appy and if yer want any washin' done 'is women will do it."

Pike looked down upon Terry Mack with disapproval. The little man was not his idea of a dignified interpreter.

"Tell the Chief thanks very much but we have our own laundry. Also tell him I would like to know the disease situation on Nikki."

"The disease situation?"

Terry Mack was openly bewildered. His good eye sought the sky for a suitable answer.

"Yes. I want to know about typhoid, any fevers, and are the women infected?"

Pike glanced significantly at the group of young women who had gathered at a respectable distance behind Tanni. They met Pike's eyes frankly, and then they giggled. Hanover, the press representative, caught up their giggle and started forward. Mumbling vaguely about starting a party, he was restrained and towed back into position by Sgt. Doolan.

Albright said, "If I might suggest, Governor, your question might be rephrased more delicately."

Terry Mack said, "I caught the Guv'nor quite all right. 'E wants to know 'ave the women got the clap."

Pike snorted and his face turned the color of the new

coral beneath the wharf. But his forbidding stare failed to affect the little man. He only displayed more of his rotten teeth in a knowing smile.

"The answer is no, m'lad. And if they do get it we'll know where it come from."

Pike's face became redder. The veins in his powerful neck enlarged and his lips became a tight, thin line.

"So much for your delicate approach, Mr. Albright. I'll thank you to stay out of this from now on. Captain Michaud. Would you mind lending a hand as interpreter? If I could communicate with the Chief in French we could get rid of this renegade. I can't say I care for his attitude."

Terry Mack stood his ground. He said, "The Chief don't savvy French, m'lad."

"Then let me straighten you out on a few things. . . . In the first place I am not your lad. I am the duly appointed Governor of our settlement on Nikki and as such I am the senior representative of the United States Government. You will address me with the respect that position deserves."

"Righto, Guv'nor."

Terry Mack seemed honestly contrite. He wiped his nose on the back of his hand, scratched at his beard, and seemed delighted with Pike's rebuke.

"In the second place your duty as an interpreter is to faithfully translate the remarks of the two parties involved and not insert your own opinions. Now is that clear?"

"Clear as the sky, Guv'nor. But I've seen you Yank blokes before and you bring a lot more trouble than you take away."

Pike exploded.

"I don't give a damn what you happen to think! You stick to your business and tell the Chief this is not in any sense a military operation—"

"Then what is that soldier 'angin' about with you?"

"He's *not* a soldier, dammit! He's a marine! He and four of his men merely have the duty of keeping order in our colony."

"Knowing Yanks I should think that's 'ardly enough . . ."

"Shut up!"

Pike swerved and looked at Albright. "This is impossible! This impudent clown is deliberately insulting us."

"You instructed me to stay out of this, sir. But if I am free to make an observation, I would suggest patience."

"Maybe he's a Russian spy," Hanover mumbled.

Pike turned back and tried to split a smile at the Chief and a glare at Terry Mack. The result was confusing. After a moment he managed to continue although his words came with ominous slowness.

"You tell the Chief that we are normal, law-abiding people. Our population includes several married couples and their children. We have as well some of the most distinguished scientists in the world and the representatives of France, England, and Japan. This is merely a courtesy visit. We have not the slightest desire to interfere with the Chief's village or his people in any way, shape, or form. I have given the strictest orders that no one shall cross the channel, although if the Chief or any of his people wish to visit us, they will be most welcome. Now is that all clear? Do you think you can get it across without making a botch of it?"

Terry Mack shrugged his shoulders and said innocently, "Why not?"

Then while Pike fidgeted he turned to Tanni and spoke with many gestures in the Polynesian manner.

When Terry Mack concluded his speech there was silence while Tanni thoughtfully examined the face of each man in Pike's party. There was no emotion in his large brown eyes. He seemed to be looking into the men rather than at them, neither approving nor disapproving. Pike clasped his hands uncertainly behind his back and assumed an at-ease posture. Capt. Michaud reached for a pack of cigarettes in his shirt pocket and then, thinking better of it, dropped his hand. Dr. Case, suddenly uncomfortable beneath Tanni's searching look, tried a half-smile and abandoned it almost instantly. Albright experimented with his balance as was his habit. Hanover, suddenly sobered, wiped the perspiration from the pouches beneath his eyes and worked his dry tongue across his lips. Doolan alone appeared unaffected by the Chief's examination. He stood rigidly at attention and stared at a red tin roof he had selected as a target at the end of the village street.

At last Tanni seemed satisfied with what he had seen. He beckoned lazily toward one of the women who moved quickly forward and held out a large, cardboard box. Tanni reached into the box and drew out a necklace of sea shells. The shells were a mottled brown and highly polished, so much so they glittered in the sunlight as he placed the necklace around Pike's neck. Then he moved solemnly among his visitors and presented each one with a necklace from the box. When he had finished, he returned to his position and spoke briefly to Terry Mack.

"The Chief sez yer welcome to Nikki, and 'e 'opes yer women will like the shells. You ought to. It takes a long time to get that particular kind."

"Tell the Chief we deeply appreciate his gifts. Albright! Why the hell didn't you tell me this sort of thing was goin' to happen? We should have brought something for these people."

"I'll see that a launch brings over something appropriate this afternoon."

"The Chief sez would you like to see the village?"

"We would be honored," Pike said.

And so Tanni and Pike, with Terry Mack trotting along between them, led the procession along the sun-baked street which was the only one in Nikki. They saw the Mormon church and admired its crudely painted glass windows; and they entered the Catholic church, which was smaller but more serene beneath a cluster of palms. Dr. Case observed that the Atlas Construction Company seemed to have remembered everything but a church in their own establishment, and Pike said yes, that was wrong and that he would do something about it. They saw the Chinese store of Fat Sue, whose wares consisted of canned goods, fishhooks, and needles and thread, and they saw the store of Charlie Yip Kee who sold exactly the same thing. They saw the post office and pretended to admire M. DeLage's antiquated wireless equipment. They inspected a line of sheds in which copra was drying, and Tanni ordered two boys to open enough coconuts so they could each have a drink of the milk. Hanover tried bravely to swallow the liquid but was almost immediately forced to retire behind a tree, where he gagged noisily for such a long time that Pike ventured a frown of disapproval when he finally returned.

The tour of the village took less than an hour in spite of Hanover's lagging, and the re-embarkation into the launch went off without incident. As the launch pulled away from the wharf, Pike stood erect in the stern and waved his hand at the assembled crowd. He reserved a final salute for Tanni. The departure was robbed of some dignity by Terry Mack, who called after them with the maximum effort of his lungs, "Keep yer friggin' nose clean, Guv'nor!"

The question of a name for their settlement troubled the people who now occupied the buildings set up by the Atlas Construction Company. They could not call the place Nikki because that was already the name of the native village across the channel and, furthermore, it identified the entire atoll. Yet everyone seemed to feel the need of a name suitable to their new home. Debates on the subject flourished in the mess hall and at times almost led to violence. There were innumerable suggestions and no one from Pike to little Floyd Dunbar hesitated to voice his opinion. Sue-Anne Pike, who managed to be present at the closing of the bar each night, said she didn't give a hollerin' hoot in hell what the place was finally named if they didn't call it "Bourbonville." Her selection won some support among the more carefree settlers who waited for the bar to open at five each day and were invariably present when it closed at ten.

Others were inclined to be more conservative. Professor Tasamachi, the Japanese observer, suggested "Babylon" because, as he pointed out, it would not be in existence for long. Pete Walsacki, the boss plumber, liked "Little Toledo." He was able to persuade Barney Dunbar, the boss carpenter, Pinkey Riley, the baker, and Ellsworth Tompkins, the chief of mechanical maintenance, to his way of thinking. This was a powerful coalition.

There were independents particularly among the scientific team now resident on Nikki. Dr. H. P. V. Callandar, the physicist, inserted the problem in his IBM-machine brain and after several days of almost audible clicking came up with "Station Sixty-One." His choice aroused so little enthusiasm he never had an opportunity to explain why the number so appealed to him. Dr. Herman Keim, the astronomer, said why not just call the place Nikki and let confusion reign; it was always stimulating. He could enlist no support whatever and brooded for several days on what he called the "human yearning for special identity."

The matter was settled for everyone by a mandate which came down from Tuamani. The message danced across the Pacific sky and found its way down to the prefabricated shack which served as the communications center. It was Sunnie Mandel who saw it first on the number three radioteletype machine.

"Well, whaddya know. We got a name!"

She turned to Margaret Trumpey, who shared the work in the center and pointed at the still-clacking machine. Sunnie blew out her cheeks and said, "Wait until Herbert Zebulon Pike gets a load of this! One of those big brains on Tuamani has fractured a cell! Ya just gotta be dippy to think up such stuff. . . ."

Margaret joined her before the machine. Standing side by side, the two became as much a contrast as Nikki atoll and the island of Tuamani, where the message had originated. Sunnie Mandel was so thin that in certain lights her skin gave the impression of being translucent, and only the lively sparkle in her eyes rescued her from appearing sickly.

Margaret would have made two of Sunnie. Her facial features were lovely, her eyes wide-set and intelligent, her mouth well formed and inviting. And when she smiled it was impossible not to admire her perfect teeth. Her complexion was a striking heritage, and when struck by sunlight, her tawny hair became like well-polished gold.

Unfortunately, Margaret's beauty ended abruptly at her neck, which was all too sturdy. Her neck matched her body and her powerful legs. She would have fitted perfectly into a nineteenth-century landscape stacking grain or crushing grapes with her bare feet. An artist who had once dined at Margaret's home in Beloit, Wisconsin, said that Margaret had not been born like other girls, but had really escaped from a Rubens painting. The next day Margaret went to the library and spent almost an hour studying Rubens. She was both embarrassed and sad. For the artist had been right. He only neglected to mention that fashions in the female figure had changed and that to people who were not artists, and especially to the young men of Beloit, Margaret Trumpey was just overweight. This was untrue. She could not have lost a pound if she tried. She was simply peasant-husky. Yet few young men in Beloit, conditioned by a generation which believed the deliberate malformation of the female figure to be a supreme social duty, understood or appreciated Margaret's honest and graceful proportions. Which was why she was not very unhappy to find herself so far away from home.

Now standing beside Sunnie Mandel, a quiet smile crept along her lips as she watched the last stutters of the machine.

DIRECT URGENT PIKE

FOR CONVENIENCE COMMUNICATIONS YOU NOW CLASSIFIED CODE NAME PISTOL TWO PERIOD OA TITIA ATOLL WILL BE DESIGNATED OA AND EXPLOSION SITE TRIGGER PERIOD

COMPLY IMMEDIATELY AND FROM NOW ON SO DESIGNATE
PERIOD ALL CONCERNED AIRCRAFT AND SHIPS ADVISED PE-
RIOD SIGNED KEATING

The machine paused and then clacked off EOM, for
end of message. Sunnie pulled the yellow paper upward
and tore it off below the signature name. She said,
"Which one of us is going to risk her life delivering this
to His Majesty? Last I heard the Governor was bound
and determined to name us Pike City just in case somebody might forget who's boss."

Margaret said, "I'll take it over. I have to pick up the
weather map anyway."

"Lucky you."

Margaret paused as she folded the message into an
envelope.

"How do you mean?"

"That weather guy. He's pretty cute . . . for a jerk.
That is, his face is kind of cute, you know, sort of
Abraham Lincoln-y without the beard, you know, sort
of the kind that shoulda been a minister, or could be if
he turned his collar around. But he's so quiet! He don't
talk. Maybe because he's living with an important secret
. . . like he was in the Foreign Legion, or he has a wife
who is in a T.B. sanatorium, or maybe really he's a
counterintelligence man . . . or, you know . . . Cripes,
I never met anybody like him either back in Nyack or
none of the other projects I worked on. Like NATO . . .
Well, there was a few fellows in Frankfort who used
to come down and sniff around the machines and keep
their mouths shut until they got around to sex, and when
I was in Japan with the WAC's there was this lieutenant
who never said much either, but he danced like a wild
man, which was kind of strange until we found out he

used to be in a Broadway show and was as queer as a thirteen-dollar bill. . . . But this weather guy is a character, believe me. Maybe he was tortured by the Chinese or something and they cut out his tongue."

At the door Margaret said, "He talks to me every time I go for the map."

"Yeah? What's he say?"

"Hello. Sometimes he even says good-by."

"He must be in love with you. Maybe that's it. He made some kind of a oath with himself which keeps him Silent Sam until he meets the woman he will love. She will wear some kind of a special sign, like a crysanthemum or a pearl in her right ear or . . ."

Margaret laughed. "Sunnie, if I had your imagination!"

Sunnie's face saddened and the expression was so rare, Margaret waited at the door.

"You don't have to make with the compliment talk, Margaret. I don't really have any imagination. I'm just repeating the kind of talk that's pretty standard in the Ree-Jay Club. I'm sort of a charter member and it seems like now that smart-aleck yak has become a part of me. But then, I can see from your face you never heard of the Ree-Jay Club."

"I've never been much of a joiner."

"Well, don't ever join the Ree-Jays. There's too many of us now. It's sort of a poor girl's Junior League. I can spot a member a mile off. To qualify you got to be just naturally ugly."

Sunnie glanced at Margaret's legs and then she looked quickly at her face again. Their eyes met, understood, and turned away. Sunnie started to talk again, but she now spoke uncertainly as if she were seeking a convenient exit from what she had begun.

"Well, mainly, there's got to be something about your

personality men don't like and which all the Listerine in the world won't help. Maybe the girl has a little mustache on her upper lip, or happens to be eight feet tall, or maybe she's all skin and bones like me. The funny thing is some of the nicest gals in the world belong to the Ree-Jays, only I guess it isn't really very funny. Because no one but ourselves ever bothers to find that out."

"I'm beginning to feel like I'm missing something worth while."

"Oh no, you're not. Don't go and get ideas like that, for heaven's sake! Ree-Jay is our laugh-clown-laugh way of saying *reject*. These government projects are full of us. The best training ground is the WAC's, where you learn to lie in your bunk at night in the dark and cry inside and know that every other girl in the room will know just how you feel. Sometimes it gets to be a regular and sympathetic chorus and in your heart you can hear it as plain and loud as the Salt Lake Tabernacle Choir. I've known Ree-Jays who were thirty years old and never had a date in their lives. They never even had a chance to louse one up. Nobody wants them hanging around home if they ever had a home to begin with, and the competition is too rough in the average business firm. So what does a Ree-Jay do? She signs up to go overseas with some outfit and the good old government is usually the only outfit who'll take her. Overseas, see, things are supposed to be different, and maybe the men aren't so particular because they're supposed to be lonely. Malarkey! The men get with the native girls whether they're slant-eyed, brown-skinned, or what. The men know a reject when they see one, and if they're going to marry anybody, it's Little Nell back home, or Fräulein Schmeercase in Europe, or Madame Butterfly if they get real good and desperate in the Far East. One thing is good about being a Ree-Jay. You get a lot of readin' done and you go to lots of movies . . . by yourself. Which is how I get all those crazy ideas I just spouted about that weather guy. And if you think I'm feeling sorry for myself, well, I am. I do it every once in a while. It's purifying."

Margaret looked at Sunnie and saw that there was not a trace of bitterness in her eyes. Then she said, "I'm awfully glad you're here, Sunnie. I have a lot to learn."

The weather office was housed in the same building as the photo lab and was situated diagonally across the main street from the communications center. Margaret was still squinting from the brilliant sunshine when she opened the screen door. She saw Adam Smith standing before his drafting board, and for a moment she watched in silence as he marked down a series of arrows and numbers on the large chart. Finally she said, "It's eleven o'clock, Mr. Smith."

He raised his head a moment, glanced at the Navy clock on the wall as if to confirm her statement, and then signed his name along the bottom of the chart. He rolled it carefully and handed it to Margaret. Then he smiled and said, "Good-by."

On her way out of the office Margaret said, "Think it will snow today?"

"Nope."

"See you around."

"Sure."

Margaret stepped into the sunlight and began walking down the main street, which had now been labeled Broadway. She walked slowly because she wanted to think . . . mostly about Nikki and a lot about what Sunnie Mandel had said. So? Ree-Jay. At least that was a new way of putting it. Back in Beloit no one had ever heard of a Ree-Jay. A girl who failed to conform to a rigid set of physical standards was known in Beloit as a "dog." She might be a "nice dog" or a "good-head dog" or at worst could be an "awesome dog," but once classified in the canine status a dog remained a dog until she either moved away or enough time passed so that all interest in her was lost. Not, Margaret supposed, that Beloit was any different than other places. She could remember now that the young and eligible men in Beloit had actually been kind to her. Overly kind in one instance. Her mouth twisted into a little smile when she remembered Luther Kidd, who was thirty-two and already owned half of a lumber yard. No one had ever questioned the activities of Luther Kidd. He was the most eligible young man in Beloit, yet he had the grace and intelligence not to show that he knew it. The Junior Chamber of Commerce held an annual picnic which was a lot more than just potato salad and sandwiches and beer and singing. It was an ancient rite in Beloit, as fixed in routine, Margaret thought, as a black mass. The young wives who were already mothers remained in one cluster and talked about their babies and what a relief it was, oh dear, to get away for an afternoon. The young wives who were not yet mothers, but soon would be, or even hoped to be, were allowed to pass through this cluster; in and out without pausing too long, like needles on a loom. If they were obviously pregnant they were permitted to remain in the cluster for as long as they wished, the supposition being that by mere exposure to the chatter, because they were never encouraged to speak, they might absorb the wisdom of those who knew their potties and pablum.

All of the wives at these picnics were still attractive

to look upon although a few showed signs of early deterioration. They were the more sophisticated young matrons, who laughed long and loudly about their roles as mothers. They pretended openly and without blushing that their most recent conception had been an accident and that they would just have soon waited a few more years. Most of these wives read the *New Yorker* and were very keen on progressive jazz. If there was enough sex in it, they would actually read a best seller. They were all deeply involved in various charity drives, often at considerable pain to their immediate families, who wound up with peanut-butter sandwiches for dinner because there just wasn't time to make anything else. There was, however, always time to pose for promotional photographs which inevitably found their way into the newspapers wherein the young matrons were identified as Mesdames.

Now, walking slowly down the sunlit street on Nikki, Margaret could almost hear the feminine laughter at the picnic, and hear it echoed by the husbands who stood nearby in their own cluster with their sleeves rolled up to remind everyone and also themselves that their muscles were still hard; well, fairly so, considering. They would laugh about that and suck in their stomachs unnaturally because their waistlines were not often so publicly exposed. And they would be looking down into their glasses pretty solemnly while they talked about the high cost of building even a modest house, and ho-ho-hoing just a little louder than the next man when some wit reminded all of them that it really hadn't been so long since they attended these picnics as free men.

Yes indeed, she thought, remembering she had better stop daydreaming and get on to General Pike's house. Yes indeed, there was always an invisible dividing line at those picnics even though almost everyone knew everyone else. To cross that line was asking for trouble. It separated the mated from the not yet mated, or the never-would-be mated, as surely as an electrically charged fence.

There were no dogs among the young mothers and wives. Junior Chamber of Commerce men did not marry dogs. They married the best, and a great many so-called lifetime partnerships had begun on the picnics. If a bachelor just wanted a date, regardless of his design or intentions, he did *not* take her to the Junior Chamber Picnic. There were too many inquisitive eyes focused on both the young man and the girl, and a lot of those eyes could make things tough or easy in a business way.

Then why, everybody wanted to know, did a good catch like Luther Kidd bring Margaret Trumpey?

Now, so far from the sound of any music, she tried to separate just a few of the parties at which she had sat as an unpaid entertainer and played the piano. Those parties were now ancient history, and here on Nikki each melted into the other until they seemed a single affair. The keyboards of all pianos looked very much the same and so did the faces which hung over the piano nursing their drinks, half-screened by cigarette smoke, and their voices were the same, saying, "That's for me, Marge. Play it again," or, "Can you do tum-tum-dee-dee-dum," or, "Why don't you rest a minute, finish your drink and then maybe you'd feel like playing something we could *all* dance to, huh?" The "all" never included Margaret Trumpey. Some of the men leaned far enough over the piano so they could more openly study her breasts. A drunk once said he would like to walk across them in his bare feet. Everybody around the piano laughed.

But it was fun being at the parties anyway. It was fun

watching people have a good time, or think they were having a good time, and it was sort of satisfying to think they maybe wouldn't have quite such a good time if you weren't there.

She was thinking about the picnic and why Luther Kidd had taken her when she passed the building which quartered the scientific team and which was already known as "Brains Bungalow." Dr. Herman Keim, the astronomer assigned to Nikki, sat on the concrete stoop which led to the door. Margaret had sat beside him twice in the mess hall and found him delightfully grumpy. He reminded her of a Humpty Dumpty illustration in one of her children's books, and his vast belly sagged in such a way she thought it most nearly resembled a kangaroo's pouch. Since his arrival on Nikki he had grown a walrus mustache which well suited his heavy jowls. Smiling at him, Margaret thought that in the brilliant sunlight his nose was almost as red as his hair.

"Good morning, Dr. Keim."

"What's good about it?"

"Didn't all the stars behave themselves last night?"

"They continue to twinkle. Why do you trot past here with that roll of paper every morning?"

"A girl has to earn a living."

"Come on. What is it?"

"This is a weather map prepared daily for God."

Dr. Keim glanced significantly down the street toward the row of palms which nearly surrounded the Governor's house.

"I thought you ran the radioteletypes."

"We double as messengers. There are times when I could use a horse."

"Would it be violating your security oath to tell me

what the weather is going to be like today? I thought I might snoop around the east side of the lagoon and catch a fish."

"The forecaster does not discuss the weather with me in detail. Nor does he discuss anything else. He's the silent type."

"If I were younger I would discuss a great many things with you."

Margaret smiled at the sun and said, "That's the age-old excuse of a mature man who's afraid he will be caught talking to a younger girl."

"Pretty smart, aren't you? But you're wrong. I lost my chances thirty years ago when I fell in love with the stars. I could not see then that the stars would never do anything for me."

"They made you famous, didn't they?"

"Romance with a star has its limitations."

Dr. Keim scowled at the sky, patted his belly; and then as if Margaret had suddenly ceased to exist, he rose abruptly and went into the bungalow.

Margaret continued along Broadway toward Pike's house. She passed the area which had been leveled for a baseball diamond at the intersection of a narrower street labeled Second Avenue. Here, on one corner, stood the small building which housed the Marine detachment. Two marines, Peterson and Randall, labored without enthusiasm on the path which led to the door of their quarters. They were trimming each side of the path with large sea shells. They were stripped to the waist and the sun had already provoked a menacing burn on their backs. Peterson said, "Here comes that Western Union babe again. Get a load of them knockers!"

Randall did not look up from the problem which had occupied him for nearly an hour. Squatting before a pile of shells, he was trying to select a duplicate pair for each side of the doorway. That's the way Doolan wanted it and God-damned if that wasn't the way he was going to get it. Now Randall grumbled, "So what. She's old enough to be your mother. I'll bet she's thirty. What you want to do, wrestle with a Sherman tank?"

"She looks comfortable."

"Comfortable, hell. It would take a chain hoist to get her on a bed."

"Well, Jesus! A guy's got to do *somethin'!*"

"Don't get that desperate. You know what Doolan said. Lay off the local talent."

"What we supposed to do? Lay off the locals and don't go across the channel. What we supposed to do? *Starve?*"

"Affirmative."

"Anyway, her name is Trumpey. I found it out from Aubrey, the barber. He knows everything that gives in this whole Godforsaken base."

"How come you're talkin' to that pansy?"

"I got to get my hair cut, don't I? Besides, how you know he's a pansy?"

"Such ideas come to me when I see a guy lift his little finger higher than his coffee cup, and when I see him sashay along with his balloon butt, and when I hear him use words like sensational and très chic. I know."

Still watching Margaret, Peterson smiled and waved a shell in salute. She answered his wave with the roll of paper, but kept on walking. Peterson said, "Even if she is as old as thirty, even if that was so . . . I got a feeling that six months from now she'll look pretty damn good to me."

"Six months from now even Aubrey will look good to you."

Margaret passed the mess hall, which was opposite the Marine quarters.

Now, almost a year later, it was very plain why Luther Kidd had taken her to the J.C.C. picnic. And it wasn't very complimentary, no matter how you switched it around. One of the young wives made no attempt to conceal her fascination with Luther whenever she laid eyes on him. The husband was one of Luther's best customers and, furthermore, so very much liked that he had been elected president of the Chamber three times. Luther didn't dare wander loose about that picnic; and he certainly didn't want to announce his engagement to any girl officially or unofficially. So he invited Margaret Trumpey. He might be on the receiving end of a few laughs from the boys, but she made a hell of a fine shield! So be it. It was fun protecting Luther, even for that one night. It was the only genuine, dyed-in-the-wool, beginning-middle-and-end date she could remember.

Just beyond the mess hall she turned into a much smaller building which housed the establishment Pike had insisted be called the store instead of the post exchange. It also contained the post office and the barber shop. Lillian Strock, who served as clerk in the store and also as postmistress, was still sorting the mail which had arrived on the morning plane from Tuamani. Mrs. Strock was a faded blond who had lost her husband some ten years previously, a personal calamity which had left her with a constant air of martyrdom. All things in Mrs. Strock's life were verbally dated as before she lost her husband or after she lost her husband. Once begun, her adventures and trials of the before and after were difficult to silence. She only neglected to report that her husband was lost to another woman.

Now when she saw Margaret, she nodded and said, "Mornin'."

"What's for His Imperial Highness?"

Mrs. Strock handed her a large manila envelope and two smaller ones. Then she said, "What's this Pistol Two business? All the official stuff is addressed that way."

"It's our new name."

"To think I'd ever have to live in a place called Pistol Two! Why couldn't they pick a pretty name?"

"I just work here. See you, Mrs. Strock."

On her way out of the post office Margaret paused by the open door which led to the barber shop. She called a cheerful good morning to Aubrey Tinsman, who, as often as the occasion permitted, referred to his place as the beauty parlor and himself as a fashion stylist.

Aubrey said, "Good morning, my dear."

Below the waist Aubrey was considerably wider than about his shoulders, and as a result, his figure most nearly resembled a milk bottle. Now he left his barber chair, where he had been yawning over a movie magazine, and came toward her. Clasping his hands primly before him he smiled and said, "Off on your appointed rounds, my dear?"

"Through hail and sleet, nothing will stop me unless a coconut falls on my head."

Aubrey put one thin finger to his lips and looked at her appraisingly. Then he said, "I should like you to know that the sight of your statuesque beauty at this time every morning starts my day off sensationally."

"Aubrey, this is so sudden!"

Margaret laughed and raised her hand in a mock salute and went out into the street again. She walked rapidly toward the one group of palms which had been left standing in the area. She turned into the circular driveway of crushed coral, followed its course around a flag-pole, and knocked on the screen door of Pike's house. She heard him bark something unintelligible from the interior shadows and entered.

The Atlas Construction Company had done well by Herbert Zebulon Pike. Although the house was prefabricated, it managed an air of permanence, and the veranda which surrounded it on three sides was cool and spacious. Part of the veranda was designed to serve as a waiting room for those who might attend on the Governor. Here there were two benches and several chairs set about a round wicker table. Someone had already placed an array of American magazines on the table. This area, which might have been the introduction to any dentist's office, was separated from the rest of the veranda by a bamboo screen. Beyond the screen the furniture was less formally arranged and the veranda overlooked the sea.

Although she went to the Governor's house at least once every day, Margaret had seen nothing of the interior except Pike's office, which was just off the hallway to the right. This was a large room with only two attempts at decoration. An American flag stood in one corner, and on the wall opposite the veranda there was an enormous map of the Pacific. The room appealed to Pike's Spartan tastes. It reminded him of his office at Fort Sill, where he had briefly commanded a battalion of artillery. And when he thought about it, he could still hear the chink of spur chains on the bare floor as his officers reported to him. Those were good times then . . . between the big wars. There weren't a lot of damned reservists around taking all the gravy commands. It was a *regular* army then and if you weren't *regular* army you didn't stand a chance. Those were the days, he often told himself, when soldiers were soldiers. Artillery officers wore boots polished so you could see the sun in them, and they were careful that the only break in these boots was just above the ankle. They wore perfectly tailored whipcord breeches with a chamois patch inside the knee, and they wore spurs and chains even when they weren't mounted. And always there was about those men an agreeable and proper masculine aroma of whisky and horse manure. Now, in Pike's opinion, most soldiers, man and officer, smelled like garage mechanics and they looked like a bunch of God-damned civilians. In short, Pike did not know what the military was coming to.

It did not improve Pike's disposition to know that unless he declared a state of emergency, the Marine detachment on Nikki was for most purposes unavailable to him. Or that his only courier was a mere girl who slipped into his office wearing tennis shoes. He thought wistfully that his courier should be a properly booted young second lieutenant. And so now he looked up unhappily from his desk when he allowed himself to realize that Margaret stood waiting in the center of the room.

"Miss Trumpey . . . do you suppose you could knock before you enter this office?"

"I knocked at the door, sir. I thought that was enough. And you said come in."

"Never mind what I said. I don't like people creeping up on me."

"I'm sorry."

Pike extended his hand and she gave him the rolled weather map. Then she placed the three envelopes which were marked "Official" on his desk and held out the radioteletype. She turned to leave as Pike tore open the envelope.

"Just a minute, Miss Trumpey. I may want to send off a reply to this."

"I . . . doubt it . . . sir."

Displaying elaborate patience, Pike said, "Let me be the judge of that."

Then as Margaret waited in penitent silence, he read the message. And the veins in his neck stood out as she knew they would. While she tried to concentrate on the trade winds brushing the palms outside the window, she heard a low cry escape from Pike's throat. She had just time to think that it sounded like the bleat of a sick lamb back in Wisconsin when he said, "We'll see about *this!*"

"Do you want to send a reply, sir?"

Pike hesitated, and then slowly, as if the muscular effort were almost more than he could bear, his shoulders straightened. He laid the teletype down and aligned its edges with his desk blotter as carefully as if it were a directive to bombard Moscow.

"No. Go down to the carpenter shop and tell Dunbar to stop work on the two signs I ordered for the wharf. 'Welcome to Pike City' is one thing. 'Welcome to Pistol Two' is ridiculous."

"Yessir."

As Margaret crossed the veranda a man who had been waiting on one of the benches called to her.

"Miss?"

She turned in surprise to see a little man whom she vaguely remembered as a fellow passenger on the ship from Tuamani. He peered at her from beneath the brim of an enormous straw hat. He wore a brilliantly patterned hula shirt which was much too large for him and a pair of new khaki shorts long enough and wide enough to accommodate a man twice his size. Yet it was his eyes that held Margaret, for they were of a remarkable blue and now they sparkled mischievously as he smiled. He said, "Did you just leave the Governor?"

"Yes."

"What kind of a mood was he in?"

"Not good."

"Ah. That is going to make things rough."

The little man stared unhappily at the floor a moment and then the life returned to his eyes. He removed his hat and said, "I saw you on the ship and we've passed each other in the mess hall, but I never had a chance to say hello."

He bowed slightly and touched his banana-like nose as if the gesture was a part of his salute.

"The name is Pete Hildebrandt. And you are—"

"Margaret Trumpey. Hi! I work in communications."

"So? If you receive any mail for me would you return it to the sender marked 'addressee deceased'?"

Margaret laughed. "I don't have anything to do with the mail. I work in the radioteletype shack."

"Oh? Well, the same would apply to telegrams. Don't get the wrong idea. I'm not a fugitive from justice. . . . Just from my wife's family. You have no idea."

"Is that what brings you to Nikki?"

"Partly. It's as good a place to hide as any. I'm your sanitation expert. I'll bet you never knew there was the need for such a person."

"I really hadn't given it much thought."

"Few people do. Everybody knows we have to have supplies in a community like ours, but disposing of those supplies is rarely considered. So it's always easier to identify myself as your garbage man."

Again he bowed and then returned the straw hat to his head with a flourish. "I intended to discuss all that with the Governor, and if I could get a line on his mood maybe I could get some action in there. Is he alone now?"

"He was when I left."

"Then I'll take a chance. A thousand thanks for the information. If I can ever do anything for you, you'll find me in Building C. I share a room with our weatherman."

"Doesn't it get a little lonely for you sometimes?"

"He's a man of few words, all right. But sometimes we discuss music. As soon as another flute arrives I'm going to try and talk him into playing duets."

"Does he play a flute?"

Margaret tried very hard to match the little man's serious expression, but she found it almost impossible.

"No. I do. And I intend to teach Adam. You have to come by for our first recital."

"Just give me an invitation."

Pike was not prepared for Peter Hildebrandt. He was still brooding over the directive from Tuamani and trying to reconcile himself to the fact that a place named Pike City would never go down in history, when he saw Peter standing meekly in his doorway. Now, he thought, who is this clown? That shirt looks like a collapsed parachute. Oh God, what next?

"Good morning, Your Honor."

Pike answered him more crossly than he intended. It was the loss of Pike City as a name, he thought afterward. It had him all upset. He said to Peter, "I'm not a judge, sir, so the term 'Your Honor' is out of place here. Out of respect to the meaning of this office you should address me as Governor."

"Then good morning again, Governor. Can I have a few words with you about an important matter?"

"Of course," Pike said, regretting his harshness. "I'm

available for grievances at any reasonable time. What's yours?"

There, Pike thought. Go right to the core of things before the petitioner had a chance to beat around the bush. In so doing, you put subordinates on the defensive before they had a chance to justify themselves. "What is it, man? And I'd appreciate your being quick about it because I have a very busy morning scheduled."

This, Pike knew, was a considerable exaggeration, for after he had examined the weather map, which took only a few minutes, he had nothing whatever to do until lunchtime.

Peter Hildebrandt fiddled with the brim of his large hat, turning it around and around. Finally he said, "Governor, you have over two hundred people in this new community."

"I am well aware of that."

Who the hell, Pike wondered, was this fellow? He had seen him on the ship but could not place him now. Where the hell was Albright? He ought to be around at a time like this to identify visitors. Make a note. Set up regular visiting hours every morning and have Albright around to run things. "Go on," Pike said, finding it extremely difficult to give the little man his full attention. God, what a pair of shorts! Made the man look like an observation balloon. "Go on. . . ."

"These more than two hundred people are eating and drinking and opening boxes and cans several times a day. They are also defecating and urinating and washing and sweeping and, well . . . I tell you it's a problem."

"What's a problem?"

"Doing away with it all."

Pike was not certain he had heard the little man correctly. What the Sam Hill was he talking about? Was this some nut who had slipped through the Commission's screening? Make a note. Have Albright send immediately for a strait jacket. And make sure Doc Case had plenty of sedatives. Out of two hundred people someone was bound to go cuckoo sooner or later. Including myself, Pike thought ruefully. Between that fresh girl and her teletype about Pistol Two, and Sue-Anne groaning out her latest hangover down the hall . . . and now this fumbling fool . . .

"Go on, go on," Pike said impatiently.

"I want another dump, Governor."

"You what?"

"I want another dump. It's necessary."

"Sir, you are taking up a good deal of valuable time. Whatever your problem is, go see Mr. Albright."

"I did. He wasn't interested. If I may say so, Mr. Albright is not the type to explore this matter."

"Mr. Albright is my aide. He takes care of all the minor problems here."

"This is not a minor problem. If you would only listen to me . . ."

"I have been listening."

"I don't think you even know who I am."

Pike's voice rose. "And I am beginning not to care!"

Pike thought he would have to get some kind of directive from Tuamani allowing him more of a free hand with the marines. There ought to be one of them on duty outside the Governor's office. Cranks like this little man could be dangerous. His kind planted bombs and all sorts of things. There was, indeed, a mad glint in his eye. Now, without a marine in sight, the best thing to do was humor him.

Pike glanced at his wrist watch. "I am going to give

you fifteen more seconds, mister. Then you must excuse me."

"I need a lot more than fifteen seconds, Governor. This here matter will take a lot of figuring if it's going to be done right. Now . . ."

Pike was horrified to see his wife appear in the doorway. She still wore only a nightgown and her flesh was plainly visible through the filmy material. A cigarette hung from her lips and she held an ice bag in one hand. Her hair was matted on one side where she had apparently pressed the bag.

"Where'd you put the aspirin, Zebulon?"

"In the medicine chest where it belongs."

"That bottle's empty."

"Then there aren't any more. Can't you see I'm busy, Precious?"

Sue-Anne Pike looked at Peter Hildebrandt as if he were a creature just arrived from another planet. She moved across the doorway so that the light from the veranda was behind her, and Pike thought that she might just as well be naked. She cocked her head to one side, then moved very close to Peter until she was looking almost down upon him. She shook her head in disbelief, then passed her hand slowly across her eyes as if they had betrayed her. She made a pistol with her hand, raised it carefully to one eye, and pointed it at Peter. She worked her lips experimentally and swayed slightly when she said, "You look like a goblin to me. *Are* you a goblin?"

Peter made a quick little bow and in doing so contrived to step back far enough so that he would inhale a lesser concentration of bourbon.

"No, madame. I am your sanitation expert."

"Would you like to be a goblin?"

"I think maybe I would."

Sue-Anne slapped him triumphantly on the shoulder. "Good! I'll fix it up for you! I know a lot of goblins. A whole delegation came to call on me this morning."

Pike said, "If you will excuse us now, dear. Mister . . . er . . . this gentleman and I were discussing quite an important matter. Weren't we, sir?"

"Oh yes, indeed."

Peter's little eyes sparkled as he added, "This here we were talking about is something that's got to be taken care of right now. It's sort of an emergency."

"Well, I have an emergency, too. I damn well need some aspirin right now, Zebulon. How about you going down to the store and getting me some soon as you all are through talking? I got the willies."

Pike tried briefly and unsuccessfully to remember the time when Sue-Anne did not have the willies. Then he saw that Peter was watching him with open sympathy, and suddenly he was glad that he had come.

He said to Sue-Anne, "I'll see you get some aspirin in just a little while, Precious. Now if you'll excuse us . . ."

"Thank you, Zebulon. Beneath yoah stout chest beats a heart o' gold."

Moving with elaborate care she advanced on Peter. She bent down and took the lobe of his ear between her fingers. He felt the warm moisture of her breath as she whispered, "You can't fool me, mister. Don' you know you can't fool ol' Sue-Anne? I know. You're already a goblin!"

She swayed backward, took a moment to re-establish her bearings and veered off down the hall.

When she was gone, Pike sighed heavily. He was both surprised and pleased to hear Peter emit the same woeful sound.

Peter said, "You know, Governor, I've just got a hunch you'd feel better if I took a few minutes of your valuable time to tell you about my wife's family."

"Go ahead," Pike said. "Tell me."

Thus it was that Peter Hildebrandt and Herbert Zebulon Pike came to understand each other more than either one of them would ever have thought possible. It took Peter the better part of an hour to describe his wife's family. It took less than five minutes for Pike to authorize the location of a new refuse-disposal area exactly where Peter desired it.

"Peter, you just drop in and see me any time," Pike said warmly as he escorted him to the veranda.

"A cross borne by two is always lighter," Peter said.

Then he walked down the coral driveway whistling merrily. He would, he thought, create the most efficient and beautiful dump Herbert Zebulon Pike had ever seen.

3

Now that the people of Pistol Two had been in residence for nearly a month, their first enthusiasm waned and boredom settled like a heavy mist upon the colony. All activity concerned with Operation Zeus was still confined to Tuamani, and the people of Pistol Two waited their cue as minor actors forgotten by the director. Gossip provided a stimulant for many of the inhabitants, but the majority were left with a discussion of the nightly movie, complaining of the food in the mess hall, and rather apathetic fishing expeditions to the lagoon.

In Building C, Peter Hildebrandt began his first letter to his wife since his departure from the United States. Letters to Rose were always difficult, and now Peter frequently wet the stub of his pencil and paused for a considerable time between sentences. He wrote down, "Dear Rose . . ." and then he gazed out the screen window over his bunk until he had at last achieved a state of near hypnosis. It helped when writing to Rose.

Well, here I am on Nikki and I'm glad you're not here too. . . .

Astonished at the force of his subconscious, he erased the last part and substituted a wish that Rose could be with him.

but I guess you can't leave Helen who I guess is still ailing and after all she is your sister and probably you wouldn't be satisfied knowing that Eugene didn't have a place to eat where he could get home cooking. After all Eugene is your brother as you always point out. Just don't feed him steaks too often even if he does love them—unless he should just happen to pick one up from the grocery store and bring it back to the house at his own expense. I don't think it would be fair to Eugene if he became too accustomed to steaks because some day he might get married even if he is nearly forty-eight and with his income it might be difficult to buy steaks for two. Give my regards to your father and wish him a happy eighty-fifth birthday when it comes which I think is soon—but tell him I suggest he doesn't try to drink a whole fifth of my Scotch like he did last year to celebrate because #1 —I doubt if there's any Scotch left if Eugene is still there and #2—your father is getting on and I don't care what the doctors say about Scotch being good for his circulation. #3—It would be better if he took such medical treatment in his own home and why doesn't he try it just once? Also give my regards to your Aunt Grace. Tell her she can play any of my records she wants but please not my

Brandenburg Concertos. Those are the ones I bought after she let her cat play with my other albums.

Regards to your cousins, India and also Bessie. When India borrows my Ford again to go to the Gray Ladies will you remind her to put a few gallons of gas in the tank? I know about India's war with the oil companies and all about how the officials stay up nights figuring out ways especially to get her just because she sold Sinclair short in 1930 and how she wouldn't buy another drop of any oil product no matter what, *but the car won't run without it.* Tell her to charge the few gallons to me. It's cheaper than a push which cost sixty-six dollars for a new fender like last time.

And regards to all the rest of your family who were pretty nice about coming over to the house and saying good-by. I forget how many stayed for drinks and dinner but I vaguely remember there were eleven. Oh, and thanks to Max for bringing back my overcoat he borrowed last year. Of course, I really don't need it out here. And special thanks to your Uncle Stanley who brought along that pint of peach brandy as a bon voyage gift. I broke it out on the ship and it made me sicker than a dog but I know he didn't intend it that way. Like he said, "One drink deserves another and if I can drink your Scotch it's only right you should have some of my brew."

Peter's pencil now required sharpening and he spent as long as he could in the process. It was almost five o'clock and soon his roommate would return from the showers.

When he had brought his pencil to a needle-like point, Peter carefully picked up the shavings and threw them into the metal wastebasket. Then he returned to the window, where he stood for several minutes admiring his new dump which he could see in the distance at the end of the airstrip. At first Peter had been dubious about placing the dump so near the airstrip. The smoke, he thought, might interfere with landing airplanes. But he had talked with Dana Wood, who flew down with the mail every day from Tuamani, and he had said that the dump was no hindrance at all. Actually he claimed that since the control tower was not yet manned, the smoke was a great aid in determining the wind force and direction, and, said Dana, he could often see it miles away.

Peter was pleased about that. It was sort of satisfying to know the dump served a dual purpose and that a lonely airman over the sea might first become aware of Nikki through Peter Hildebrandt's work. Sort of a lighthouse, he mused. People just didn't know all the things that went into shooting off one single bomb like Zeus.

Peter left the window reluctantly and sat down on his bunk. He fiddled with his pencil a moment and then wrote rapidly.

Well Rose, I guess that's about it for now. This is a nice island and all of the people who came down here at the same time I did seem very nice indeed. In a way you could say it's a typical American community. Not very big maybe, but we have all the same problems except parking.

I live with a nice young fellow named Adam Smith. He's the weatherman here. I'm still not sure whether he's just shy or what, but he certainly is a great one for keeping to himself. He's from some place in Vermont. I sort of feel sorry for him because most of the time he's alone and when he does sit down with a bunch of the fellows in the mess hall they give him a terrible kidding about the weather. Just seems that when he says it's going to rain it doesn't and if he says it will be a nice night for the movies it rains cats and dogs. Of course these tropical rains never last more than a few minutes but it's enough to soak everybody. I've sent for another flute, (Sears Roebuck) and he says he's willing to try learning to play it. Maybe it will loosen him up a bit, like joining in music sometimes does. Shyness doesn't last long if there's good music around.

Enough for now. I guess winter has pretty well set in back there. Don't forget to drain the toilet in the garage. If the pipes bust you'll have to hire a plumber and even with the fancy pay I get out here you know we can't afford luxuries like plumbers.

I'll write again soon.

Knowing that he would not, Peter scrawled a "Love to all" across the bottom of his writing pad, signed his name, and slipped the paper in an envelope. He was licking the flap when Adam Smith entered the room.

Adam wore only a bath towel and turned his back when he slipped into his pants.

"Good shower?"

"Yup."

"How about a flute session? I could sort of break you in on mine until yours gets here."

"I . . . don't have the time tonight."

Puzzled, Peter watched him take a fresh khaki shirt from his locker. What was this no-time business? When he was through with his nightly forecast Adam should have all the time in the world. So did everybody else on Nikki until Zeus really started cranking up. Now Peter saw that he buttoned his shirt with unusual care and brushed his short hair as if it actually made a difference. Peter was disappointed. He had been looking forward to giving a flute lesson.

"Out on the town tonight, friend?"

"Sort of."

"I don't wear this long nose for nothing. My wife calls it my radar because it's always poking into other people's business. So I'm obliged to ask you . . . what's her name, or rather, since I assume you're not mixed up with the Governor's wife . . . which one is it?"

"You wouldn't know her."

"But I would. A talented scavenger can't help knowing a lot of things. People throw away their immediate past you might say. And I pick it up. You'd be surprised at the things I knew about people back home when I was supervisor of fourteen trucks. Why, I knew who was drinking too much, and who was trying to meet their household budget and who just had a new baby, and who was on a diet and so on and so on. Lots of people think being a scavenger is disgusting. I always thought it was very interesting if you kept your eyes open. By the time you reach my age, keeping your eyes open gets to be a habit . . . which is why I'm ninety-five per cent sure I know the young lady you have in mind."

Adam smiled, but he remained silent as he bent over and tied his shoes.

"It would be that girl who works in communications . . . the one with the bowling pin legs . . . the one who's got sense enough to know she doesn't need make-up. I met her at the Governor's house one day. Nice kid. But you aren't going to get very far with her."

Adam paused in lacing his shoes. His hands remained still for a moment, but he did not look up. Then slowly he resumed his lacing. He said, "Oh?"

"No sir, you won't get anywhere and I'll tell you why if you'll just listen to an old man for a minute."

Adam straightened and, looking at Peter, he forced a half-smile. Then he turned his back and began transferring matches, pipe, and tobacco pouch to his new pants.

"I haven't the slightest desire to *get* anywhere with her."

"What're you taking her out for then . . . a political discussion? You need a button sewed on or something? Next thing you're going to tell me is that there are other things besides sex."

"There are."

"Don't you believe it. That idea was invented by people who can't get it. What are you going to talk about—Zeus?"

"Maybe."

"If you do it will be the last you'll see of her. That girl's got a sense of humor and you better develop one quick."

"I'll see what I can do."

"And wipe that sad look off your face. You look like a pallbearer."

"I've had a bad day."

"Tell your troubles to me. Then you won't to her."

"Our Governor Pike."

"What's his strain . . . besides his wife?"

"He has a very low opinion of all meteorologists . . . especially me. . . ."

Adam paused and for a moment Peter saw a flash of true anger in his eyes. This, he thought, was encouraging. Deep within Adam there was spirit then, and something was eating at that spirit. Just now he reminded Peter of a young man whose house he had once serviced. He had been a quiet young man held in complete domination by his wife. And it was he who meekly lined the garbage pails with paper every morning before he went to the office. And Peter had several times heard him give what he was sure was a standard answer to his wife, "Yes, dear." Then one day Peter read about the young man and knew he had lost an account. His customer had embezzled fifty-thousand dollars from his firm and run off with what the newspapers called a honey-haired matron

. . . who just happened to be his boss's wife. So you never knew. And what's more, Peter thought with strange satisfaction, they never caught the young man, either. He was probably having a hell of a time. His mind drifted back to Adam.

"Why let Pike's opinion bother you?"

"In the beginning I didn't. But he keeps needling me. He says he would rather depend on his neuritis than my maps. All this because he happened to get rained on twice in the movies! Golly, I can't tell when one of these tropical cumulus is going to let go. Nobody can! It's a matter of dew point and temperature for each individual cloud and I can't fly around like a sea gull taking readings on every cloud. He won't even read my forecasts any more."

"Can't you just say, possible showers? That's what the experts always say back home. Either way, they're right."

"Not with Pike. He damn well wants to know exactly what's going to happen and I'm tired of telling him only God knows that. You'd think the whole of Operation Zeus depended on my daily weather analysis for this one little stinking atoll."

"It does *not* stink. I've seen to that. And yet I can't say I've received any fan mail for my efforts."

Adam's sudden anger subsided as he lit his pipe. He glanced at his watch, then strode to the window, where he stood silently watching the trade-wind clouds flow past the edge of the roof. Then as if he were speaking to the clouds rather than to Peter, he said slowly, "I dunno . . . I don't care what a man does, he likes to be proud of it; and if he tries hard he likes to be at least respected for trying. Meteorology is supposed to be a science, which it is, but no science will prove itself out consistently unless you know the exact behavior of all the elements involved. So a lot of times meteorology becomes a guessing game and that's where the trouble comes with people like Pike. For that matter there are more jokes about the weatherman than any other profession I can think of. . . ."

"I don't suppose you've ever heard a joke about the garbage man?"

"You don't hear jokes about chemists, engineers, musicians, or, let's say, architects . . . at least not as direct insults to their professional ability. That's what finally gets you down. . . ."

"You're working in futures. That always gives someone else a chance at hindsight."

"If Pike tosses my forecast in the wastebasket once more or sends over a message like 'Tell that fumbling wizard to get himself a new crystal ball,' or says that the whole weather setup here ought to be eliminated to save the taxpayers' money and he ought to get his forecasts teletyped down from Tuamani, where they know their business . . . if he keeps on like that I'm going to blow my top."

"Good. It's long past time. Maybe it will make you more of a human being."

"Just what do you mean by that?"

"I never saw a young fellow with so damn many complexes! Where the hell did you acquire them all? Keep on the way you are and someday you'll bust wide open."

"I'm doing all right."

Peter snorted. He would have been happier, he thought, if the whole conversation had never started. But it was too late to retreat now.

"*Sure*, you're doing all right! You don't say six words to anybody on this whole atoll all day. You work alone and you walk to the mess hall alone unless I deliberately tag along, and you might as well be eating alone because you sit there like a Sing Sing prisoner. It doesn't cost anything to be pleasant to people. They won't bite if you say good morning or good night or even go to hell."

"I haven't anything especially to say."

"Well, find something! You must have said something to make a date with that communications girl."

"No. . . ."

"Well, then will you kindly explain to this ignorant old man how you managed to arrange a rendezvous? Or did you employ sign language?"

"I don't really have a date with her. It's just your idea that I have."

Peter regarded him solemnly for a moment. Finally he said, "I see. You aren't going to be a complete damn fool and try to cross the channel, are you? I somehow don't picture you as swimming the Hellespont."

"No. Nothing like that. I take walks down to the wharf occasionally. I like it down there. You get a good view of the sea. Can I help it if she seems to like it down there, too?"

"So you just sort of *happen* to run into each other down there. Is that it?"

"That's it. That's all there is to it."

"Do you hold a small conversation?"

"Not so far."

"Try it. Pass the time of day and send the bill to me. Try something original like, 'It sure is a nice evening,' as an opener."

When Adam left, Peter stood in the middle of the room and stared at the floor for a long time. And he was not, to his surprise, very lonely, because he was so involved in thinking about Adam. What a dull fellow! What a nothing! And then he remembered the young man who had stolen the wife and the fifty-thousand dollars . . . also, Peter recalled, an astonishingly dull fellow.

He stepped to the metal cabinet at the foot of Adam's bed. It was exactly like his own and served as a combination clothes locker and dresser. He opened the two top drawers and peered hopefully inside. He was disappointed for he could find nothing of any interest. The blindest man could go through my locker, he mused, and come away with at least some line on my personality. Among other things he would find a stack of pennies, two boy-scout knives, a compass, foot powder, fishline, two extra pairs of glasses, a red necktie still folded in its gift box, and, of course, my flute.

Yet here, in Adam's locker, there was nothing but clothes—neatly folded, if that meant anything. Peter closed the drawers in disgust. The man was a cipher! But then so was that rascal with the fifty-thousand dollars and his boss's wife.

Deep in thought, Peter crossed the room to his own locker and almost automatically took out his flute. He sat down gingerly on the end of his bed and wet his lips. As he raised the flute toward his mouth, his eyebrows and playing fingers also ascended as if they were attached to the instrument. He took a deep breath and poised himself for the opening notes of his favorite movement in the Vivaldi sonata.

He hesitated, and for a moment his mind lost all contact with the music. Wasn't it so that banks were never robbed by forceful men? And corporation officers almost never embezzled; it was always some obscure little clerk? And the reasons were not always financial, for they sometimes confessed they simply didn't understand what it was that compelled them to take the money. Who committed hatchet murders? Big, roaring men with primeval tempers? Never. The pictures in the paper always revealed some mouse of a citizen, previously notorious only for mowing his lawn on the Sabbath.

He decided he would have to do some more thinking about Adam Smith. A cipher was not always a circle with nothing in the middle.

He puckered his lips and changed his mind about the Vivaldi sonata. No! The mood was all wrong. He would stimulate his thinking apparatus with a little Mozart. Much better! He took a deep breath and tootled happily until long after the sun had set.

By increasing his pace slightly Adam managed to arrive in front of the carpenter shop just ahead of Margaret. And when it became obvious they would be the only people walking along the street which led down to the wharf, he said, "Good evening."

And he thought that if she was surprised she certainly didn't show it, nor did she seem to mind when he fell into step beside her. She simply said, "Well, good evening, Mr. Smith. And how are you?"

"You don't have to call me Mr. Smith, do you?"

"I guess not. What should I call you?"

"Adam."

"My name is Margaret."

"I know that."

They walked slowly toward the wharf, and after Adam had cleared his throat experimentally, he finally said that Margaret looked different to him.

"Well, I'm wearing lipstick if that's what's different. And I never wear this dress to work."

Adam said he didn't think it was the lipstick or the dress, but maybe it was the way they were walking along together just like they might as well be strolling down the street of some little town in the States, and in some ways it was sort of surprising to him that they couldn't stop in somewhere and have an ice-cream soda.

And Margaret said that yes, she had the same feeling, and wasn't it strange that here they were five thousand miles from anywhere and doing just what people did at home and that it was hard to believe it would all be over in less than a year, and everything just left to wither away in the trade winds.

Adam thought for a while and finally agreed that was a pretty good way of putting things all right because it was picturesque to think of the whole settlement just completely empty of people and having no purpose any more and the buildings standing there in the evening light just like now and wind whistling through the empty buildings just like she said.

Margaret replied that it was a sure thing Adam hadn't made such a long speech ever since he came to Nikki, and he laughed and agreed that maybe it was, and added that he was sorry he just had to think things out before he said anything and since he was a very slow thinker people sometimes just gave up and departed before they heard what he had to say.

Then they were both silent for a long time and remained so even after they reached the wharf. All the way from the carpenter shop they had walked very slowly, and when they reached the wharf Adam found two boxes near the warehouses and set them upright so they could have something cleaner than the creosoted planks to sit on. As he placed them side by side he saw that Margaret was smiling at him.

"Please," he said, adjusting one of the boxes so that it faced the sea.

"Oh, thank you," Margaret said. She sat down quickly.

Adam moved his box a few inches farther away from her and lowered himself to it cautiously. His knees were almost level with his chin.

"You have the longest legs," Margaret said.

"In school they used to call me the stork."

Adam lit his pipe, and again there was a long silence between them. They watched the sun dip into the sea and listened to the swift water in the channel gurgling among the pilings of the wharf and they heard a bell tolling in the village across the water.

Looking at the sun, Adam finally said, "There may be a green flash tonight."

"What do you mean by that?"

"Sometimes in the tropics when it's a clear evening like this and conditions are just right otherwise, you'll see a bright green flash in the sky just after the sun goes down. But you have to watch carefully. It only lasts a second or so."

"You like the sky, don't you, Adam?"

"I do."

"Where I come from there's a lot of it."

"There's a lot of sky everywhere. The trouble is, people spend most of their time looking down instead of up."

"It does prevent stumbling."

"Yeah. But they miss so much. Now. . . . Watch!"

Adam nodded at the bronze glow on the horizon which lingered after the sun. Then, far above it, the sky suddenly became a vivid green. The coloring endured for so short a time, Margaret was not certain she had actually seen it. Yet, glancing quickly at Adam's face, she saw a look of such genuine pleasure she knew he would be disappointed if she had missed the spectacle. And so she said softly, "I liked it very much."

"Pretty spectacular, huh?"

"I like what it does to you. You communicate with the outside world. You talk to people like me. I was beginning to think you were pretty much of a snob."

Even as she said it Margaret regretted it. For she saw the look of contentment die on Adam's face and he seemed visibly to withdraw within himself. Why had she said it? Why take a crack at Adam Smith, who was just another young man and not a very imposing one at that? In Beloit there were a lot of Adam Smiths and even if they lacked the color of a movie hero, or seemed obsessed by money and sex, there was no reason to spit in their eye. Smart girls sighed and told them they were wonderful. And they lived happily ever after. At least most of them tried to act like they did.

Now watching Adam she was almost certain of what he would say even before he stood up.

"Well," he said, turning his back to the twilight, "I guess that's that."

Trying to hide her disappointment Margaret rose beside him and thought that only Adam's legs justified any comparison with a stork. She looked up into his face, appreciating the bones and the crevices which might have been expected in a much older man, and she was certain she saw great inner strength. She said halfheartedly, "If we're going to get any chow we'd better go now. I guess it'll be pork chops tonight because it's Tuesday."

"Okay."

She thought, Well, it's sure a romantic setting down here on the wharf anyway.

He stepped to the edge of the wharf and looked down at the swirling water. It was almost black now and the eddies and whirlpools melted together until the whole surface of the channel appeared violently disturbed. As he stood watching the water, Margaret realized that he was smiling.

"What's so funny?"

"Nothing. I was just looking at those little whirlpools down there and getting some ideas."

At least, Margaret thought, he's not laughing at me. And she thought, too, that they were both terribly clumsy with each other and so nothing would come of this meeting. But then why should she expect anything to come of it?

Finally, when she was sure he had forgotten her, Adam turned and took a step toward her, and the expression on his face was so strange that for one panic-stricken second she thought he was going to kiss her. And then she saw that it was a trick of the dusk light about his face and that what she had mistaken for lust was only a mischievous grin. She was not sure whether she should feel pleased or sorry.

"When you take my weather map to Pike in the mornings . . . does he ever say anything in particular?"

Margaret was trying to remember the last time she had been kissed and was amazed that she could not. She knew that it had to be in high school, but she could not remember either the boy or the event. And now I am twenty-nine!

"How do you mean, does he say anything in particular?" She heard her own voice echo so softly in the dusk it seemed to come from another person. The thought of standing in Adam's arms caused her whole body to become moist very suddenly and she thought, Well, so this is what it's like and why should I be so affected when I don't even know him?

Adam said, "So you won't talk."

". . . about what?"

"About Pike."

"Oh, he's all right. His bark is just a lot worse than his bite."

Cliché—cliché! Oh, you're a great conversationalist, Margaret! Continue and you will fascinate the man, as you have so many others!

"I didn't ask after his health. He can choke during one of his tantrums for all I care. I just wanted to know if when you take the map to him in the morning does he read it, or change it, or toss it away?"

Is this all we can find to talk about . . . on a wharf? On a tropical evening? Margaret desperately searched her memory. She could remember nothing Pike might have said which would be of the slightest interest. Why did Adam care so much what Pike said? After a moment she was amazed to find herself saying, "Well, one morning he allowed as how there was nothing like having a good weather map around."

Adam placed his hands on her shoulders, and the touch of his fingers on her flesh completely destroyed her surface calm.

"You're not telling the truth."

"No. I'm not. Why is it so important, Adam?"

"One of the most important things about this whole operation is the weather analysis. Conditions have to be just right before the explosion takes place; otherwise, there could be hell to pay. If we get the wind wrong, I hate to think of the damage that godawful firecracker can do for thousands of miles around. It's not the scientists who will decide when Zeus blows its top. It's us . . . the meteorologists."

"I should think that would make you feel quite proud."

"It might, even if this is only an auxiliary station. The

trouble is Pike has made up his mind all meteorologists are crazy. He has never even been down to the weather office. He ignores my reports and makes up his own according to the way his neuritis behaves. I'm helpless now and I could be helpless when explosion day rolls around. That just might not be very funny, and Pike could turn out to be the greatest villain in history. Unfortunately, I would be hung with him."

His hands were still on her bare shoulders and she found that she wanted them to stay there. She tipped her head back just a trifle, just enough so that if he did decide to kiss her, well, maybe it wouldn't turn out to be a complete disaster. But he did not move. Instead he said insistently, "Tell me the truth. Have you ever actually seen Pike read one of my forecasts? Does he change the summary I make up for Tuamani?"

She waited. Now his hands seemed cold and she wanted to twist away from them. She sought his eyes, trying to discover in them what she thought she had seen before. But the quick tropical twilight had gone and his face was only a silhouette against the sky.

"Is that why you spoke to me tonight, Adam? Is that why we talked? You just wanted information?"

"Well, partly . . . sure. My neck is long enough now. It doesn't need stretching."

"Good night, Adam."

She turned away from him very suddenly and ran along the wharf until she came to the place where it met the street. The sound of her shoes hitting the crushed coral was easier than it had been on the planks of the wharf, and she was very aware of it and grateful for the softer sound, because now, she thought, I don't sound so much like another husky girl running away from the truth. And I must not sound that way—*ever!*

Adam looked after her, and when she had disappeared he reached for his pipe and clamped down on the stem hard with his teeth. You can see what happens when you open your big mouth, he said to the dark whirlpools in the channel. Now how can I tell her I'm sorry and that she took what I said the wrong way? Or at least not the way I meant it. Because for one thing, I guess I like her a lot more than any girl I've ever met.

He stood watching the dark, swiftly moving water for a long time. Finally from across the channel, he heard the sound of hymn-singing. He found peace in its easygoing rhythm, and so he sat down on the box and looked at the few lights across the channel and listened, and wished Margaret were still sitting beside him.

4

The Mormon church was the largest structure in the village of Nikki. It was built of plaster. The roof and gables were of red corrugated iron and the design was straight New England. There was a graveyard behind the church, and a wooden shed. During the daytime the interior of the church was illuminated by windows which had been opaqued in squares with varicolored paints so that they resembled stained glass. When they were pushed open, the sea and the coconut palms, lashing softly in the trade wind, were visible to the congregation. During the evening service the interior of the church was less spirited because the congregation was sleepy and the illumination came from a single bare bulb hanging from the high ceiling. It took energy from a generator powered by a one-cylinder gasoline engine and housed in a wooden shed. The exhaust of the motor had rusted through and now it made a terrible racket, at times overwhelming the soft and lazy hymns which the people of Nikki liked to sing.

"Onward, Christian Soldiers" had never been popular on Nikki. It was too strident, too energetic, and altogether unsuited to the Polynesian way of cherishing a note and letting it develop fully and enthusiastically in the throat until of its own variation it became another note and then another, each melting into the other, until the moment required for breathing became a mystery. The devout on Nikki much preferred the slower hymns, and they further slowed the original rhythms until their voices rose and fell as easily and peacefully as the wind outside the windows. Thus such medium-paced standards as "The Church in the Wildwood" became so lethargic and soothing that both the elders sitting before the altar and the congregation in their pews were often mesmerized. Only the noise of the generator motor kept them alert enough to follow the service.

And so the task of arousing her fellow worshipers often fell upon the woman Huahenga, who was exceedingly well qualified. For when Huahenga lifted her head and almost visibly captured the trade wind beneath her vast bosom, her beginning notes of song could be heard even by the night fishers prowling the coral at the far end of the channel. Huahenga weighed three hundred pounds. She invariably clothed her body in spotless white and the total effect was that of a cumulus cloud which had somehow descended into the church and found itself joyous with voice.

Once Huahenga had shocked the congregation with an introductory note, then assistance flowed toward her from various places among the pews. Karara, who was the star of her Bible class and who braided her pigtails so cleverly the gray hairs were almost invisible, liked to join Huahenga on the second note of the hymn, although she invariably chose an octave lower. Subsequently her friend Apakura would rise and spread her bare feet wide so that the floor breeze could billow the hem of her moo-moo gown and pass easily upward to cool her bottom. And she would tip back her head and shout out a rhythmic counterpoint which never varied, but which seemed to fit every hymn perfectly.

The total effect was satisfying to the elders. For the younger women of Nikki would stop fiddling with their hair and close their French movie magazines and sing, and the children of Nikki would cache the bubble gum they had bought at Yip Kee's and they would sing, and the older men of Nikki would rouse themselves from their dreams and sing, and even the few young men who were in the church because they had cut a toe on the coral, or had a sorry belly from drinking too much soda pop, or were otherwise incapacitated from fishing in the lagoon, would stand up and brace their powerful shoulders, and they would allow their embarrassed voices to make a humming sound beneath the melody.

It was inevitable that the young marines, Randall and Peterson, would first be drawn to the source of so much noise and light. They swam the channel because they had been told not to swim the channel and because they were young and had joined the Marines to see the world and because they were convinced that the relative darkness in the native village only served to conceal certain mysteries in which they would very much like to participate.

"Listen!" Randall said, as they stood gazing across the channel. "Listen to that singing . . . only it ain't singing.

It's like you call a chant, and right now I bet they're getting all squared away for one of those orgies where the girls run around naked or maybe just carrying a torch!"

Peterson coughed, trying to conceal the hunger in his voice. Then he said, "Pike claims they don't do things like that."

"To hell with what Pike says! How's he know what goes on over there? You think they tell *him?* Why, I bet they have ancient ceremonies nobody ever seen, and here we stand like a couple of jerks when we could be dancin' and drinkin' and doin' things we could be tellin' people about for the next hundred years!"

Peterson looked down at the swift black current and said that he wouldn't mind at all being the father of some kid who was maybe a little dark-skinned and had a tow-head like his own; he would even send money from the United States after he got back there, and also he had heard for damn sure that such an arrangement was exactly what all the natives in the South Seas wanted; in fact, they wanted it so much that sometimes they would actually pay a white man to sleep with one of their daughters, or at least, if they were short of cash, they would feed him and treat him like a king and make him so comfortable he just never wanted to go home. "I read it in a book," he said, to establish his information as a fact.

"Well, then let's get the hell over there! We can wade halfway across if we start farther up by the little point. Then we drift down with the current, only we don't drift, we swim like we never swum before, and we wind up right in front of the village! There ain't really nothin' to it."

"There will be somethin' to it if Doolan catches us," Peterson said mournfully. "Or the sharks like white meat."

"What can Doolan do? Ship us back home. Is that bad?"

"I don't want a dishonorable discharge."

"Who's gonna get a dishonorable? If we do get sent home we can just say Doolan is a friggin' fiend and we was abused. That's all there is to it. But we won't get caught. All we got to do is swim over there, see an orgy, swim back before dawn, and say good mornin', Sergeant Doolan, you dumb son of a bitch and don't you wish you were all unfrustrated like us?"

"It will be better if we keep our mouths shut and don't say nothin'."

Now Peterson and Randall, still breathing heavily from their swim, stood in the shadows outside the Mormon church. They wore only their T shirts and pants, which were soaking wet. They were so cold they had difficulty keeping their teeth from chattering. The water in the channel had proved much colder than they had expected, and the distance to swim was much greater because the current had carried them almost to the mouth of the channel, where it met the ocean. As they made their way slowly toward the church and paused beneath a palm, the wind passing through their garments caused enough evaporation to chill them thoroughly.

And inside the fire of their youth was even colder.

"That," said Peterson, standing on his toes so he could see through the open doorway of the church, "is not exactly what I would call an orgy."

"Well, it *sounded* like it, didn't it? How can anybody tell when they sing like that?"

"Where, Mister Wise Guy, is all the dames running around with no clothes on and carryin' torches? Go ahead. I risked my life gettin' here. Now show me."

"Well," Randall said in a voice that had lost all conviction. "Maybe something will turn up."

"Like a cigrett? You can't even buy a cigrett in this

creep town. They probably arrest you if they catch you smokin' a cigrett. I heard about these Mormons. They don't allow anybody to have fun. Not even theirselves."

"I heard a guy can have a hundred wives if he wants. How about that, Pete? How would you like to have a hundred wives?"

Peterson did not answer for a moment. He moved cautiously toward the church door so that he could see more of the interior, and he thought that he would sure as hell feel a lot easier about things if he was wearing his boondockers instead of being barefooted because you never could tell what people like those inside were going to do. They might take a dim view of a guy like Randall doing night patrol on their front lawn wearing just his skivvies and that awful smile he used every time he saw a woman, no matter if she was ten or seventy years old.

Peterson ventured even further toward the doorway until he almost stood in the light. Now he could see the whole interior of the church and the elders sitting before the altar, and he decided that it looked pretty much like a Tuesday evening back in the Methodist church in Elmira, New York, where he wished he was right this minute. Except that the people were dark, of course, and the only organ seemed to be a built-in job which was wearing a white dress. And for a moment, listening to Huahenga's voice soar to the roof and reverberate down again, he forgot his chill. When at last her voice subsided until it became only a delicate overtone to the others, Peterson forgot himself and leaned against the doorway entranced. He remained so, motionless, until a touch on his arm startled him.

He turned quickly and was ready to ask Randall just what the hell he thought he was up to, creeping up on him like that when he was jumpy enough already, and then he saw that it was not Randall at all, but a small man who needed a shave and a new eye. Randall was still back in the shadows, but now he came up quickly.

"Well, m'lads! Having a peep at the show?"

Terry Mack displayed his two remaining front teeth and fixed his good eye at first on Peterson and then on Randall, whose fists had automatically doubled at his side. "Now then yer wet and that's a shame. You'll catch a death."

"We was just lookin' around," Randall said defensively.

"Yeah, that's right . . . just lookin'," Peterson agreed. "We were out fishin' and our boat dumped over, and, well, here we are."

Terry Mack scratched his chest. Now since Peterson and Randall had moved so close together he could survey them both with his good eye. He said, "Balls, m'lads. I see ye swim over here. All ye Yanks is balmy. Lucky ye didn't drown."

Randall relaxed his fists and assumed his most diplomatic air, favoring Terry Mack with the smile he normally reserved for sergeants who had something on him.

"We were hot," he said. "And we just thought we'd cool off by going for a little swim. The current carried us away from the other side."

"If that's the story yer thinkin' of tellin' the Guv'nor, ye better find a fancier one," Terry advised.

"We don't want no trouble," Randall said hastily. "We'll just swim back and suppose you make like you never saw us."

"I wouldn't think of it. My woman wouldn't talk to me for twenty-eight days if I let ye lads try to swim the channel again. I'll take ye back in my canoe."

"Well, say, thanks!" Randall said, greatly relieved. Then he looked more thoughtfully at Terry Mack, surprised that his grand manner seemed to actually increase his size. In the light from the church doorway he could see his frizzy hair and the stubble of his beard and the crudely patched shirt which, with the tails out, hung almost to his knees.

"*You* have a woman?" Randall asked so directly that Peterson wanted to slink into the shadows and hide because, he thought, Randall has no damned manners at all and is always going around sticking his nose in other people's business which is how we got in this bind in the first place and now here he is doing it again.

"Of course I got a woman. Ye can't avoid 'em."

"We seem to be able to," Randall said.

"Ye want to go to church?" Terry Mack asked.

Both Randall and Peterson hesitated, and then at once they uttered unfinished sentences which, jumbled together, somehow came out as flat denials.

"I didn't think so," Terry Mack said. Then he waggled his frizzy head and added, "Not much happens here. So it's good to see you even if ye are Yanks. Come avec moi."

Terry Mack revolved as if he had been standing on a potter's wheel and without looking back set off into the darkness. Randall glanced at Peterson and the hope had returned to his eyes. "This is more like it!"

"I dunno," Peterson said doubtfully. Yet with one long step he was beside Randall, who was already pursuing the diminutive figure down the street.

The custom was easy to establish. After night had descended solidly and dependably upon the atoll, Sue-Anne Pike began to relax. This was not a physical manifestation, but a degree of mental tranquillity, which she reached as soon as she emptied her fourth bourbon. The feeling crept upon her softly, enclosing her brain in a gossamer web which allowed her to see through to the outer world and yet served as a protection. She was not drunk. Nor did she stagger, weave, or display any other evidence of physical uncertainty. Sue-Anne seldom surrendered to the "vapors" state in spite of what certain people in Pistol Two reported. She was normally too skillful a drinker and a vapors condition, during which she might miss a great many things, was very much against her desires. Therefore, she rationed herself carefully after the fourth bourbon had enclosed her consciousness in its gentle webbing.

The fifth and the sixth and the seventh drinks she sipped slowly and cautiously according to the needs of the web; when it threatened to become too finely meshed and reduce her outside visibility, she would allow a considerable time to pass so that the delicate balance might restore itself, or she would move her body, or eat a handful of popcorn, or show her charm bracelet to someone handy, or go to the bathroom, or almost anything to avoid becoming a slob. For she knew very well what she was like when she became a slob and it disgusted her. She swore and she yelled. She used four- and eleven-letter words indiscriminately; and if there was no one around who cared about restraining her, she had a well-nigh irresistible urge to remove at least part of her clothing. She insulted all other women present who would stand still long enough to hear her, accusing them of every conceivable kind of bitchery, and if their men attempted to defend them, she reviled the men also. All of which had made life very difficult for officers and wives of all ranks inferior to Pike during his years of active duty. Nor had she ever spared his superiors on these disastrous occasions, which was one of the several reasons Pike's military career had limped to such a prosaic conclusion.

"Wal, now, you and Sue-Anne had jes' better have a lil talk," was an opening phrase Pike had learned to dread. It was like a first salvo. Sue-Anne was getting the range, and once she had the target bracketed, she pounded away without mercy. She was never sorry until the next morning, at which time she loathed herself.

She strove with equal anxiety to avoid the opposite condition, wherein the mesh of the web widened for some reason and dissolved and she discovered to her horror that, in the middle of her fifth or sixth drink, she was uncomfortably sober. Then she would recognize the absurdities of others who had been drinking with her; and far worse, discover a shockingly clear vision of herself. As if emerging from a cocoon, she saw a faded blond wearing too much lipstick and such a collection of bracelets, earrings, pendants, and other odd jewelry that she jangled and bangled with every movement. She saw eyes that were vague and at the same time troubled. She beheld a multitude of tiny wrinkles which spiked downward from her eyes and the corners of her mouth, and no combination of novelty necklaces and rings could hide the crinkled skin about her neck and hands. She saw, too, and the revelation was almost more frightening than any other, that her breasts sagged and that her belly was a distinct mound. Sucking in her breath helped a little, but was limited in time, and standing up straight was too difficult to remember. It was much easier to distract attention from her belly by displaying her legs, which still merited honest appreciation.

Sue-Anne feared the sober side of the web as much as the opposite, and when she suspected approaching sobriety she swiftly downed another drink—straight. Consequently in the bar at Pistol Two she walked a constant tight rope and was not always successful in maintaining the exact status she preferred. At the same time Peterson and Randall plunged into the channel, she concluded that she had better have another drink—quick! She raised one arm and shook her charm bracelet and yelled at the bartender, who was very lonely because he was the only Filipino on Nikki and who wished he had never signed on for such a deal, no matter how much he needed the money. "Miguel! What the hell kind of a club you all running around here! Set me up with another bourbon chop-chop and . . ."

She paused and looked down at the end of the bar, where a residue of people not yet ready to start to the mess hall had accumulated. "And set all the rest of these heah clowns up, too! Big night! Charge it to the ol' man!"

Fred Hanover, lost in nostalgic memories of applejack drinking with fellow press representatives in a certain little New York bar, had been trying to satisfy himself with a series of Martinis through most of the afternoon. Now he mumbled, "Big deal, Sue-Anne. Big deal. Mighty generous at two bits a shot. Pretty high off the hog, as they say down your way."

"Shut up, you Yankee bastard. Shut up and sit up and drink up yoah gin like a good boy."

"I love you, Sue-Anne. I love you madly," Hanover said solemnly. "I love you because you are such a thorough disgrace to American womanhood."

"An' that includes both the Noath and the South," Sue-Anne said proudly. She jangled her charm bracelet and pushed her fingers through Hanover's hair until he angrily jerked his head away. The gesture almost capsized both Hanover and his bar stool, but he recovered and said, "I wish you would cut that sort of thing out. There's a time and a place for everything."

"Why not, honey? I laike yoah hair. Anytime. Anyplace. It's so naturally curly."

Looking at him even now when he could barely hold his head up, Sue-Anne thought again that he was probably the prettiest man she had ever seen. Any woman would have envied his eyelashes, and his mouth was sensitive and beautifully formed. Yet there was nothing feminine about him. It took a perceptive person to notice that God had cheated Fred Hanover in only one physical aspect. His chin was anything but firm, and when, as now, he had been drinking, it wobbled. "Cut it out," he said when she reached again for his hair. "People are watching and pretty soon they'll be talking and pretty soon after that the old man will throw me off the island and not long after that I'll get the can. I'll get the can when I get home and that will be that."

"Not you, honey. Zebulon Pike wouldn't throw *you* off this heah island. Yoah a newspaper man an' you have a story comin' up in *Life* magazine and Zebulon just won't do a thing to you no matter what kind of shenanigans you pull off. No, Fred ol' boy, not even if you pull off his wife's dress. It don'—"

"Shut up for the love of Mike!"

Sue-Anne slid off her bar stool and stood very straight before Hanover. She held her shoulders back so her breasts would stand out, and she sucked in her breath and held it for as long as she could. That last drink had done the trick; the web was just the right thickness now and if maybe it was a little too thick all of a sudden, well, the hell with it. She didn't have to care, did she? She could tell Mr. Fred Hanover just where to get off. Humph! Telling me to shut up? Just because he was a newspaper man he thought he could go around whenever he wanted, tellin' people who were minding their own business to shut up?

"Listen, you carpetbaggin' son of a bitch, who do you think you're talking to? And since when do gentlemen go around tellin' ladies to shut up? And you're supposed to be a gentleman, aren't you? You and that stuffed shirt, Albright! You both talk laike you have a mouthful o' mashed potatoes, if you ask me. Noathun intellectuals is what you are. *Noath-eastern* intellectuals and that's the *lowest* form of carpetbagger . . . lower than . . ."

"Sue-Anne. Why don't you stop fighting the Civil War?"

"Because it ain't ovah! That's why, Mr. Fred Hanover. It ain't nevah going to be over until you damn Yankees learn to act laike decent gentlemen."

"You read too many books."

"Quit insultin' me!"

Sue-Anne's voice rose in an offended contralto until it easily dominated the music from the juke box. Hanover turned back to the remains of his Martini and tried to pretend he was alone. Sue-Anne was not pleased. She grabbed a handful of popcorn from the plate on the bar and sprinkled it on his head. And throughout the process she purred softly, "Yo' all don' love me any more. That's it, Fred. Yo' all just don' care any more what happens to ol' Sue-Anne. See? It's snowing. Yoah just pushin' little ol' Sue-Anne out in the snow!"

The web was not yet so thick that Sue-Anne had lost awareness of the considerable audience gathered around the end of the bar. Which was why she reached for the popcorn. If Fred Hanover thought he could ignore Sue-Anne Pike he was mistaken. Not until she was ready anyway. "Ah'm leaving you," she said. "Ah'm leaving you because you bore me. Ah'm leaving you and taking a long trip down to the other end of the state where the gentlemen live! Jus' laike Liza crossin' the ice."

She filtered another blizzard of popcorn through her fingers and held one arm across her face as if to guard against the cold and wind. Then slanting her body against the wind, which by now she could almost feel, she picked her way carefully over an imaginary ice floe which extended to the end of the bar. She arrived among the spectators breathless and triumphant, and she took a little bow when they laughed.

"Now," she said, peering at the faces surrounding her. "Who's for some real honest-to-God deep-down rootin' and hoggin' drinkin'?"

"I will accept another beer," Carlos Reveza said.

"Yo' all don't have to be so damn condescending about it," Sue-Anne said. Then imitating him perfectly even to the intonations of his Mexican accent, she said, "I will 'ave another beer. Who are you? Pancho Villa?"

Smiling at the others, she resumed her normal voice except for a slight addition of throatiness and said, "How about that? Fatso allows as how he'll break down and have another beer. Why don't you have a man's drink? Bourbon whisky, Fatso! That's a man's drink. Come on. Sue-Anne's payin'! Miguel! . . . On target! . . . Bourbons away!"

While Miguel filled the glasses, Sue-Anne took a moment to survey her new-found companions. There were still great gaps in the web and she knew she had seen all of them before, although the only one she knew by name was Aubrey Tinsman, the barber. With what was intended as a gay gesture she jangled her bracelets in his direction and said, "Aubrey, darling! Introduce me to your friends! Don't just sit there and look wistful!"

The moment Aubrey stepped down from his stool, Sue-Anne knew that the time had come for her to watch the web closely, for a woman sat in the shadows behind him and Sue-Anne had not even seen her. She told herself that she would go very easy with this new bourbon. When people started to appear from nowhere, then you had to start being careful.

Aubrey introduced the woman, who was dark and small and, Sue-Anne noticed with relief, not too young. He said that her name was Crystal Blum and that she was in charge of the laundry. She nodded politely and Sue-Anne wondered if her lovely teeth were real.

Aubrey stepped back to reveal another man. Watch it, girl! How the hell many people were back there in the shadows?

"This is Dana Wood," Aubrey said. "He flies the mail plane."

Sue-Anne looked at him and saw that he was quite short and nearly bald-headed, and she wondered why it was that all the pilots she had ever met always looked pretty much like Dana Wood or even worse and where were the ones who looked like Gary Cooper? The next man captured her interest and her glass arrived just in time to raise it to him.

"Pete Walsacki," Aubrey was saying, and then he added something else which Sue-Anne lost in the web. Something about Mr. Walsacki's appearance caused her lips to part and she lowered her glass instead of drinking from it. Mr. Walsacki was a tall and obviously powerful man and his forearms were covered with black hair. So too, she saw at once, was his head. She resisted the temptation to stand on her tiptoes and run her fingers through it. He was grinning at her rather foolishly and his eyes were embarrassed beneath his heavy eyebrows.

"And what do you do, Mr. Walsacki? Do I have the name right?"

"Yeah. You got it right," Walsacki growled. "I'm the boss plumber on this operation."

"Oh! How nice."

Sue-Anne was confused. The web was changing every which way. One minute I'm the big lady and the next I'm a slob. She took a long pull at her glass, which would at least steady the web, and resolved to keep Mr. Walsacki in mind. What a hunk of man!

Aubrey was introducing the man she had called Fatso. Sue-Anne missed his name entirely because she was still admiring Walsacki's neck and chest, but she did manage to ask what he did.

"I am the master electrician," Carlos Raveza said. "I hope you do not mind," he added, holding up his beer can. "I prefer this."

"Pig swill," Sue-Anne said quietly. Now she was eying Crystal Blum and she was remembering that, while many men might be willing to laugh at a woman who had too much to drink, her own sex had no such tolerance. Crystal Blum was sitting there displaying perfect white teeth in what should pass for a smile. Sue-Anne was certain that in reality it was intended as a snarl. And she thought, I will knock those damned teeth down her throat.

"Is it Miss Blum or Mrs.?" Sue-Anne asked. This moment she would play the patronizing part of the Governor's wife. The web had cleared temporarily and such a question would put Madame Toothy-grin on the defensive in case the web should cloud over again.

"It's *Miss* Blum," the woman said and then, once more displaying her teeth, she repeated, "*Miss* Blum, Your Highness."

"Just what do you mean by that 'Your Highness' stuff?" The more Sue-Anne stared at the teeth and the surrounding face the less she trusted this female.

"I was only joking, Mrs. Pike. After all you are the Governor's wife."

"Pretty funny, aren't you? You made that crack with malice aforethought, I'd guess. But Ah'm a big girl an' I fo'give easy. Part of my family tradition. Where's yo' home, *Miss* Blum?"

"Hoboken."

"Hoboken? Where in Gawd's name is that?"

Aubrey Tinsman said hastily, "New York is just to the east of it."

Knowing perfectly well where Hoboken was, Sue-Anne said it again. "Hoboken?"

She mouthed the word carefully, twisting her lips around it, and the second time she said it she separated the syllables so that three distinct positions of her lips were required. She faced Pete Walsacki during this process and made sure that he was watching her mouth. Then she smiled.

"You aren't from Hoboken, are you, Mr. Walsacki?"

"No, ma'am. I'm from Toledo."

"Do all the men up Toledo way have so much hair on their chests?"

Pete Walsacki fumbled with the top button of his shirt and then took a long draw at his bourbon. He was about to say that he had never noticed the hair on other men's chests especially, when Carlos Raveza slammed his empty beer can down on the bar and shouted, "If you no drink up everybody, the mess hall close and so you starve."

"Quiet, Fatso. I was talkin' with Mr. Walsacki."

The net was nicely set now, just thick enough to see

without being seen. Whoever drank better than ol' Sue-Anne? It was the other people, the weaklings in this world, who were the slobs. If you planned carefully and knew how to handle the stuff, there was never any problem. Come to think of it, the time had come for a slight booster. Smiling an invitation, she reached out and took Pete Walsacki's empty glass from his hand.

As she turned toward the bar she knew that the web had very suddenly become too thick. She was making a mistake. Something happened to the bar. It sailed upwards and at a slant for several feet, then moved abruptly outward and bumped into her so hard she dropped both Pete Walsacki's glass and her own. There was a double crash of glass, and at the same instant the lights went out and the juke box whined down to silence and she clutched at the bar in terror, crying within herself, biting her lips so that the others would not hear her, I *am* a slob, a slob, a slob! I am a dirty, blind-drunken slob and I can't help it!

Then in amazement, she listened to the voices rising in excitement all around her. She leaned against the bar which was so unsteady and pawed at the darkness, hearing the jangle of her bracelets without being able to see them, and hearing also the voices without being able to identify them. She bit her fist in horror because she was sure they had heard her call herself a slob, and she could not tear away the web which had now brought on total darkness. Now I'm blind, she thought, as well as a slob, and the best thing to do is go jump in the channel if I can find it. Whoa! Where is that channel?

Then gradually, as the confusion eased and the bar steadied down, she understood the other voices. Pete Walsacki was saying, "Now what the hell do you know about that?"

Aubrey Tinsman said, "Oh dear, oh dear! Heaven help the poor sailors on a night like this!"

Crystal Blum began to sing "Two Cigarettes in the Dark."

Dana Wood said, "Power failure! Oh, Carlos, are you going to catch hell! Right in the middle of supper call."

Carlos Raveza's face was revealed as perfectly calm when he lit a match and held it before him.

"Impossible." He chuckled. "Still it is very dark, is it not?"

Dana Wood laughed. "You're just lucky it didn't happen during the movie. Pike would have you shot at dawn."

"I suppose it is necessary I walk over to the power-house," Carlos said. He waited hopefully as if by doing so the lights might go on again. When his match went out he sighed and said, "This is extremely inconvenient. I am in a sad mood and that is not the best time for me to tinker with machinery, electrical or otherwise."

He belched once and moved off through the darkness.

Sue-Anne fumbled for a bar stool and, when at last she found one, she sat down upon it. And she was so grateful that it was only a power failure and that she was not a blind slob, she bowed her head and began to weep again.

From the darkness at the end of the bar Fred Hanover sang in a husky whisper, "Light a candle in the winder for my wa-a-andering boy . . . !"

Zebulon Pike was en route from his house to the mess hall when the street lights went out. He came to an abrupt halt, stared for a moment at the nearest light, now so dead against the stars, and snorted.

He waited, tapping his foot and looking up at the light, as if it had personally thwarted him. He stuck his thumbs in his belt and looked all about his domain for any sign of illumination. A few candles began to appear in and between the buildings. He watched them moving about like fireflies. He heard a woman laugh and a man curse as he stumbled over something. The mess hall, vaguely outlined in the starlight and normally the origin of considerable banging and clatter at this hour, was silent.

Pike waited for approximately one minute, damn well time enough, he told himself, for any idiot to start the auxiliary generating equipment. He frowned at the outline of the powerhouse. He could detect no activity either in or near it. He waited another thirty seconds, then set off at forced-march cadence.

When he arrived at the powerhouse door, he was breathing heavily, more as a result of anger than from his exertions. The main generator was still running smoothly although it seemed to be under no strain. Why didn't the idiots turn on the lights then?

He saw a match struck and someone moving about behind the generator.

"Hallo in there!" Pike called and at once set off for the match flame. "Who's in charge here?"

"Me, unfortunately," Carlos Raveza answered.

In his haste and concentration on the match flame, Pike suffered a head-on collision with a heavy tool box and for a moment he was convinced he had broken both shins. Cringing with pain he shouted, "What the hell do you mean by leaving equipment around like that?"

The match went out and Carlos said, "Why the hell to look and mebbe be more careful where you're going?"

"This is Governor Pike speaking, I'll have you know."

"So? This is Carlos Raveza. Is there something I can do for you?"

Another match flamed and Carlos held it above his head.

"I want to know exactly when you're going to turn on the God-damned lights!"

"Señor Governor, truly I am a lazy man. If you think I prefer this method of illumination you are loco."

Still rubbing his shins, Pike limped gallantly toward him. By the time he stood facing Carlos he had recovered most of his dignity and managed to stand menacingly erect. Unfortunately, his action coincided with Carlos' burning his fingers. He whipped out the match and the effect of Pike's charge was lost. In the darkness Pike said, "Haven't you got a flashlight? Do you have to stand there lighting matches? What kind of an emergency procedure have you got set up here? Are you in charge? Who's in charge? What did you say your name was and when are we going to have *the God-damned lights!* People are eating in the dark, dammit, and I have no intention of eating in the dark, and later on there's got to be a movie!"

Carlos lit a match and Pike was astounded to see that he was smiling. Barely holding on to himself he said very slowly, "*Where*, my good man, is your flashlight?"

"Over there," Carlos said, waving the match casually toward the end of the building.

"Then why aren't you using it?"

"The batteries. Finish."

"Well, put some *new* batteries in it! Now!"

"Impossible, señor. None exist. I have make inquiries at the warehouse and also the chief of supply. They say it is one of the things forgot. Yes, so many things to forget. So even the Atlas Construction Company is not perfect."

"If I find out that's true, I'll get a boatload of batteries here immediately. If it's a lie, you're going home."

"Hooray! That would be very nice of you, señor. My contract is to be pay for one year and I much prefer not to work for the money. I will take a vacation in Cuba, perhaps go to Santo Domingo, where I have friends, then possibly stay a month or so in Venezuela, where the beer is excellent. Later I will—"

Stabbing his fingers at Carlos' belly, Pike said, "*You* have been drinking!"

"But of course, señor! It is a requirement of the soul!"

"Will you stop standing there and holding matches and talking about your soul and geography in general! Fix the confounded lights!"

"By and by I will, señor . . . with luck, that is. But I do not think it so bad a disaster to get the panic. It is better you calm down. Otherwise and for certain you will have bile in your liver."

As Pike clenched his fists helplessly, Carlos squatted before the large control panel and moved his match slowly along the array of dials and switches.

"Who is responsible for your being on Nikki? Who hired you? Who checked your qualifications for this job?"

"Nobody, señor," Carlos answered without looking up from the panel.

"How could *nobody* hire you? You don't answer my questions!"

"You ask so many at the same time it is very difficult which to prefer to answer."

Bending over the control panel, Carlos grunted. "Ah!"

"Have you found something? What's the trouble?"

"No, señor. I only permit air to escape from the lungs because it happens that I am in a very uncomfortable position. I am no longer young enough to bend over so long."

"Where are your assistants? I seem to remember there were several electricians assigned to Nikki. Where the hell are they right this minute?"

"I have two assisants, not several. At this moment they are probably asleep."

"What are they doing asleep? This is dinnertime!"

"They eat later. They must stand watch all night and relieve each other. Also they must do many other things. For example, to make sure all is well with freezers for the meat and various other machinery. Here we labor all the hours of the day and night. It is a silly arrangement. Often there is not even time for siesta."

"I fail to see what there is to check about the other machinery if the main plant is out."

"Sad but true," Carlos said, lighting another match.

Now Pike lit a match and began peering at the control board. Before it had burned halfway through he said, "What's this?"

"What is what?"

"This switch which says *off*, dammit!"

Carlos brought his match, held it beside Pike's. "Ah," he said. "But of *course!*"

"Of course *what?* Has this switch anything to do with the trouble?"

"Most certainly. Without a question of a doubt. Witness, please."

Carlos held the switch down to the ON position. At once the main generator slowed momentarily and then, as if gathering strength, began to labor with a heavy, solid rhythm. The lights hanging from the powerhouse ceiling took on an amber glow and gradually brightened.

"It is the main circuit-breaker!" Carlos yelled above the new pounding of the motor. "She kick out because of an overload, I am proud to state. Automatic!"

"That's all that was wrong and *I* had to find it?" Pike gasped.

"You are a very intelligent man," Carlos said. "I regret that you were troubled."

Pike shook his head in disbelief when Carlos pointed up at the lights and calmly inquired if they could not be considered both efficient and beautiful. "What kind of an electrician," he said through clenched teeth, "are you?"

Still looking up at the light, Carlos smiled thoughtfully. "Not the best, señor. You may be sure of that."

Pike dropped his match on the floor and made his way slowly to the door. He went out into the night without looking back at Carlos Raveza, and he walked all the way to the mess hall in stunned silence. Those who saw him en route failed at first to recognize him, for his normally alert eyes were glazed and his broad shoulders were slumped as if a cannon ball had struck him in the chest.

When he entered the mess hall, Albright looked up from his plate and wondered if Pike had suffered a heart attack.

It was so that things seemed to come in pairs on Nikki atoll. For on the other side of the channel Peterson and Randall were also engaged in an electrical problem. Terry Mack did not lead them, as Randall had hoped, to a bamboo pavilion inhabited by maidens whose sole purpose in life was to satisfy the desires of men. Instead Terry Mack escorted them to the store of Yip Kee, a simple establishment which matched in every respect that owned by Nikki's other Chinese, Fat Sue.

It was the intention of Yip Kee that the similarity between his own and Fat Sue's store should be brought to an end. In fact it would bring no tears to either Yip Kee or his wife or his six children if Fat Sue went bankrupt and was forced to leave the atoll forever. Nikki was too small and the native inhabitants too prudent to bear the exploitation of two merchants. It had proved to be that rare perch in the broad Pacific where not even a Chinese could make a profit. Yip Kee wanted to join with the thousands of other Chinese in Polynesia, Micronesia, and Melanesia and at least get one of his carefully manicured fingers around the financial neck of the Pacific. In time he realized that the most logical way to begin such an ambitious program was to eliminate his nearest competitor. Since the results of violence were always unpredictable, Yip Kee resolved to employ cunning. Which was the reason Peterson and Randall were guided to his store before they were permitted any deviation. Terry Mack was also using his cunning. He was after a reward of five cans of salmon, a delicacy much preferred to the variety of fresh fish the lagoon offered. Any native of Nikki knew that whatever came in a can must be superior to anything found in its natural state.

Yip Kee greeted Peterson and Randall with considerable warmth. Two wooden chairs were placed in the center of the store for them, and they were handed bottles of orange-colored pop which had been kept in cool water. Peterson held up his pop bottle, and after he had taken a sip and the bubbles stung his tongue with unaccustomed warmth, he pointed the end of the bottle at Randall and said sourly, "Yeah. Let's go drinkin'! We can tell people about this here orgy for a hundred years!"

Randall asked him sotto voce to lay off and added that obviously their hosts were only trying to be nice.

As they sipped without enthusiasm at their pop, Yip Kee set before them two coils of wire and the units of a wind generator. They were part of his scheme to eliminate his business competition, for if his store could furnish electric light, he reasoned that all of Fat Sue's customers would be attracted to him. Yet since its arrival the contrivance had not produced a glimmer of light, though the trade winds blew faithfully and the propeller spun industriously on the roof. After endless experiment the reason for the generator's failure became obvious. The instructions for hooking it up were printed in English, a language not even Terry Mack pretended to read.

"Now, m'lads," Terry Mack said, allowing his good eye to rove along the shelves of canned goods. "Do ye think ye could read the words a bit and make things proper? Ye *can* read, can't ye?"

"Naturally," Peterson said, accepting the sheet of instructions. He was, he thought, willing to do almost anything to stop sipping pop. Randall leaned to read over his shoulder, and Yip Kee hopefully held the kerosene lantern between their heads so that they would enjoy a maximum of light.

When they were finished Randall and Peterson looked at each other and then down at the units of the generator. They set down their pop bottles and rose simultaneously.

"Can ye fix it?" Terry Mack asked eagerly.

Peterson smiled wearily and said, "If you have a screw driver it is so simple your friend will have light in five minutes."

A shiny new screw driver was produced instantly, and like two young Americans lost in the intricacies of a hot rod, Peterson and Randall began connecting the wires to the units. There was a reverent silence as they worked.

The mess hall was the largest single structure in Pistol Two and was also the only building with a rounded roof of corrugated iron. From a distance it resembled an old-fashioned aircraft hangar and hence was not an object of beauty. The Atlas Construction Company had erected many such buildings from the Arctic to the tropics and had at last developed what they considered to be a purely functional design. The semicircle of roof shed heavy rain and snow, the concrete floor could be laid in one day, and the sides could be easily adapted to keep out cold, or, as in the case of Pistol Two, screened and left open to admit cooling breezes without subjecting the occupants to the direct rays of the sun. It was fortunate for the Atlas designers that they were never required to dine in their creations for extended periods. They might have been less satisfied, for the round metal roof and the cement floor combined to produce acoustical pandemonium. A fork dropped at one end of the hall sounded more like a falling anvil at the opposite end. Conversation at meal times among the diners was necessarily keyed in competition with noises from the kitchen, which caused considerable hollering even when two people sat side by side.

The kitchen was at one end of the mess hall behind a cafeteria-style serving counter and was firmly governed by a despot known as Clara to those who ignored the grease in her stew, and as Mrs. Riley to those who were courageous enough to complain about it. Clara was of Swedish descent and had cooked for such projects from Greenland to Texas. She took the name Riley when she married one Pinkey Riley, who now served as Pistol Two's baker. He was a very good baker when he was sober, which was seldom.

There were twenty long tables set in two rows along both sides of the mess hall. Normally only fifteen of these were required. The others had been provided to accommodate casual trade which might become involved on Nikki for several days.

Before the first three meals had been served on Nikki certain amenities came to be observed, and within a few days the social structure at dining time became as fixed as a beehive's. The table directly opposite the door and closest to the ice-water dispensing machine became Pike's private board as surely as if there had been a sign forbidding transgressions upon it. Here he had a solitary breakfast and at noon, lunch with Sue-Anne; and when she was not too long detained in the recreation-building bar so that she missed the meal entirely, they had supper together. No one thought it odd that, while the table could easily accommodate fifteen persons, the only other occupant ever seen at the table was Albright. As Pike's aide his presence there was understood and thought correct, an impression which would not have prevailed had anyone else elected to dine with the Governor.

The next table, which was second both numerically and socially, was almost as firmly established as Pike's. It was occupied by the members of the scientific team and the foreign observers. Dr. Case also sat at this table more or less permanently and sometimes Fred Hanover would bring his tray, although he was likely to wander aimlessly about the mess hall for some time before he found a place which pleased him. Impelled by curiosity a stranger from the masses would occasionally make the mistake of sitting at this table, a stranger in the person of a carpenter, or mechanic, or Crystal Blum. And they were made as welcome as the regular occupants were able, which was of little avail because the conversation invariably branched off into subjects not easily followed by people who were merely hungry. Thus, the few who had tried it never returned, and after a few weeks the faces at this table were always the same.

The complement of the next table was more involved and subject to more change than any other. For here sat those who were independent workers or who, through official directive, held positions of authority. As chief electrician Carlos Raveza found himself comfortable at this table. So did Dana Wood, the mail-plane pilot, when he remained on Nikki for dinner. Peter Hildebrandt sat here as did Sgt. Doolan; and sometimes, to Doolan's disgust, Aubrey Tinsman found it inviting. Adam Smith always ate at this table. When it was possible he chose a seat at the end. In nature this became a bachelor's table, although from time to time it would be invaded by the Chief of Commissary Supplies and his wife, or by Alice Summer, the schoolteacher.

The other tables, which stretched to the end of the hall, were voluntarily occupied by the more ordinary citizens of Pistol Two. They usually dined in family groups although there was, for variety's sake, a considerable interchange of children among the tables. Here sat the boss carpenter, Barney Dunbar, and his family, the Pete Walsackis, the Harry McAdoos, and the Ellsworth Tompkins. Here Margaret Trumpey would also be found, and Sunnie Mandel, the marines, the movie projectionist, the paymaster, the man in charge of sports equipment, the photolab technicians, Miguel, who doubled as bartender and librarian, and an assortment of men all of whom were abnormally muscular and copiously tattooed. These last were the straight laborers who were required to do almost anything on Pistol Two from maintaining the streets to moving supplies. Most of these men had been employed on overseas projects from Arabia to Alaska, and many had not spent a full month in the United States for over ten years. Those who had saved their money against the day when they would permanently return to their homeland had formidable bank accounts. Those who did not had equally imposing beer bellies.

The noise level in this section of the mess hall was several hundred decibels above any other.

When Pike left the mess-hall doorway, he moved toward his table as if he had not yet awakened from a heavy sleep. He whipped up his napkin, glanced at the bowl of celery, and sat down with a thump. Albright was so unnerved by his behavior he could only toy with his pork chops. He sensed a crisis in the making, and he hoped that somehow he could finish his meal and depart before Sue-Anne descended upon the table. She was already so late Pike might explode when she eventually walked into the mess hall; and since Sue-Anne performed best before an audience, Albright knew that his chances of leaving would be very slim indeed. *He* would be the audience and he dreaded what the role might do to his sensitive digestion.

Normally when Pike sat down to his meal he smiled expansively and waved at those subjects among the farther tables who might be looking his way. It was a part of his regular now-we-are-just-boys-and-girls-together routine. Then he would pass the time of day or discuss the merits of the actors in the night's movie, and he would sit very straight in his chair and make a point of commenting on the excellence of whatever came out of the kitchen. He would say that people were mighty lucky to enjoy such food at no cost to themselves and that Napoleon was right when he said an army marched on its stomach. This would bring him to a brief review of the responsibilities of the American nation to the world in general and further exploration of his pet theory that, unless a careful check-rein were kept on all Americans, they were sure going to hell just like the Romans did and that very soon a nation accustomed to a more Spartan existence would take over the world and then, by God, you would see. All of which Albright considered nonsense in an electronic age as well as being a frightful bore.

Peering at Pike through the stand of celery, Albright saw that he was sweating profusely and he thought that his face was like a steak broiled very rare. He accepted his plate of pork chops without comment and, seizing his knife and fork, manipulated them with such ferocity Albright was certain the instruments, which were Navy surplus anyway, would bend and collapse beneath the strain.

Pike was a meticulous eater, an observation, Albright thought wistfully, he was most certainly qualified to make since he bore witness to the exhibition three times a day. Normally he marched through a meal with admirable dignity and when he had finished not a crumb remained at his place. In Albright's opinion Pike lacked several important attributes of a true gentleman, but he was willing to admit that at one time in his life his table manners must have been properly supervised. For which Albright was most grateful.

Now, therefore, Pike shocked him. He stuffed enormous chunks of pork chop into his face, splattering his shirt with gravy in the process, and there were lumps on both cheeks as he chewed like a busy squirrel. When he pointed his fork at Albright and began to speak without waiting to swallow, Albright momentarily lost all sense of superiority.

"Look here," Pike said without the slightest regard for the fact that in gesturing at Albright his bare elbow dipped into his butter plate. "There are going to be some changes made around here! Believe you me, there are going to be some changes made and that's starting tomorrow morning!"

"Just what seems to be the trouble, Governor?" Albright asked cautiously.

"I am surrounded by inefficiency! I have never seen such

loose, fumbling control since I took over the 326th from poor old Chubby Steel."

The 326th, Albright knew only too well, was an artillery regiment which had fallen on evil days back in 1920, allegedly because the often-mentioned Chubby Steel had been assigned to Armenian relief after World War One. It seemed that he had taken to smoking hashish, a habit which he maintained on his return to America and the 326th, and was eventually found unfit to command. Albright had long hoped that he would never hear another word about the 326th's troubles or Pike's solution of them, but now he wished he would stay with the subject in lieu of an unknown something which threatened to be more immediate. He was disappointed.

"I am surrounded by a pack of idiots," Pike went on. "How in the name of God did some of these people get assigned to Zeus?"

"Just which people are you referring to, sir?"

"To our master electrician for one. I will have you know that *I . . . me,* mind you, had to fix his equipment when the God-damned lights went out a little while ago!"

"Couldn't he fix it?"

"No. He could not. And we would still be stumbling around in the dark if it was up to him. Oh, he was frank enough! He admitted he didn't know what the hell he was doing."

"I'll check up on him in the morning."

Pike shoved an enormous forkful of mashed potatoes into his mouth. Albright studied his nails.

"I want a full report on that man's qualifications . . . how he got the job and why."

"Yessir."

"And furthermore I want a marine stationed outside my

office during business hours. In guard uniform and equipment."

"May I ask why, sir? As you know they are an independent unit and I would have to obtain authority from their duty officer on Tuamani. I doubt if Sergeant Doolan would have the authority or would be willing to assume the responsibility. My recollection of the directive was that the Marines functioned as police only . . . except, of course, they would be under your direct command in a state of emergency."

"This *is* an emergency! How do I know what that idiot will do after I practically called him a liar?"

"Did you, sir?"

"He said there was not a flashlight battery to be had on the base. I said if he was lying I would send him home."

"And what was his reaction, sir?"

"He said hooray."

Albright, having thoroughly examined his nails, turned his hands over and stared at his palms.

"If you will permit me to say so, that hardly seems to constitute an emergency. It would be very difficult to put into a teletype to Tuamani. I'll go see Mr. Raveza and smooth things over. If he doesn't seem amenable to reason, I'll let you know at once."

"We might not have had a movie tonight if I hadn't gone to the powerhouse!"

Albright glanced up at Pike's eyes. He almost took the risk and said that the loss of a movie could certainly be classed an emergency when he noticed that Pike's attention had wandered. Furthermore he had stopped eating and placed his knife and fork carefully in line on his plate.

Mother of God, Albright thought. This will be Sue-Anne coming to dine. Perhaps I *had* better call out the Marines.

Albright turned to follow Pike's eyes and was instantly relieved to discover it was not Sue-Anne, but that weather chap who had so captured Pike's attention. He was bound toward the door and Albright noticed that he held a toothpick between his teeth. It made Albright slightly ill.

"And there goes Jack of the beanstalk, the king of my idiots," Pike said. "Look here, I'll prove something to you."

Then he called out in a voice that easily overcame the clatter of dishes. Albright assumed that such a voice, which he had never heard before, could only have been developed over the roar of a cannon. He found his mind unable to resist quoting the opening stanza of Tennyson's "Light Brigade" and he found it easy to visualize Zebulon Pike leading the charge.

"Mr. Smith! Will you come here a moment!"

Adam Smith halted as if he had been lassoed by Pike's voice. He turned to look at Pike and thoughtfully removed the toothpick from his mouth. He hesitated and then walked slowly toward the table. Nodding to both men, he said good evening in a voice which was barely audible. Pike ignored the greeting.

"Mr. Smith," he said, "I would like to ask you a question."

"Sure," Adam said.

"Did you enjoy your dinner?"

Albright was astonished to observe a crafty gleam in Pike's eyes. Of all the characteristics which Albright had discovered in Pike, he thought that deception or a fondness for guile was most certainly not one of them. In Albright's estimation the man was a great plodding oaf, a military hack who would have been eaten alive in the civilian world. Even in the Army, Albright thought, he would have been a hopelessly lost and confused bull if he had not sprung from the sacred womb of West Point.

That brass ring on his finger was, and had been, his shield against reality. It was as much a part of his body as his nose. Throughout the major portion of his life, when ordinary men were heavily engaged in open war with economics, that ring had constantly established its owner's seniority, and from seniority all blessings automatically flowed. And so during this period of growth and gestation and final maturity, keenness of mind was superfluous for Pike and might in some cases have been an actual handicap. There was no need for cajoling or gentle persuasion in a military order, written or verbal. Albright was convinced that constant exposure to military directives petrified any natural facility for the subtle approach. And so now he watched Pike in fascination, as though he had suddenly betrayed not only himself, but his kind.

"Why yes, Governor," Adam Smith was saying, "I enjoyed my dinner very much. Something wrong with yours?"

Pike smiled benignly up at him and leaned far back in his chair.

"No, indeed. I was only checking up. The well-being of our people here is part of my job, you know. I want to be sure that even our parasites are content."

"I'm not sure just what you mean by that, Governor."

Pike placed his hands on his broad chest and carefully moved his finger tips together so that they formed an isosceles triangle. He beamed on the structure as if it were a trick not easily mastered.

"I mean nothing by it especially, except that every project of this magnitude is like establishing a separate society. There are the workers and the truly skilled. . . . And then there are the . . . shall we say, drones, and even incompetents who must be carried along with the others. In the Army we counted on such weaknesses and provided for them. In battle the weak elements were sent to the rear, although, of course, we continued to feed them. . . ."

"Just what has all this got to do with my dinner?"

"Another question. Is it going to rain and spoil our movie tonight?"

"It might and it might not."

Pike separated his hands and spread them palm upward in a gesture of hopeless finality. "There you are!"

Though he took on the most forlorn expression, it was obvious to Albright that he was enjoying himself thoroughly. Yet there was no cruelty in his manner; only, Albright thought, a sort of silly flexing of his muscles, the garish performance of an iron-headed bully who was not really a bully because the last thing in the world he would do would be to actually strike anyone. He was certain now that Pike just wanted to roar a little and pace up and down in his cage and perhaps frighten any captive spectators. Albright was also certain that the Governor would retreat whimpering to a neutral corner if anyone so much as went boo at him, but he doubted if Adam Smith knew it.

"Correct me if I'm wrong, Governor, but I don't think you like me," Adam said.

"My dear fellow, I am not permitted any personal likes or dislikes in this community. I must regard each individual in the same light no matter how my personal feelings may be involved. I was merely remarking, and I thought you might do some thinking about it, that one's mere *presence* on this island does not establish one's value. In your case I am beginning to wonder if I haven't been perhaps . . . overly tolerant?"

Albright saw Adam's face redden, and his lips became a thin, hard-pressed line. Whatever the circumstances, he thought Pike had chosen a poor time to chastise this Smith chap even if he deserved it. Albright was framing a soothing interruption when Adam said, "You don't like me, Governor, because you don't like my weather. Has it ever occurred to you that I don't make the weather?"

"You have officially stated on four separate occasions that it was not going to rain. Unfortunately, those statements proved to be one hundred per cent in error."

"Those were *not* official forecasts, Governor. I would never attempt to forecast the occurrence of local rain squalls, particularly in the tropics. A single cloud can open up any time. It's a question of dew point and temperature."

"Don't try to confuse the issue with technicalities, Mr. Smith. The fact remains that you are being fed well and paid well to forecast the weather and in my opinion you are doing a most haphazard job of it. I realize that our nightly enjoyment of a movie is unimportant, or even the fact that our people must walk home soaked to the skin. . . . After all, Project Zeus is far more important than any individual's comfort or enjoyment. But it is exactly Zeus which concerns me. How, when the big time comes, when every detail of this vast enterprise must click like a drill team . . . how can I trust your winds-aloft report when you have twice missed on that?"

"Any meteorologist misses once in a while. It just happens."

"Well, it can't happen here, Mr. Smith. It *must* not happen here, do you understand? As I've mentioned before, my neuritis has proved to be much more reliable than your past reports. Some improvement must be shown in your record very soon or I shall be forced to . . . Well, I think you understand?"

"I understand perfectly."

Adams said it quietly and apparently without anger. Then he turned and walked to the ice-water machine. He bent over the spigot and took a long drink. Without looking back at Pike he passed the back of his hand across his wet lips and went out the door.

Adam stood in the middle of the coral street for several minutes, looking up at the stars and listening to the night sounds of Pistol Two. The banging and clattering of the mess hall formed a solid background for other sounds which he took a strange pleasure in identifying. He could distinctly hear the juke box playing in the recreation building. There was the steady whirring sound from the powerhouse, and somewhere far down the street he heard a small boy fighting off Indians. Adam wondered if it was Floyd Dunbar. Since their first meeting he had seen him only once. Floyd was on his way to school and there was only time for an exchange of "Hi's." By listening carefully Adam could hear the sea brushing along the beach and the intermittent thwacking of the palm fronds in the wind. And finally it seemed to him that he could hear Governor Pike's voice still roaring in the mess hall although he knew the notion was ridiculous.

He walked slowly down the street, thinking first of Pike and then of Margaret Trumpey. Well, it certainly hadn't been a very good night! Golly! Maybe Peter Hildebrandt was right and he should strive to be more pleasant. But how could you come right out and say to a girl like Margaret that things were on the lonesome side and you thought maybe it might be for her, too, and that maybe it would be a good idea if the two of you sort of went places together in Pistol Two like to the movies or even over to the bar in the recreation building for a drink before dinner, and maybe it wouldn't be too obvious if once in a while you sat at the same table and at least had dinner together? How did you get the ball rolling on something like that when probably a girl like Margaret had half the men on Nikki asking her to do this and that all the time, because after all there was a terrible shortage of women, and, well, there you were?

Adam halted at the intersection of the main street and the one which led to his quarters. He was uncertain why he stopped at just that moment and place, but very suddenly in his thinking about Margaret Trumpey, the memory of the channel's black swirling waters returned to him, and it brought on the same wild feeling he had known in the mess hall only a few minutes before. It was like a whirlpool stirring within him and it was so compelling that, when Pike finished his speech, he had almost reached out and seized that thick neck between his two hands.

Now, standing in the street, his hands rose involuntarily and formed into fists which he shook at the night even though he knew it was innocent. How could that ignoramus be appointed Governor! Pike and his crazy neuritis! He didn't understand the first thing about meteorology because he didn't *want* to understand! He wanted someone he could kick around, some handy joker he could make eat humble pie whenever he felt like it because he knew his power was temporary and he had to taste all of it. And the joker was Adam Smith!

Why not put into reality the idea which had flashed across his mind when he stood on the pier with Margaret Trumpey? Who besides Adam Smith would ever know the truth when it was all over? No harm done and it would be Major General Zebulon Pike, or whatever kind of a general he was, quaking in his boots and running around in circles and looking silly instead of Adam Smith.

A smile crept across his face and he favored the night sky with it instead of his fists. He started to walk rapidly

121

toward his office and by the time he had passed "Brains Bungalow" he could hardly refrain from breaking into a run. His thoughts were still far from organized, but they were churning like the black waters of the channel. He would have to calm himself, separate the sudden wild notions which had come to him. The best place to attempt this would be in complete solitude. In the night. In his office. For they were not mere notions. They were inspirations, all the more intriguing because it was possible to base them upon scientific fact.

Beneath the third street light he passed two young men walking in the opposite direction whom he recognized as part of the Marine detachment.

"Hi!" Adam said almost gaily, and he thought it rather remarkable that neither of the marines seemed to sense the exhilarating activity in his mind.

"Hi," Randall said.

"Hi," Peterson said.

He continued on, his mind much too busy to query the disheveled appearance of the normally neat marines. In two days, perhaps three, if he actually had the nerve, Pike just might have something to take his mind off rain at movie time.

5

Sue-Anne was in a melancholy mood when she left the bar. To hell with it. To hell with everybody. Nobody loved lil ol' Sue-Anne!

She moved through the soft night uncertainly, pausing at times to stare at the lights in the scattered buildings, moving on again when she had seen enough, standing in the dark places between the street lights to look up at the stars. And then, somewhere between the bar and her own house, she lost track of things. She would stand for long periods, either in the light or the dark, weaving as she stood, and trying to focus upon something definite. It was not easy. After a while a sense of peace possessed her and she could not imagine the reason until she discovered that, when she stopped, the bangle and the jangle of her charm bracelets also ceased. So experimenting, she would take a few steps swinging her arms and she would listen to the jangle. Then she would stop. And again there would be silence.

I sound like the lead team of one of Zebulon's batteries, she thought. I chink, chink along . . . no, not like the lead, but more like the wheel team! And suddenly remembering the harmonious clinking of the chains which were so much a part of the horse-drawn artillery, she was young again. The notion so exhilarated her she kicked off her patent-leather pumps and ran along the coral road, not feeling the cuts on her feet. She spread out her arms, embracing the night, seeing not the stars or the lighted buildings which fled past like the sides of a bewildering canyon, but only herself. She was laughing and she wore a tremendous hat to shade her young face against the Oklahoma sun. For it was hot at Fort Sill. And she wore a print dress and she was sitting in the reviewing stand while Captain Zebulon Pike rode past. The battery of seventy-fives chinked along behind him and the caissons followed, rumbling and chinking, too, with the enlisted men sitting, arms folded smartly, like dolls taken for a ride. Everybody loved Sue-Anne Pike then. She could depend on it. The Colonel loved her and said so, and after the review they went back to his quarters and loaded up on Okalihau which the Colonel had preserved from his Hawaiian service, because, of course, it was Prohibition then. She could depend on the Colonel saying that he adored her right in front of his wife. Who was old. Forty!

Sue-Anne laughed at the night. Forty! It never occurred to her then that one day she would be so old, much less fifty!

Chink, chink. Halt! Who goes there? Sue-Anne Pike,

formerly, only two years before, Sue-Anne Spencer.
Daughter of the regiment! Really daughter of Orville
Spencer, who would have been astounded to learn that
according to his little Sue-Anne, he was quite wealthy.
He would have been just as surprised to hear how his
modest frame dwelling in Memphis had been described
as a vast plantation, and as a lifetime foe of alcohol he
would have been distressed to know that, according to
his daughter, not an evening was allowed to pass without
his mint juleps brought by a colored man who had been
with the Spencers since birth. Orville Spencer had never
in his life spent a morning on his bay mare riding through
his cotton fields. He owned neither a mare nor a cotton
field. And he did not eat a long luncheon at home off
silver preserved in the Spencer family since pre-Revolu-
tionary days. It was all he could do to afford the streetcar
fare down to his small hardware store, and he took his
lunch along with him in a cigar box.

Sue-Anne had described her father and his plantation
so many times that both had long since ceased to be
imaginary. So firm was the vision fixed in her mind that,
when Zebulon Pike asked her to marry him, she almost
suggested the ceremony be held in the formal gardens
which surrounded her father's mansion. Her hostess at
Fort Sill, who was a high-school friend and who had arranged the meeting with Captain Pike in the first place,
suggested that the less said about her background the
better. And for once, Sue-Anne listened . . . until the
swords crossed over their heads.

Ah, Zebulon! He was so beautiful then! Straight as one
of his own shell cases, lean and hard, and his uniform
fitted as if it had been plastered on his body. In the polo
games he rode like a wild man, coming past her at the
end of a chukker with his helmet tipped back just far

enough to show his blue eyes. And he would flip her a little salute, or lift his mallet in a very private signal of pleasure when he had played well. Oh fun, with every officer's wife on the Base envying her! Oh fun, as long as they didn't have to spend long hours alone with Captain Zebulon Pike; and slowly, like the creeping of a volcanic ooze, suspect, and then know for certain, that while Zebulon Pike was certainly beautiful, he was also most certainly an absolute dumbbell.

"Alas!" she sighed dramatically. "Alas, alas . . . alas! I am married to an ass!"

With her arms spread wide she twirled along the coral street, jangling and bangling to the music which suddenly swept her being; for now, this moment, she was a long way from Nikki. She was a ballerina of international fame twirling her way homeward through the streets of Vienna. And spinning along the street she sang in waltz tempo, La-tum-ta-ta-tum-ta-ta-tum . . . until suddenly she fell against the porch door of her own house and knocked a section of the wire screening out. Things were very misty for a moment. She drifted helplessly though pleasantly and she could not seem to lift the veil. Then there she was, not in Vienna at all but on Nikki, and Zebulon was holding her about the waist while he disengaged her arm from the screen door.

"Easy now, Precious," he said. "No sense in cutting yourself any more."

The blood did it. She stared at her arm and saw the bloody scratches, and decided it was time to be sick. Good ol' Zebulon! Take me down to the ball game. . . . No, take me down to the flag pole where I can barf.

He held her head and encircled her waist with his arm for solid support while she vomited. And over and over again he said, "Easy, Precious."

At last he led her into the house and cleaned the little cuts on her arm, and he was a long time at it because one of her bracelets proved difficult to remove and he considered it a possible source of infection.

"Why don't you call Dr. Case?" she asked. "You don't have to do this, Zebulon."

"I know I don't. But it isn't serious and I'd just as soon keep Dr. Case out of this case."

"Haw, Zebulon! You made a funny!"

Now that her equilibrium had been restored, she found it was very pleasant to lie back in the big wicker chair on the porch while Zebulon methodically bathed her wounds. He brought a bucket and filled it with a peroxide-and-water solution. He dipped her feet in it and very carefully cleaned the tiny coral cuts with a cotton swab.

"Good ol' Zebulon," she said, looking down the length of her body as he worked over her feet. "Good ol' Zebulon, you are just laike a great big ol' St. Bernard dog. Only one trouble. Yo' come to the rescue but you forgot the rum."

"Why do you do this to yourself, Sue-Anne?"

"Because I laike to. Where else can you get good bourbon at two bits a shot?"

Zebulon nodded his head and for a moment, before he bent over her feet again, she saw his face very clearly. The veil seemed to swing completely away, and there was that same handsome visage which she thought would surely befit a Roman centurion better than it did a general who no longer had any occasion to put on a uniform.

"Zebulon?" she said, lowering her voice until it was hardly more than a whisper.

"Yes, Precious?"

His interruption of her thought was too much for her

to surmount just then. The thought became stillborn and she pressed her eyes closed trying to recapture it. But all she could find in her mind was a lingering objection to his familiar "Precious." Why did he always use it, she thought, or almost always, just when he should take me off in the bedroom and beat the living tarnashin out of me? What kind of a man would let his wife in the house when she was stewed to the gills and then get down on his knees and bathe her feet just like he was a plantation slave?

"Zebulon, you are a fool."

She said it very quietly and slowly and flatly. He did not reply, but he looked up at her just for a moment, and then he went back to his swabbing. The light was behind the big chair and she could plainly see down the length of her legs to his iron-gray hair, but she could not see his eyes. She wondered if he cared what she had said, or had even heard her. She turned her head away from the sight of him and looked through the screens at the line of coconut palms along the beach and finally, as if twenty-seven years of resentment demanded the same immediate exit as the whisky beside the flag pole, she spoke again. She wept a little as she rambled on and her words were often slurred and she hated the words which came out of her mouth, but she could not seem to stop them.

"You are the biggest fool in the world, Zebulon. A genuine jerk. Nobody evah tol' you that did they, Zebulon? Because they were scared of you. God only knows what they were scared of because you wouldn't hurt a fly. . . . No siree. Not a fly. We have plenty of flies in this crazy place to hurt, but you wouldn't . . . would you, Zebulon Pike? Par'rm me . . . *General* Pike! Lil ol' Sue-Anne knows. You bet she knows. Maybe you can fool the public by stomping around and making laike a real general but you can't fool lil ol' Sue-Anne. On account I know you haven't got the guts of a feather duster. When you were a platoon commander you were scared of your captain and when you were a captain you were scared of Major Miller, and when you were a major you were scared silly every time ol' Colonel Boyd opened his mouth. No wonder they decided the best place for you to fight a war was runnin' an arsenal. Ol' chicken-on-his-shoulders Zebulon Pike stomping around a bunch of concrete warehouses and brewing up a storm of papers. Ol' Sue-Anne knows. . . . Sue-Anne knows you didn't put in for transfer to combat laike you let everybody think you did. Sue-Anne knows because she got good an' loaded one night in the club with ol' Spang, who if you just happen to remember was Division Commander then, and he said that, hell no, he didn't see any reason why I should look for smaller quarters because no request had ever come in from you to go anywhere. He said he remembered way back when you managed to wheedle out of even foreign service in the Philippines. . . ."

"What did you do with your shoes?" Pike said.

"Tossed them up in the air. Threw them away like I ought to do with a lot of other things."

"We'd better find them before somebody else does. They might recognize those shoes and maybe they might get the wrong idea."

"Oh for Christ's sake, Zebulon! Don't give me that Sherlock Holmes business. I haven't been out in the bushes with anybody. I've been down in the bar gettin' good and drunk laike a lady. You about done with my feet?"

"Yes. You'd better stay off them for a few days. They're going to be very uncomfortable."

"Why don't you order me to bed and order me to stay there, General? What the hell's the matter with you? You can't make your own wife behave! I'll tell you why, Zebulon . . . because you never were a real general. They shoved that star through for you two weeks before you were due to retire, so they weren't taking any chances. And they shoved it through 'cause Frank Hoover really deserved a star and they couldn't very well bang him without including you. Just one trouble out of the whole thing, Zebulon. They made you a general in the wrong service. It should have been the Salvation Army."

"All right," Pike said quietly as he lowered her feet to the floor. "The cuts weren't really deep and they're good and clean now. I'll take another look at them in the morning."

She pushed herself out of the chair and stood up. She kept her feet well apart and managed to remain quite steady until she reached up to brush back a lock of hair that had fallen over one eye. The gesture almost capsized her. Before she fell against the screen Pike caught her, and for a moment she hung limp in his arms. She peered at him thoughtfully, the lids of her eyes almost closed.

"Why do you do this, Zebulon? Why do you take care of me?"

"Come," he said.

He led her to the bedroom and laid her gently on the bed. He pulled the sheet up to her neck because the trades were strong even through the screens, and turned out the light. As he started for the door she called after him.

"Where y'all goin'?"

"To the movies."

"Have a good time, Zebulon."

"Yes."

He closed the door with great care and almost tiptoed down the hall. Before he reached the front door he heard a sound that caused him to halt very suddenly. He listened and his lips gradually tightened. It was raining—hard.

When Fred Hanover had consumed enough Martinis to deaden any errant pangs of conscience he went back to his quarters and sat down before his typewriter. He was already two days late in producing the weekly piece he was supposed to send from Nikki, and he just simply had to put something in Dana Wood's mail pouch before he flew up to Tuamani in the morning.

It was not going to be easy for, as far as Hanover could see, things had come to an absolute standstill. Typing out, "No movie tonight raises Pike's Pique," just wouldn't do. And no matter what he wrote, it had to be siphoned through press relations on Tuamani. When you wrote for or about the colossus A.E.C., you had anywhere from five to fifty editors. Hanover thought that it was worse than his stint on *Time*. Never mind the news, grind the axes and above all mold opinion. And the colossus was so big it was like writing about the Indian rice problem. Only much bigger. Here was an isolated enterprise, only one of many, and the climax of this one would begin and end in less than a second. And would cost at least fifty million dollars. Just the plant investment of the A.E.C. was more than eight billion dollars! How could you put such figures into words and expect comprehension from anyone except Aristotle Onassis?

On *Time* magazine you could take up a cause, or one of the masterminds would throw a cause in your lap, and you could hammer away at it with a lot of smart-aleck phrase inventions until the subject died a natural death, or somebody made a dull Italian movie that would be given the two-page masterpiece treatment, or some idiot made a series of paintings using the lobe of his ear as a brush and attached honeydew melons to his nudes, in which case he would be solemnly given the genius treatment. You could do such things on *Time* according to your departmental niche, but, by God, Hanover thought, you could not so blithely monkey around with the Atomic Energy Commission or its endeavors. Presumably Operation Zeus was going to be the most terrifying cataclysm ever conceived by human beings if it was a success, and a simply unbelievable waste of talent, energy, and money if it was a failure. "Which," Hanover murmured aloud, "I hope it is."

But you couldn't write that. Tuamani would never pass such opinions if you did write them down. And if it ever did pass, the public would never read the stuff anyway. People did not *like* to read such things; and he, Frederick Payson Hanover, the poor man's Patrick Henry, the Amherst boy who couldn't even make the grade on *Time* . . . did not blame people in the least.

There was only one solution, and for the past few days he had been working at it with such energy as he could muster. He had even made a few notes. Flipping through them now, he smiled sourly when he noticed that he had unconsciously reverted to *Time* style in making the notes. He was trying the only approach left open to him—the personality angle. On Nikki, with even the lowest-magnitude celebrity far below the horizon, using the personality approach was tricky, and after investigation, showed an alarming tendency to prove a dry well.

. . . Pert, vivacious, piano-playing bachelor girl Margaret Trumpey of Beloit, Wisconsin, may signal the end of mankind with finger tips trained to the delicate cadence of Bach. . . .

Nuts! Margaret Trumpey was anything but pert. She hadn't been particularly vivacious when Hanover talked to her, and she certainly was not going to signal the fate of mankind with her finger tips. She sent out weather reports and could, if authorized, signal for additional cartons of canned milk, but most of the messages were coming her way and they were dull beyond description. The only factual thing about the notes was that Margaret was unwed, which was not exactly surprising, and that she came from Beloit. Beloit papers, if there happened to be more than one, please copy.

So much for Margaret Trumpey. She was a nice girl, *but,* Hanover thought, I am not being paid to write about nice girls. Such material was expertly enough handled by *Cosmopolitan* and *Redbook* writers. Glowering at the rain cascading past his screen window, Hanover remembered that those nice magazine girls were almost invariably in grievous trouble. Which the Trumpey girl was not.

"No!" he muttered at the rain. "My job, if it can be so designated, is to write about the creation of the most vicious, insulting slap in the face that God has ever received from the hand of man! Not really write about it . . . just make it easy to swallow!"

Hanover bent his head and closed his eyes. He discovered to his horror that he was gnawing at his knuckles, and he wished that he had not consumed so many Martinis. Since when, he thought, have I taken off on this religious kick? It is going to get me into trouble because I'm not equipped either by training or inclination to explore spiritual urges and, furthermore, it just will not make good copy. I am thirty-five years old. I smoke too much and I drink too much. I am educated after a fashion and generally conform to certain rules set down by the particular society into which I was born. I do not violate those rules because I am aware that to do so will get me in endless trouble . . . and yet, I am partner to the greatest social violation in known history. I prod my flabby brain, which has only become a hunk of punk, to convince others that this violation is perfectly all right, and there is nothing to get concerned about . . . worse yet, that there will be trouble if we *don't* commit the violation. I must even imply that through some mysterious process, about which I can be as vague as I please, this tragedy is somehow going to benefit society. Holy Mackerel! *This* is making a living? *This* is justifying my existence?

He looked at his notes again.

. . . high-domed scientists and brawny-armed laborers worked feverishly side by side on the flyspeck of an atoll to do their part in making Operation Zeus the biggest, most fantastic firecracker of them all. . . .

Hooey!

No one on Nikki was working up the slightest fever, side by side or in any other position. The laborers spent most of their time lying in their bunks reading comic books when they weren't drinking beer. No one knew what the scientists were up to, but it certainly wasn't much. Maybe, he thought, I ought to fly up to Tuamani, where things are supposed to be happening. But I wasn't assigned to Tuamani. I was assigned to Nikki and I either make something out of it or go home.

. . . Bar-straight, hammer-jawed veteran soldier, General Herbert Zebulon Pike, establishing proper diplomatic relations with Nikki natives, found the presumed savages had outdevoted his model town in the middle of nowhere. Score two to nothing. The native area of his atoll boasts two churches. Pike's pulsing model of American habitation —none. By teletype roared God-fearing Zebulon Pike: URGENT. SEND ONE CHURCH!

Religion sections please copy. Otherwise dull stuff.

And Pike would be justifiably mad because the omission of a church wasn't his fault anyway and he shouldn't have the credit of creating Pistol Two, if indeed, any credit was deserved. The whole thing was Atlas Construction. Also it was very possible he sent that wire more out of a sense of being cheated rather than a need for spiritual dedication.

Hanover lit a cigarette and walked to the window. The wind which had first come with the rain was gone now, and the smoke from his cigarette was drawn straight out through the screen. Across and down the street he could see the weather office, and he was surprised to notice that the light was on and that Abraham Lincoln sat over a drawing board. How about that guy? Maybe he was Honest Abe's great grandson, or nephew, or *something*? Maybe there was a piece in him. Jesus, if he even came from Illinois you could sort of work it around!

The rain came down heavier and the weather office became a dull blob of light. What was his name? . . . Smith! Why the hell couldn't it be Lincoln? Maybe he could at least be persuaded to grow a tuft of beard. A photo story on look-alikes maybe? Local contest? Phooey!

Hanover turned around to face his typewriter. He stood motionless, staring at it for a long time. Why didn't the contraption write its own stories? They invented every other kind of a machine. . . . Give enough information to an electronic brain and a machine could translate an income-tax report into Russian in a few minutes. Why not just feed an idea to a machine, go smoke a cigarette, and come back to read the story? Ask one of the boys in "Brains Bungalow" about such a machine in the morning. Make a fortune.

He sighed. All right, admit your brain is dead. Go for a walk in the rain. Get some fresh air. For lack of anything better to do, stop by and see that fellow Smith. At least he seemed to be able to find something to keep him busy nights. Maybe he was rewriting the Gettysburg Address.

Adam had almost forgotten about Pike. For over an hour he had been lost in the large map on his drawing table, and the lines and symbols which he had drawn upon it were now as real as the rain outside. He was working over one of the standard printed weather maps which he used as the basic form for each day's weather analysis. The principal islands and atolls of the area were represented by rough approximations of their shapes in faint brown ink. Nikki atoll was placed a few inches from the bottom of the map; Tuamani was three hundred miles to the northeast; Oa Titia atoll, which like Nikki was an auxiliary to Operation Zeus, was near the very top. One hundred and fifty miles to the west of Tuamani a small atoll was indicated and marked with an X. This, when the time came, would be the actual explosion site. The meridians of longitude and the parallels of latitude were printed in a fine blue overlay and covered the entire map.

Normally, Adam drew in such weather fronts as might be present in the area, basing his drawings on information teletyped from Tuamani and his own observations. Some freedom and imagination were both permissible and necessary in sketching in the isobars and isotherms because it was impossible to obtain a reading from every section of the area. Pressure, temperature, and wind reports from ships, radiosonde balloons, airplanes, Tuamani, and Oa Titia served only as guideposts when plotting on the map. Connecting them produced various line patterns; and, while Adam wished there were more reporting points, yet he saw no reason for Pike or anyone else to question the general accuracy of his work. The area was vast and there were bound to be local disturbances which would never appear on his maps or anyone else's, but the general pattern of the weather and, particularly, the all-important behavior of the winds aloft were based upon a known system which rarely betrayed a trained meteorologist.

So Adam told himself that he was only allowing his thoughts to simmer down when he first began doodling a portrait of his storm. He was just blowing off steam, that was all, and trying to forget about Pike in the mess hall. His pencil moved idly over the map, barely sketching, making what in the beginning appeared to be meaningless circles, one around the other. He was not really concentrating on a storm pattern in the beginning. He was thinking more about Margaret Trumpey and wondering how he could approach her again without sounding like a dunce. The map was fresh and clean, ready for his next morning's work, when he sat down quietly before it, and it *was* quiet he needed, not Peter Hildebrandt's tootling on his flute. He sat listening to the rain, the arrival of which only proved that Pike had ceased to read his forecasts. He had predicted it as a result of a mild front presently passing to the north of Tuamani.

And then suddenly . . . there it was! Now Adam stared at what he had drawn and for a moment he wondered about the power of the human subconscious. Certainly he remembered drawing it. For that matter his pencil was still poised above the series of concentric circles which, to anyone with the slightest knowledge of weather, would indicate a hurricane. And he had, without too much thought or intention, located the center of his circles about a hundred and fifty miles to the southwest of Nikki . . . actually in the middle of nowhere.

Smiling at his fancy, he started to label the hurricane MARGARET; then he stopped and erased the letters. Just for the hell of it, where would a hurricane go? How would it move if there *really* were one to the southwest of Nikki? There was no reasonable basis for prediction. Maybe the natives on the other side of the channel would know, but that was questionable because it had been a long time since anything of the sort had come anywhere near Nikki. It might, Adam thought, hang around in the vicinity for days, in which case—

Adam moved the pencil slowly in an arc around Nikki; then his hand swept off to the northwest on the map. In which case, he thought, it might reverse its course, make a lazy giant circle and become lost in the umpteen square miles of the Pacific. Cocking his head to one side, he again followed the course of his imaginary monster and decided that as long as he was momentarily in control of the elements he would feel better if the thing moved very slowly. It struck him that he had a fine name for such a slow-moving storm. Where he had erased Margaret's name, he solemnly printed LAZY ETHEL in bold letters.

Now thoroughly absorbed in his fancy he began to write a summary. A summary with a smile, he thought.

"A tropical disturbance of hurricane character is approaching Nikki atoll. Further references this storm will be coded Lazy Ethel. Center is estimated one hundred and fifty miles southwest and moving slowly in a north-easterly direction. . . ."

He hesitated, wondering what Pike's face would look like if he read such an analysis. He might even challenge the rights of the elements to make such a commotion and command them to cease.

Ah, well . . . it had been fun anyway. And he was feeling much better about everything—even General Zebulon Pike. He yawned. Now perhaps he could sleep. He was about to crumple up the summary and throw it on the floor when he heard the screen door slam behind him. He turned to see Fred Hanover standing in two rapidly forming pools of water.

"Hi!"

"Hi!"

Hanover smiled and wiped the water from his face and his hair. "Kind of wet outside," he said.

"Yeah."

"Is this going to last all night?"

"Probably."

Hanover advanced a few paces toward the drawing table and wondered how, with being out in the rain and all, he could still feel those Martinis. He fished in his shirt pocket and brought out a sodden pack of cigarettes.

"Don't happen to have a cigarette, do you? Mine seem to be pretty damp."

"Sorry. I only smoke a pipe."

"Oh."

Hanover hesitated, then placed a limp cigarette between his lips. Adam struck a match and he leaned over the drawing table to accept the light. He puffed for several seconds without success and he wondered later if it was because his mind was, very suddenly, not on smoking. He straightened up finally and said, "The hell with it."

He tossed the cigarette into the wastebasket beneath the drawing board. "I hope you don't mind my barging in on you like this?"

"Nope."

"I've seen you around, but no one ever bothered to introduce us. Hanover . . . Fred Hanover's the name. I'm in press relations, which probably doesn't mean much to you."

"Well, not exactly."

"No matter. I just thought I'd stop by for a talk. . . . Seeing you sort of left a candle in the window."

"I guess I'm not much of a talker, but you're welcome anyway."

Hanover glanced at the drawing board again and then looked carefully at Adam. "What's cooking . . . generally?"

"How do you mean?"

"I mean who, what, and where? You know. People like me have to make a living like everyone else. Nikki is a very easy place to get stuck for a story, I can tell you!"

"I suppose it is."

This fellow, Hanover thought, is like playing badminton with a balloon. You hit the object, swing through the air, and nothing comes back. A very smart character, and who did he think he was kidding? Martinis or no, Fred Hanover had twenty-twenty vision and he had seen that drawing board. He could still see it.

"Nothing special at all, huh?"

"Not as far as I know."

Oh, you lying bastard! I'm looking right *at it!* Are you going to sit there with pie on your face and tell me there isn't anything going on? Not as far as you know? Who the hell *else* would know about a little newsy item which seemed to be labeled Lazy Ethel and which certainly did not appear to be very far from a certain atoll known as Nikki? Except maybe Pike, who must already know about it, which, of course, explained why he was in such a flap when he left the mess hall.

"Not a thing doing, huh?"

"Nope."

"I suppose it does get pretty dull weatherwise around here. The Pacific being the Pacific and all that."

"Occasionally, it is pretty interesting," Adam said matter-of-factly. "You'd be surprised."

"Yes. I guess I would."

Hanover looked about the office and his eyes came to the written summary. He took a step closer to the drawing board and was grateful again for his perfect vision. He could easily read the words Adam had written.

"Could you," he said slowly, "give me some idea what the weather will be like tomorrow? I was thinking I might go fishing in the lagoon."

"It should be very nice."

Hanover pressed his lips together and made a humming sound. He was both uneasy and uncertain. If he told this Class A dullard that he knew very well he was sitting on the best story ever to come out of Nikki, he might get to Pike and manage to stop it. And he could just about guess why Mr. Dullard was being so cagey. Also why he was working nights.

"Well," Hanover said. "Nice to talk to you. If you find out anything that might be of interest newswise . . . let me know, will you? I live over behind Brains Bungalow."

"Sure. Good fishing."

Hanover walked slowly to the door. He opened it, looked back over his shoulder and suppressed a sudden urge to wink at Adam. He said, "This rain doesn't mean anything special . . . is that right?"

"Correct."

"Good night. Thanks for the hospitality."

"You're welcome."

Hanover stepped out into the rain. When he moved away from the glow of light he turned and saw that Adam was again bent over his drawing board. He watched him only a moment, then trotted toward his quarters. He still had plenty of time to crank out a story before Dana Wood flew back to Tuamani. And the chances were very good indeed, what with the hour and all, that his little piece would hit the desks in Tuamani even before Abe Lincoln's technical manifesto found its normal way through the morning teletype.

This, Hanover decided, would put press relations in its proper place where press damn well belonged—at the head of the line. What a flap! The brass on Tuamani getting their first dope on a little item called Lazy Ethel from a mere journalist! A journalist who just happened to be in the doghouse more or less. Yes, sir. A journalist who had been exiled to the bush league island of Project Zeus because he allegedly drank too much, but now by God in heaven they would have to admit that, drunk or sober, one Fred Hanover was very much on the job.

He hummed tunelessly yet happily as the rain spattered on his head. Stories, he thought smiling, are where you find them.

6

Pike rose before the sun as was his custom. He set his wrist watch on the wash basin and spent exactly twenty-one minutes brushing his teeth, shaving, and showering. He brushed his stiff hair vigorously for exactly fifty strokes, then took up his watch again. He glanced at it with considerable satisfaction, then strode into his bedroom. There he stood before the open doorway which led onto the porch and began those ritualistic movements which had, with rare exceptions, officially introduced his day ever since his graduation from the Point. He began, as always, with his push-ups, stiffly executing twenty before he jumped to an erect position again. Pike was methodical and realistic about his push-ups. When he was thirty he had done forty every morning and at forty, in the interest of his heart, he had deliberately cut the effort to thirty. Now, for the past five years twenty push-ups seemed quite enough and he was considering cutting things down to fifteen. The forced reduction did not depress him. He glanced at his watch again before he did twenty bends, touching the palms of his hands to the floor each time. He was also thinking of cutting these bends to fifteen. After all.

Then he rested, red in the face, yet breathing only slightly faster than normal. He rested with his feet together and his hands at his sides in a posture of attention, although on this morning his head was bent in contemplation of his nakedness. His feet were still good and well formed, but lately the veins in his legs were becoming too prominent, standing out like small purple ropes entwining his muscles. Yet his belly was firm and showed no signs of becoming a pot.

Regarding his body with honest curiosity, he began to wonder if he would ever again lose himself in Sue-Anne's passionate embrace. It had been a very long time, so long, in fact, that the preliminary maneuvers which always seemed so necessary, now presented an almost insurmountable wall between them. How, presuming Sue-Anne was in the mood, which she never seemed to be any more; how could he possibly start things off? How could he, without embarrassment, without making a damned fool of himself, without having Sue-Anne burst out laughing and say for criminy sakes Zebulon, *what* in tarnashin you trying to do, how could he begin? Supposing he went through the door and into her room now, right now in the morning when he was so charged with energy? Supposing he slipped into her bed and began, as they had on so many mornings for so many years? Would she welcome him, or submit with bored indifference as she had done the last time, which would now be over two years ago; or would she laugh? And if she laughed that would be the end. Forever.

He decided not to risk it. Certainly not on this morning. The cuts on Sue-Anne's feet were going to hurt and she was going to have a terrible hangover. It would be much smarter to stay out of her way for the rest of the day.

He raised his arms above his head, taking a deep breath as he did so and standing on his tiptoes. He repeated this process fifteen times, staring vacantly straight ahead at the row of palm trees beyond the porch and at the sunrays which were now just touching their tops. As he breathed he thought about Sue-Anne sprawled on the bed in the next room, and he wondered why it was that he had never even considered spending himself within the body of another woman. No. That would never be the answer. Half-smiling at the morning, very much awake now, he murmured, I guess I'm just a one-man dog.

He dressed rapidly and with mechanical efficiency. No old soldier would have been ashamed of Zebulon Pike when he had finished, for somewhere in his career he had mastered the tricks of smartness until every shirt and pair of pants he possessed seemed to be faded just the right amount, and they fitted his torso as if most expensively tailored. His starched khaki shirt hung perfectly on his shoulders. The pockets were creased and always buttoned, his service belt was scrubbed, and the brass buckle shone as if his fingers had never touched it. The jodhpur shoes which he chose to wear on this morning were old and well broken, yet so carefully polished and preserved it was almost impossible to detect any wear.

He made his bed with equal efficiency, turning the top sheet down precisely eight inches and snapping the pillow slip until it was quite smooth. When he tucked in the ends and swept his hand swiftly across the top sheet, there was hardly any evidence that the bed had been occupied. Then he snapped on his wrist watch and saw that the entire operation since his first push-up had taken twelve minutes. As it always did. Holding his shoulders well back so that his shirt and pants appeared to be a sort of secondary skin, he strode out of the room. The time was exactly six-thirty.

He quick-marched to the mess hall and ate his breakfast in solitude. This displeased him, not because he was particularly anxious to talk with anyone over his Sanka, but he thought that Albright, in his position as aide, should be up and about before hoi polloi. The brass, Pike had long been firmly convinced, should be brass in every connotation of the word. They were entitled to certain privileges, but there were also certain penalties attached to those privileges. Brass should lead, in effort as well as time. It was not seemly for those common laborers at the far end of the mess hall to be all through with their breakfast and ready to go to work when the brass, or a part of it in the person of Albright, was still lolly-dollying around in bed. The result of poor training, Pike thought, as he drained the last of his Sanka. Intellectual parents, no doubt, too much money, doting mother, Eastern school, unmarried irresponsibility, no experience with military discipline; all that. Very well, he would speak to Albright about this getting-up business. It would be the second such address and most certainly the last one.

He stood up and carefully patted his mouth with his paper napkin, which had remained unsoiled and folded. He was, as soon as he had revisited his bathroom, ready for what he was determined must be a very busy and fruitful day.

School for the children of Pistol Two began at seven o'clock with a ceremony carefully prescribed by Pike. He considered that he had rather cleverly circumvented an early and primary directive set down by his superiors. Normally Pike had a reverence for any directive which might arrive through channels. He was convinced there was only one way to run an organization and that was by a strict allegiance to tables of organization, plus absolute obedience to any directive worthy of being placed on paper. There was not, there never had been, and there never could be, any other way to control any given number of people from a squad to the entire population of an occupied country. A properly authorized directive was *not* just red tape, whether it covered the invasion of a hostile beach or stated the number of wastebaskets required per square foot of office space. Without directives, in Pike's solemn opinion, any organization of more than two people was automatically doomed to chaos. Furthermore, a good and well-written directive left no opportunity for personal interpretation. It stated bare facts, nothing more. Which was why Pike considered he had not taken undue liberties with that certain directive A-12 which stated, in what he thought were rather ineffectual terms, that "it must be remembered the A.E.C. is in no sense a military organization or even a branch of the military. While we co-operate and in turn receive co-operation from all branches of the armed services and employ ex-service personnel, we function purely as a civilian organization. Direct identity with any branch of the armed services could be detrimental to our authorized functions and could easily result in adverse public reaction to our basic goals. Therefore all those to whom this directive is addressed will avoid any act or procedure which might possibly be considered as of a military nature and/or originating from military authority."

Pike almost knew the directive by heart and it had come as a profound shock to him. But it was still a directive, innocently denying its theme by being set down and mimeographed in the best military form with suitable space for acknowledging initials, and it was signed by the Director himself. Therefore Pike had no hesitation in complying. He believed that he was within the bounds of propriety, however, in the business of the flag.

It would, of course, be in direct violation of the directive to have the Marine detachment hoist the American flag over Pistol Two every morning, or take it down at sunset. Yet Pistol Two was as much an outpost as Fort Ticonderoga back in the seventeen hundreds. The thought of beginning or ending a day without the good old Stars and Stripes troubled Pike, and he was determined that any place commanded by himself was going to observe the ceremony.

He believed that he had solved the problem neatly. The school children would raise the flag in the morning and a special honor detail, based upon their grades and behavior, would lower the flag at night. Ho—ho! Who could ever accuse school children of representing the military?

And so every morning before school began the flag was raised and every evening it descended, albeit without bugle or gun, which Pike could not see any way of providing. And every morning the Governor of Pistol Two stood at rigid attention while Alice Summers, the school-teacher, saw to it that her charges displayed a minimum of restlessness during the ceremony. When the flag was up and the halyard made fast, Pike beamed on the assemblage gathered about the pole and he watched with enormous satisfaction as they filed into the schoolhouse. Like so many childless men a great yearning welled up within him whenever he saw the issue of others, and when they were particularly well behaved as they always were at this fresh time of day, it was all he could do to refrain from following them into the building and patting the more likable students on the head.

Yessir, he thought, as the last pair of scrawny legs disappeared through the school's screen door. There is nothing like the little ones! Nothing was too good for them and within the physical limits of Pistol Two he had provided well. He had seen to it that the carpenters made teeter-totters from leftover dock planks and had authorized the plumbers to use all excess pipe for Jungle-Jim bars. He had personally designed the six swings now hanging motionless in the morning sunlight and had subjected them to the most strenuous tests himself by swinging nearly to the horizontal and performing a wild "chain snap" fifteen feet off the ground, for which he was resoundingly cheered. Now in the afternoon when school was out, he could hear the distant playground cries and shouts of delight in his office and he found it the most rewarding experience since he first beheld Nikki atoll.

He stood for a moment looking at the playground and regretting the fact that no amount of technical ingenuity had been able to furnish a proper slide or trampolin. If I had more money, he thought, I'd send for a trampolin myself and that would be the end of it. But he didn't have the money, and the two request letters he had sent to Tuamani for such equipment had so far been ignored. He would write again today. Dammit, millions to explode a bomb and the A.E.C. couldn't spare a hundred dollars for a kid's slide! There was no directive to cover such items, or he would long since have allocated the amount out of settlement funds.

He turned away from the school and set off briskly on what he had come to think of as his daily reconnoitering patrol. This consisted of a fast-paced tour throughout the environs of Pistol Two. It took him the better part of an hour. Leaving the school yard he walked through the equipment park, noting as he passed that the tractors, fork lifts, emergency cranes, jeeps and carryalls were properly aligned and covered with tarpaulins. Leaving the park he glanced at the wharf and the warehouse, about which there was rarely any activity at this hour, and then he proceeded down the center of Broadway. He passed the carpenter shop and saw that Barney Dunbar was still tinkering with his power saw, but he did not slow his pace lest Barney again beg him to order another. There was a limit to the equipment even the A.E.C could provide at this distance from the States, and Pike had heard quite enough whining about that damned saw. He hardly glanced at the weather office as he passed around the corner of it, but he did note that it was still unoccupied. Of course that weather fellow would be lolly-dollying around in bed.

He passed the movie, noting grimly that the benches were still wet from the night's rain. Leaving the road he cut across an open area which would lead him between the laundry and the building which housed the foreign observers. Hanover was quartered in the same building, and the room at the far end was Albright's . . . who would, of course, still be lolly-dollying around in bed.

Pike halted briefly outside Albright's window. He listened for any sound of activity and, hearing none, considered entering the room and hauling Albright out of bed by the ears. Finally he dismissed the project as beneath his dignity. He would handle Mr. Albright later.

He swung off again without a backward glance and turned up the narrow coral road marked Second Avenue. Where it intersected with Broadway he passed the Marine quarters and saw that they were engaged in swabbing down the floor or "deck" as Sgt. Doolan would have put it, and he saw that Doolan himself was in charge. Pike approved, even though Doolan seemed to take a secret pleasure in withholding a salute. He was within his rights, of course. Marines did not salute civilians and Pike was a civilian. But Doolan did throw away his cigarette and assume a posture which at least resembled attention, and he said, "Good morning, Governor," smartly enough. There was neither affection nor resentment in his voice, and if there had been either intonation, Pike would have followed old instinct and stopped to find out what was wrong.

Pike continued up Second Avenue, passing the deserted ball park and the recreation building, which was locked at this hour. On the opposite side of the street he noted that the space between the two buildings which housed the single ladies had again been selected as a place to dry their laundry. He frowned at the two pairs of panties hanging from a line and assured himself that if the buildings had quartered WAC's, he would most certainly have spoken sharply to their lieutenant. Under the circumstances about all he could do was maintain his frown until the thoroughly unmilitary spectacle was far behind him and he had reached the hospital.

Now, because almost a week had gone by since he had

inspected this particular building in his domain, Pike halted again, executed a smart right face, and entered the doorway. Dr. Case, who had his own rather spacious quarters in the rear of the hospital, was brewing a pot of coffee on his sterilizer. He looked up when he heard the door slam and regarded Pike without any sign of welcome. He was still in his pajamas, which Pike thought were not particularly clean for a doctor, and he muttered good morning in such a way Pike wondered if he was still asleep. Probably lolly-dollying around in bed, Pike thought, when he should have been up polishing his instruments, or going over some old X rays, or something since there were not, so far as he knew, any sick to heal in Pistol Two.

"Good morning to you, Doctor!" Pike boomed, aware now that Case was flapping about in his bare feet, which was probably most unsanitary. And he was smoking a cigarette before breakfast, which anyone knew was extremely unhealthy.

"Have a cup of coffee, Governor?" Case offered without enthusiasm.

"No, thank you. Never touch it."

"Why?"

"I don't think stimulants, artificial that is, do the body any good."

"It's possible that, taken in moderation, they don't do any harm, either."

"You're the doctor. Ho. Ho!"

Pike could not understand why Case seemed to wince at this instant. Actually the sentence, which had slipped out of him before he had really thought about it, seemed worthy of an echoing ho-ho from Case. His dour look, now, was disappointing. The man obviously had no sense of humor. As a matter of fact there were a great many things about Dr. Case which were puzzling. Reaching into his file-case mind, Pike clearly recalled their original interview, which had occurred in the ship. He had bluntly asked Case why he had abandoned his practice in Oregon and taken the assignment with Operation Zeus.

"If you'll sit still and listen for a week or so I'll tell you in about a hundred thousand words," Case had said. "It could be because I refused to join a new high priesthood which makes the Spanish inquisitors look like a bunch of amateurs. You must remember, Governor, that in America at least, a doctor is more than a professional man. He is a holy man, an untouchable, of whom one speaks only in whispers, or the most reverent tones. A part of this aura of greatness has been created by the doctors themselves, but for the most part it is the tribute of ordinary citizens who would not so respect the President of the United States or even one of the latter-day saints. The secret hero of every woman over thirty-five is her doctor, and otherwise sensible men often prostrate themselves before these new tin gods. I could not go along with this nonsense. I called some doctors fatheads publicly. I asked and accepted advice from outside the priesthood. I admitted openly that there were times when I didn't know what the hell I was doing. No one could seem to convince me that a code known as 'medical ethics' gave any man license to put those in his care through the torture of the damned. So I took this job because I finally gathered up enough courage to do some thinking, and a Pacific island seemed to be a pretty good place to do it. Frankly, I get too wrapped up in my patients' emotions to make a very good doctor. I found that I was unconsciously looking for gratitude, which is wrong. Jesus cured eleven lepers and only one returned to thank him. You see, a good doctor should never admit to himself that his patient might have recovered from two medicines . . . time and the will to live. If he does, he becomes inept from doubt, or conscience-stricken from sending his bill, or both. Well, sir, that's what was happening to me and that's why I'm here."

Looking at him now in his wrinkled and slightly soiled pajamas, Pike thought the man presented nothing to inspire confidence. All right for cuts and bruises perhaps, but he wouldn't have made buck sergeant in the Medical Corps.

"Don't you like our mess-hall coffee?" Pike asked.

"No, sir, I do not."

"What's the matter with it?"

"It tastes and looks like urine. Sometimes it even smells like it."

"I'll look into the matter."

"Do," Case said, scratching his bald head. "In the meantime what's your trouble?"

"I don't have any troubles . . . physically at least. I just dropped by for a checkup."

"Heart bothering you?"

"No. Not that kind of a checkup. I'm in fine shape. Always have been and intend to stay that way. It's another . . ."

Dr. Case peered at him from beneath his eyebrows, which in contrast to his bald head were as bushy as a mustache. He took a puff at his cigarette, which brought on such a fit of coughing Pike allowed time for it to subside before he continued.

"I just dropped by to check up on you and the hospital. Quite a community we have here, you know, Doctor. I like to look in on everything now and then . . . keep things at my finger tips."

"I suppose it would be too much to ask if you'd schedule your visits a little later in the day. I'm not at my best in the mornings. As a matter of fact I prefer absolute silence. It's better for thinking. That's why my office hours are in the afternoon."

Case engaged in another fit of coughing while he poured himself a cup of coffee. He sipped at it hungrily and said, "However, since you're here, I'll give you a brief run-down on the medical situation in Pistol Two. When it ceases to fascinate you, you are at liberty to stop me. Floyd Dunbar, who is eight years old, was punched in the face by one Herbert Fry, who is nine years old, at approximately sixteen hundred hours yesterday and arrived here with a bloody nose. Patient treated and dismissed after being held thirty minutes for observation and a mild lecture on the folly of picking on people who are bigger than you are. A Mrs. Pickering, I think that's her name, came in and wanted her gall bladder removed. I questioned this patient at some length in an attempt to find out why she considered such an operation necessary and she advised that she had been trying to get said gall bladder removed for some time and this seemed like an ideal opportunity since the government would assume all expense of the operation. Patient was otherwise obscure about her desire to have operation performed except to state that she had previously, and at her own expense, had her tonsils, adenoids, and appendix removed, and since all of those fixtures were hangovers from primeval man, she assumed she could get along very well without her gall bladder as well. Patient dismissed after medication. Two aspirin. A man with the rather interesting name of Jellico came in to complain about his back. It seems he drives one of the bulldozers and they give him such a rough ride he often slips a disc in his spine. After considerable conversation about where in the name of God he inherited a name like Jellico, which incidentally he never explained to my complete satisfaction, I took what turned out to be a pretty good guess and diagnosed his trouble as rheumatoid arthritis. He then admitted to me that he had been under treatment for that disease for several years and had graduated cum laude from courses in traction, physiotherapy, cortisone derivatives, aspirin, and frog's left ears captured and swallowed only by the light of a full moon. After we got through all that we spent about twenty minutes bemoaning the fact that doctors didn't know a damn thing about arthritis including the two most elementary facts which would be how it's caused, or how to cure it, and we both felt a hell of a lot better. He's an interesting man, that Jellico . . . and a brave one. Care to hear more?"

"No, thanks," Pike said, wishing he had never stopped by the hospital in the first place. Convinced that Dr. Case was "peculiar" if not actually a little crazy, he turned for the door. Then suddenly he faced about and, trying to avoid looking directly into Case's piercing eyes, he said, "By the way, Doctor. I don't suppose they included any strait jackets in your medical equipment?"

Pike forced his attention to remain on the ceiling so as to appear entirely casual, as if the question of strait jackets was only a demonstration of his devotion to detail.

"Strait jackets! What the hell for?"

"You know. Among so many people, and all civilians, there are bound to be a few . . . unfortunates. Perhaps I should say a few who lack stability . . ."

"Is that so?"

"Matter of fact, a man called on me not long ago whom I at first considered as somewhat unbalanced. It turned out that he was perfectly all right . . . matter of fact, very intelligent man . . . but it set me to thinking."

There was a moment's silence while Dr. Case explored the contents of his coffee cup. And again Pike wished he had not stopped by the hospital. Finally Case said, "Well, Governor, there are still a lot of boxes in the store-room I haven't looked at. Maybe one of them contains a strait jacket. I don't know and I don't much care. But if the need for such a thing arises, there are other methods these days to keep a patient quiet. Medicine hasn't made much progress in the last fifty years, but it has made some."

"Thank you, Doctor. I have complete confidence you could handle any such situation."

"I can always borrow a baseball bat," Dr. Case said and broke into a violent fit of coughing.

Pike retreated two steps to the door and fled. He passed along the side of the hospital as quickly as he could without actually breaking into a run. He had spent entirely too much time in the hospital and it had been wasted time at that. So instead of taking the long way back to his office, which would have permitted at least a cursory inspection of the airstrip, the garage, machine shop, and water-evaporation plant, he cut directly across an open area behind the store and barber shop. He marched with new determination, chin up, shoulders well back, arms swinging to match his full stride; for now the real business of this day would begin and he was more than anxious to begin.

7

He passed through the grove of palm trees which surrounded his own quarters. On the supposition that any governor and his lady would automatically be sensitive to natural beauty, these had been allowed to stand, but on this morning Pike was not to be diverted by natural beauty. He entered a small building marked PLUMBING SHOP and asked for Pete Walsacki. A thin, yawning youth, who looked so young Pike wondered at once why he was on Nikki instead of in the Army, said that Pete Walsacki had just used up his last hacksaw blade and had gone to the warehouse for a new supply and would be back any minute. Pike also noted that the young man was smoking a cigarette and wondered if he had as yet had breakfast.

"Tell him to come over to my place as soon as he arrives," Pike ordered.

"Something busted?"

Pike hesitated. Nosy young man. Better find out more about him. "My shower," he said. "It needs repair. Tell him to be sure and bring his tools."

"Okay."

"Tell him to come to my office first and I'll explain what's wrong."

"Okay."

"Have you ever been in the Army, young man?"

"Unh-uh."

"A few years wouldn't do you any harm. You might learn that there is an English word commonly used in addressing your elders or those in authority. That word is *sir*."

"Ya, sir."

Pike left the plumbing shop, crossed through the palm grove, where he paused momentarily to pick a single flower, and then continued until he reached his front porch. He took the steps two at a time. He glanced at his watch when he entered his office. It was exactly one minute past eight. Twirling the flower between his fingers, he circled his desk impatiently. Then he went down the hallway and stopped before Sue-Anne's door.

He carefully turned the knob and entered the room on tiptoe. He saw with some disappointment that she was still asleep. And he saw, too, that the morning sun which now shafted through the veranda doors was unkind to her and all that surrounded her sleeping figure. The pillow was smeared with lipstick. An ash tray containing eight cigarette butts was on the floor within easy reach of her hand. Her charm bracelets were strewn about in little piles on the night table. One of them encircled an unopened jar of cold cream. Another had been placed around a glass of water. Her dress was a collapsed oval of Shantung on the opposite side of the bed, and her slip had somehow been tossed onto the porch. Pike remembered her shoes. He would have to retrieve those today and he would have to do it himself. When she awakened she could tell him where to start looking.

Still twirling his flower, he tiptoed to the porch. He picked up the slip and placed it on the bureau. Then he carefully closed the porch shutters. Moving cautiously through the dim light in the room, he picked up the ash trays, emptied them in the wastebasket, and placed the flower in a glass of water. Finally he bent down and gently shook his wife. He said, "Good morning, Precious."

"What the hell do *you* want?"

"I just wanted to tell you that you're going to have plumbing trouble."

"Now, Zebulon! I'm in no mood or condition for yoah bum jokes. Go 'way."

"Just you rest, Precious. But if anyone should ask you, we *did* have plumbing trouble. Shower wouldn't drain. It was fixed this morning. In fact I don't care if you drop that little bit of information when you go to the mess hall or the hairdresser or whatever."

Sue-Anne tried to raise her head, then eased it back to the pillow again. "Zebulon? What in tarnashin you talking about?"

"Pete Walsacki. He's on his way over to fix the shower drain."

"But there's nothing wrong with . . . Wait a second. Did you say Pete Walsacki? That big fellow?"

"Yes. He's the boss plumber."

Some of the glaze removed itself from Sue-Anne's eyes. "Oh ye-yes!"

She spoke with an enthusiasm Pike made no attempt to understand.

"Of course he really won't fix it. I just wanted you to know about it in case someone asked what he was doing here. . . . Then you would have an explanation that made sense."

"Why won't he fix it? Zebulon, *you* aren't making any sense . . . which only surprises me because I'm not awake yet."

"The shower is perfectly all right."

"Then what . . . ?"

"Never you mind, Precious. Now you know, and you can go back to sleep. I'll see you for lunch."

He left the doorway and returned down the hallway. He did not hear Sue-Anne say that she was certainly not going back to sleep if Pete Walsacki was going to pay a call. And he would have been amazed at the speed with which she left her bed.

Pike sat down at his desk; and, after he had arranged his two pens and several pencils precisely behind the small triangular sign which spelled out ZEBULON PIKE, he tipped back in his chair and waited for Pete Walsacki. How long did it take to get a hacksaw blade, dammit? On this particular morning, time was of the essence.

His fingers moved automatically to his gold class ring and he pushed it slowly around and around, musing on the devices worn almost smooth; the crossed rifles, the sabers, the crest, and the spread eagle. And he saw himself a plebe at the Point again, frightened and terribly anxious to please his upperclassmen. He saw the cold, gray battlement-encrusted buildings with the Hudson flowing beneath them, and he heard the high-pitched cries of day orders echoing down the barrack halls. Swiftly, as though the intervening years were like a moment's sleep, he heard the flat explosion of the reveille cannon outside his barracks window, and the more distant, lilting notes of the day's first bugle. And somehow then, it became a Sunday morning. There he sat on the gray blanket which covered his iron cot, and across his knees was spread the blouse of his dress uniform. There were, including those adorning the sleeves and the claw-hammer tail, forty-eight brass buttons on that blouse, each shaped like a small ball and arranged in lines. He heard the clicking as he slipped the metal "button board" over the first row so the polish would not stain the fabric, and he could smell the peculiar tang of the polish itself as he vigorously massaged the protruding buttons. Cadet H. Zebulon Pike never received a single demerit for neglect of uniform. The device on his shako, the rectangular plate which clipped to the intersection of his white shoulder straps, the insignia on his patent-leather cartridge case, all glistened; not only on Sunday morning, but every morning of every year he had been at the Point. Cadet Pike may have graduated in the lower third of his class and had his troubles with algebra, but no one could ever say he had not been a good soldier.

Then, Pike suddenly found himself asking, what happened? What went wrong between the time he was a second lieutenant and the time he reached his majority? There were a lot of years in between those commissions and they were not nearly as clear as his cadet days. And after he had pinned on a major's leaves, was there anything to remember except a string of posts around the country, all somehow very much alike until it was impossible now to distinguish any feature about them save the difference in climate? Fort Sill, Snelling, Ethan Allen . . . Monmouth, Plattsburg, the remount station at Riley, Funston, Sam Houston, and finally, for an all-too-brief tour of duty, the Presidio. A house, a "dog-robber," prisoners raking leaves in the yard . . . whisky, horses, Sue-Anne talking huskily and endlessly on the telephone to other officers' wives . . . and debts. For what officer above the rank of captain ever managed to live within his income? And all of those years the most dangerous exposure was summertime maneuvers. And when it was all over, a star. No ribbons, no medals, just a star which there had never really been an opportunity to display in active service. Those two weeks before retirement could not honestly be counted. The star was a reward for honest, if not distinguished service, thoughtfully arranged by a few surviving contemporaries who had been at the Point with Zebulon Pike. Seeing that old Pike got his star, which would, of course, increase his retirement pay, was a matter of class honor. There were also certain elements of self-preservation involved since those recommending the star were looking forward to at least equivalent consideration upon their own separation from the service.

So I became a general! Pike grunted audibly at the thought and swung around in his chair to stare at the palm trees beyond the window. Sue-Anne was right. It could just as well have been the Salvation Army.

He heard the screen door slam and heavy steps in the hallway. He whirled around to face his desk again and assumed his most formidable pose. When Pete Walsacki appeared in the doorway, Pike was more than ready for him.

"Close the door," he said quickly. Then he arched one eyebrow and his voice took on a conspiratorial tone. "Good. You look exactly like a plumber."

Walsacki smiled and thoughtfully scratched at the black hair on his powerful forearms. "I am," he said.

"Where are your tools?"

"On the porch. I didn't think you'd want me to lug them in here."

"No. . . . No. Of course not. That wouldn't be really necessary." He pointed to the visitor's chair beside his desk.

"Walsacki," he began gravely, "we have trouble."

Reaching into his desk drawer he pulled out a sheaf of papers. He wet the end of his thumb and flipped through the papers until he came upon one which caused his eyes to narrow until they were mere slits. By God, when Zebulon Pike read a paper he remembered what was on it! Every last word and item!

"Yessir! *There* is the item on the manifest, plain as day . . . item number 2605 dash J . . . flashlight batteries . . . four cases."

He handed the sheaf of papers to Walsacki, who accepted it without the slightest sign of interest.

"What do you make of *that?*" Pike asked.

Walsacki hesitated. "Well . . . it looks like somebody thought of everything and ordered four cases of flashlight batteries."

"Exactly. But there are no batteries in Pistol Two. I was so informed last night. They have disappeared. Gone!"

Beneath the black fibers which covered Walsacki's neck under the open shirt an experimental rumbling occurred as if the man behind the matting had unsuccessfully attempted to start a reciprocating engine. "That's too bad," Walsacki finally said.

"Too bad? It's theft of government property, that's what it is! Therefore it becomes your baby."

"Why mine?"

"You're the F.B.I. agent here, aren't you? Unless I have been misinformed this is a straight F.B.I. matter. Theft of government property is strictly the province of your agency."

Walsacki forced a smile and looked disbelievingly into Pike's eager eyes. He stuck one finger into his ear and wiggled it vigorously as if he would erase the words he had heard. "Look, Governor. You have not been misinformed. Theft of government property is and always has been a function of the Bureau—"

"Then catch the bastard!" Pike broke in triumphantly.

"I was about to say that while you are legally correct, these things sometimes have to be viewed with regard to the overall picture. I am fairly certain that no one on this island but yourself knows I'm with the Bureau. A great deal of my effectiveness, if not all of it, would be lost if it was generally known that I was not just a plumber."

"To hell with the overall picture! I want those flashlight batteries and I especially want the bastard who stole them! Who knows what he'll make off with next?"

"Whatever it might be, may I suggest that he can't go very far? Assuming the batteries were stolen in the first place and not just misplaced or really never arrived, don't you think it would be rather unfortunate to jeopardize my primary function by kicking up a fuss about flashlight batteries? Wouldn't it be a lot easier to just order some more batteries?"

"Your primary function is to protect government property and act as my deputy in so doing. You know as well as I do that I'm charged with every damned thing on this base from toothpicks to dock pilings. I was in the Army too long, Walsacki. Nobody's going to hang Zeb Pike with a paperwork noose."

Walsacki wiggled his finger in his ear again and took a long moment to re-establish his patience.

"Governor," he said finally. "While you are technically

correct, the Bureau did not send me here to investigate petty thievery."

"Then what the hell are you here for?"

"If you were not informed, then I must assume you are not supposed to know."

Walsacki kept his voice so controlled and polite he could have been talking to a nun.

Pike pressed his lips together until they vanished. His short-cropped hair seemed to bristle as if it were on the back of an angry dog and the thousands of tiny veins in his face became as suddenly visible as if he had turned an electric switch. It was with some difficulty that he refrained from pounding his fist on the desk.

"I am supposed to know *everything* that goes on here! *Everything*, do you hear?"

"I hear you very well."

"Apparently there is something I do not know. You will tell me at once."

"I am sorry, sir."

Pike rose abruptly and brought his hands together behind him with a loud smack. He paced across the room and did an about-face just before he collided with the flag standard.

"If you were a soldier I'd let you think this over in a stockade!"

"I am sorry, sir, but I am not a soldier."

"Nonsense! We are all soldiers here. We have to be. Only way to get the job done. Perhaps we don't salute or wear uniforms, but by God we are all soldiers in the cause of democracy!"

Liking the sound of what he had said, Pike turned and gave Walsacki his full Sunday-morning-before-chapel-battery-inspection glare.

"Frankly, I don't like your attitude, Walsacki. I will

not tolerate any Gestapo-like activities on this base as long as I'm Governor. I will not have you snooping around in other people's business and informing Washington or anywhere else as to their politics. I know you cloak-and-dagger fellows! Ho! Ho! Well, you just remember this is a little bit of America here and I intend to keep it that way."

"The Bureau functions in America, Governor. I don't think anyone except people who prefer another type of government consider us a secret police."

"Dammitall, I didn't call you over here to engage in a political discussion! I want those flashlight batteries and I want to lay my hands on the man who stole them."

Pike clasped his hands before him and cracked his knuckles as if they were the disintegrating vertebrae of a handy battery thief.

Walsacki said, "Well, Governor, about the only suggestion I can make is that you have the marines or somebody like that check over on the other side of the channel. Whoever made off with your batteries might find the trading pretty good over there. There certainly isn't any place to dispose of them here. It would be most unwise at this time . . ."

Walsacki sighed with visible relief when a sharp knock on the door interrupted him. Pike at once brought a precautionary finger to his lips and glanced at the door.

"Yes? Who is it?"

"Teletype, sir."

Recognizing the voice, Pike relaxed slightly. That damned girl. She had a genius for appearing at the wrong moment. She was not due until she brought the weather map.

"Come back with it at your regular time," he said as mildly as he could.

"The message is designated Urgent First Priority, sir. It's from Tuamani."

Pike hesitated uncertainly. Walsacki and the flashlight batteries were important, but this was the first time any such message had come through. He stalked thoughtfully to the door and yanked it open. Margaret Trumpey handed him a sealed manila envelope.

"Do you want me to wait?" she asked.

"No. Yes . . . maybe you'd better."

Pike tore the envelope open and squinted angrily at the enclosed message. The first time he read it his mind was still on Walsacki and the flashlight batteries, so the words were nearly unintelligible. Then slowly, as he began a second reading, his mind which had never shifted easily from subject to subject, began to assimilate some meaning from the words.

PIKE PISTOL TWO

WE ARE MUCH DISTURBED OVER FAILURE YOUR MET OFFICE TO FILE REPORT ON LAZY ETHEL THROUGH NORMAL CHANNELS PERIOD THIS NOT ONLY EMBARRASSING FOR ALL CONCERNED BUT RENDERS IT IMPOSSIBLE TO PROVIDE YOU AID AND ADVICE PERIOD ARE YOU TAKING MEASURES TO EVACUATE QUESTION MARK WHAT HELP WILL YOU REQUIRE QUESTION MARK WEATHER CHARTS HERE SHOW NO INDICATION ANY SUCH PRESSURE AREA NEAR YOU PERIOD INSTRUCT YOUR METEOROLOGIST ADVISE US IN FULL OF PROGNOSTIC SITUATION PERIOD REPEAT ADVISE IMMEDIATELY AND MAINTAIN COMMUNICATION THIS STATION LONG AS YOU ARE ABLE PERIOD GOOD LUCK PERIOD

KEATING

Shaking his head in honest bewilderment, Pike again read the message, even more slowly this time, trying to forget that Margaret Trumpey and Pete Walsacki were watching him. The girl, the damned girl, knew what was in the message, of course. She must have typed it herself. How many other people knew what was in the message, which, if he had translated it correctly, accused him of withholding information on some kind of storm now threatening Pistol Two; a storm about which he knew absolutely nothing? Lazy Ethel? Good luck? What the hell was going on?

He passed his hand slowly across his forehead, scanned the message once more, then refolded it very carefully. Oh this *was* a morning, all right, and it was already filled with deceit and treachery! So *that* was the way the ball bounced! Ho, ho! Not only were people stealing flashlight batteries and the complete duties of certain staff members were being kept secret from him, but now a minor functionary had contrived to put him on the spot because of a fancied personal insult which any reasonable man would have considered merely a sound suggestion for improvement. That weather fellow! So! This sort of thing was precisely what he had feared when a group of people were required to work together under a system, or lack of system, wherein there was no recognized table of command, reward, or even punishment. It showed exactly what would happen without a proper manual or written regulations. Jealousies, personal animosities, ambition for attention, scheming, undermining of morale. . . . Pike could think of innumerable evils all sparked by a single glaring fault, lack of firm authority and lack of authority to exercise authority, dammit. The result was a restless, inefficient rabble of which one individual now stood out like a blank shell in an otherwise full caisson! Well, sir, Zeb Pike knew how to nip such craftiness in the bud. He glowered at Margaret Trumpey and said, "How fast can you run?"

"Fast enough."

"Then get down to the weather office. Tell that fellow Smith or whatever his name is, to report here on the double."

"On the double?"

"As fast as he can make it."

"Yessir."

"And after you've seen him, find Mr. Albright. Tell him to come here immediately."

"Also on the double?"

"Yes. On the double. And . . ."

Pike seized Margaret's arm before she turned away. He pressed it firmly and lowered his voice so that Walsacki would not hear him.

"Now listen to me, young lady. I want to make sure, *very* sure, that nothing is known of this message anywhere. *You* know what it is, but under no circumstances are you to repeat the contents of this message . . . *to anyone* . . . understand? Forget you ever saw it, do you understand me thoroughly?"

"Yes, General . . . I mean, Governor. I understand."

"Absolutely no one. This is between you and me and that damned teletype machine."

"Yessir."

After Margaret Trumpey had left, Pike turned back to Pete Walsacki. And in the very act of turning he felt a sharp pain in his shoulder. His neuritis again. Ye gods! It was better than any barometer or sad-faced weather experts with all their charts and instruments. He prodded that part of his shoulder where his neuritis seemed to be the worst as he faced Pete Walsacki and said, "Now about those damned flashlight batteries!"

8

Adam was just taking his first upper-wind observation with his theodolite, and the balloon had gone up so straight he had a crick in his neck from tracking it, when Margaret came to his side and said in a strangely breathless way, "Good morning."

Adam looked down at her, quite willing to let the balloon rise to infinity since there was no wind anyway. Remembering their all-too-short meeting on the wharf, he said, "Well, it's a dull morning, but you brighten it considerably."

Then he locked off his theodolite and cleared his throat nervously, and said, "I didn't really mean the way I sounded last night. I was sorry when you left. So I would like to apologize. I guess that in a lot of ways, I'm a total loss. I seem to have a special way of antagonizing people."

"You sure do," Margaret said. "Pike is about ready to blow his top. He wants to see you on the double."

"What's his trouble now?"

"Don't you know? How cagey can you get?"

Adam looked into her eyes and saw, or thought he saw, a suggestion of mistrust, even accusation, and he wished that he could remember everything he had said on the wharf so that he could apologize in more detail.

She said, very calmly, almost as if she were addressing an inanimate object, "You'd better trot along. There is drool on his chops. It looked to me like heads are going to roll."

"Pike swung his ax my way again last night. I am not exactly his favorite citizen. In fact it's beginning to look like I'm in a lot of people's doghouses. I'd like to have you know it's not because I want to be."

"Can I make a suggestion?"

"Sure."

"Remember he's got a colony to run. Good or bad, he's the boss and so he has a right to know what's going on."

"I'm not keeping anything from him. Neither is anyone else that I know about."

Again the look. The thing to do was take her back to the wharf and get everything straightened out in the same atmosphere. He said, "Are you going down to the wharf tonight?"

"I might. If it's still there. I should think it might depend on the . . . prognostic situation."

Adam wanted to ask her just exactly what she meant by that, but she was gone before he could say anything more. She was walking, almost running, toward the quarters at the end of Second Avenue. Watching her, Adam thought she moved with particular grace. He was vaguely disappointed when she did not look back. What was this, "If it's still there." He sighed and thought that it was no wonder his success with women was anything but distinguished. How did you ever know where you stood with the creatures? They were more complicated than the adiabatic lapse rate. No matter what you said it turned out to be the wrong thing.

Furthermore, they could with one little change of expression scare hell out of you. Still looking after Margaret, he decided that he wanted very much to be a success with her.

As he mounted the steps of Pike's front porch Adam remembered a phrase which had stayed with him since his school days. "I have often regretted what I have said, but never my silence." He could not recall the originator of the words in spite of the fact that they had long influenced his social behavior. Of all times, he warned himself, he must remember those words now. Otherwise Pike was certain to provoke him into saying things he really didn't want to say, and as Margaret had pointed out, good or bad, he was the boss. He could fire Adam very quickly if he so decided and pack him off on the very next airplane for Tuamani and home. I will not give him that satisfaction, Adam thought. I will leave this job only when it is done and I will leave in good order. I will not let a petty tyrant rattle me and capsize everything I've worked for. No matter what he says, I'm going to hold my peace. It is the greatest weapon ever created when properly used, and almost impossible to conquer. I will co-operate and I will keep my mouth shut. I must.

So armed, Adam crossed the porch in two long strides. He opened the screen door, and waited a moment for his eyes to accustom themselves to the shadowed hall-way. Then, uncertain as to which door opened on Pike's office, he took a few cautious steps down the hall. Pike's voice rang out and brought him up as if he had been lassoed.

"In here!"

Adam turned into the office. Now careful, he remembered, be very careful what you say. And say as little as possible. You, not Pike, will be the victor if you can leave this room with your job.

"You wanted to see me?" Adam said, approaching Pike's desk casually, as if a meeting in this office was an everyday event.

Pike tipped back in his chair and, looking steadily at Adam, manipulated his fingers into his favorite isosceles triangle. His voice was much more controlled than Adam had anticipated.

"Does that surprise you?"

"Well, yes . . . sort of."

"You don't think, then, that there is any special reason why I might want to see you on this particular morning?"

"No. . . ."

There was a long silence between them, and Adam could hear the palm fronds softly clicking outside the window as he met Pike's eyes. Then he knew. They were going to go over the fact that the movies had been called off on account of rain again. Ah, well.

"I'm sorry about the rain last night, Governor. As I explained to you before, I just don't make the weather."

He tried to smile, half-hoping Pike might join him.

"I did not think that you did make the weather, Mister Smith. For some reason you seem to believe that I'm not quite bright. Well, sir, I make no claim to being a mental giant or even to being in the same league with some of the scientists we have on this island, but I am not an utter fool, either. In the past I have only questioned your *interpretation* of the weather from time to time, more or less with a view to urging improvement on your part. I have helped a great many younger men in my time and I've long since discovered that in certain men, soft words do more harm than good. In your case I seem to have taken the wrong approach. I have only succeeded in offending you."

"I wouldn't say that."

"You wouldn't?"

Feigning enormous surprise, Pike raised his eyebrows and allowed his isosceles triangle to collapse. He poked one finger experimentally at the neuritis spot on his shoulder and winced.

"What *would* you say then, Mister Smith? Would you say that my efforts, however misguided they may have been, were based on honest concern for the welfare of this community and the successful completion of our project? Would you say that, accepting criticism in the spirit with which it was intended, you have in return made every effort to co-operate with your fellow workers and satisfactorily perform your duties?"

"I've done my job to the best of my ability . . . sir."

"Have you indeed."

Pike said the words not as a question, but as a flat statement. He reached into his desk drawer and pulled out a manila folder. He placed it unopened before him.

"Do you know what is in this folder?"

"No."

"I do. Even though I give you my word that I haven't looked inside of it for more than two months. This happens to be your personal folder, Mister Smith . . . your past record, your application for employment on Project Zeus, comments, letters of recommendation and so forth. Let us see how many of the more vital facts contained in that folder I can recall. Other than a certain vanity, I have a special reason for doing this now, a part of which I hope will become apparent to you as I proceed."

Prodding his neuritis spot as if the pain would stimulate his memory, Pike deliberately looked out the window and recited tonelessly, "You were born Adam Smith . . . no middle name or initial given. In Rollins, Vermont. Mother deceased at time of application. Your brother operates a drug store in Providence. You were attached to Air Transport Command during Korean War. . . . I *suppose* that might be considered military service. Graduated University of Vermont. . . . I won't take this morning's precious time to remember the year, but I assure you I could if I had to. Subsequently took one year postgraduate work at M.I.T. . . . Employed Continental Airlines as meteorologist 1954. . . . Presently on leave of absence. . . . All references good. Loyalty oath signed and political slate clean. Salary according to A.E.C. standard category D-12, at $7200 for year's contract. Have I made any errors so far, Smith?"

"You have a remarkable memory, Governor."

"If it's on paper I'll remember it. I could go on, including the fact that your father's name was Matthew, which, judging from the choice of Biblical names in your family, would suggest to me that you came from a good and God-fearing American family of solid background. Admirable. There is nothing in your file to indicate a rebellious nature or suggest that you might wish to sabotage authority."

"Now just one minute, Governor!" Adam suddenly clamped his lips together. There you go, he thought, squeezing his fists tight lest he continue. There you almost went shooting off your mouth when you didn't know what this was all about yet. Pike was licking his chops, all right. He was clearly just waiting for a chance to pounce.

"Yes, Smith?"

"I was about to say that . . . well, somewhere along the line we just don't seem to understand each other."

"I should say we do not. The reason for my little recitation of your file was to convince you once and for all that I take my duties here very seriously. It is a part of my duty to know the people in my charge and for the key positions, of which yours happens to be one, I can quote their records just as I have yours. Now, Smith, you have very clearly demonstrated, for reasons which you have so far not had the courage to explain . . . demonstrated that you would like to see me placed on a very hot spot and, possibly, if things work out just right, you might even see me removed from this office. You have been clever enough to realize that anything of a major nature which might affect this base is my responsibility and should a real foul-up occur, it would be me and not you who would bear the consequences. And, Mister Smith. . . ."

Pike pronounced the word *Mister* as if an aspirin tablet were dissolving on his tongue. He placed his thumbs in his belt and leaned far forward so that his resolute chin was halfway across his desk. "And, Mister Smith, I'm not going to let you get away with it."

Adam was completely bewildered. I don't care, he thought suddenly. I don't give a damn about the job or what a mess it is going to be back at Continental Airlines trying to explain why I have been given the sack. This man is crazy!

"Get away with *what?* Governor, I just don't know what the hell you're talking about!"

"Lazy Ethel."

"Lazy Ethel? What . . . ?"

Pike jumped to his feet. He was truly angry now and the intricate designs formed by the tiny red veins in his face flowed together until they became heavy splotches.

"Yes, *Mister* Smith! Lazy Ethel. I don't know how long you've known anything about that storm, but you have not seen fit to notify me of its existence, or more important, that it constitutes a threat to the safety of this base!"

"Governor!"

"You have deliberately withheld vital information from me in the hope I would be caught flat-footed. If it's any satisfaction to you, you almost succeeded!"

"Governor! You're away off . . ."

"You obviously had no intention of informing me until it was too late or you would have said something the moment you walked into this room. Oh, I gave you every chance, Smith! You just didn't have the good sense to take it."

"Governor, will you please listen to me?"

Adam was smiling now, a reaction which further infuriated Pike. "Just listen to me a minute, please. There *isn't* any storm. I just dreamed it up. I haven't the faintest idea how anyone found out about it."

"Don't tell me that, Smith! You're just getting yourself in deeper. I know God-damned well there's a storm around here somewhere. Not only is my neuritis killing me, but I have been so advised from Tuamani!"

"This is ridiculous . . . er, sir!"

"Ridiculous, is it? Ridiculous, all right, if I'm caught with my pants down and Lazy Ethel hits this island! I'll be the one who looks ridiculous if that expensive new wharf plus warehouse gets washed out to sea, or if every damned piece of GI property on this island gets blown to hell and gone because we weren't prepared! What was Pike doing when the thing was on its way? Sitting on his ass? Drunk? Gone fishing? Several people hurt or even killed maybe, and what was Pike doing? *You* think up some of the answers to those questions, Smith, because I just might have to answer them! And wipe that smile off your face while you're thinking!"

"Governor, look. I was fooling around on my plotting board last night and for some reason . . ."

Adam knew that he was floundering, but what else was there to say? Talking to Pike under the best of circumstances was not easy and it was very apparent that he was not in a listening mood now. But a lot of things were clear, anyway, especially that peculiar look in Margaret Trumpey's eyes. ". . . I was fooling around. . . . Why I drew in a hurricane I just can't explain, and for some other reason I can't seem to explain I named it Lazy Ethel . . . it's customary to name very low pressure areas, you know, but usually you start a season with an A. Now as to Tuamani finding out about it . . . Well . . ."

Adam's voice faded into indistinctness, for he saw that, though Pike was regarding him with rapt attention, his anger had been replaced by a coldness which was far more ominous, and there was, too, a look of cunning in his eyes. If I suggested that it must have been that press representative . . . ?

"So you still persist? Right to the end, eh? Oh, you're a smart fellow, Smith. You were just fooling around and you just can't explain why. It seems there are a great many things you can't explain and one of them, I have no doubt, includes Tuamani's knowledge of this storm. Amazing, I must say, Mister Smith. Truly, *truly* amazing!"

"I know it sounds sort of strange, but—"

"Not at all! On the contrary. Very logical. The pieces all fit in perfectly, that is, once you've been so obliging as to give me the key. You maintain that the storm is non-existent. I believe you. I am lulled into a sense of security. My acute neuritic pains are meaningless. Meanwhile you cover yourself by allowing Tuamani to know what I do not know. Then, out of nowhere, the storm which, of course, does not exist, arrives. It is then very much too late for argument. Ho, ho! I'm going to recommend you for Naval Intelligence!"

Accompanying his steps with a series of diminishing ho-ho's, Pike circled his desk. He wagged his head and poked at his neuritic spot and only occasionally glanced at Adam. Then it was a look clearly designed to assure Adam that he was not only overwhelmed by his treachery, but was torn between his bounden duty, which was to exact some kind of penalty, and since he was a man of great wisdom, experience, patience, and intelligence, perhaps a final effort at a peaceful compromise.

At last he halted before Adam and, clasping his hands behind him, assumed parade rest. He would have been much more imposing if he had not had to look up at Adam, yet by remaining absolutely motionless his stature seemed to increase until Adam found himself deliberately slumping. Pike compressed his lips and, recognizing it as a danger signal, Adam was certain that unless he could somehow think of a more logical explanation for Lazy Ethel, his employment on Nikki atoll was as good as finished. Along with a lot of other things, he reminded himself, including an association with a girl named Margaret which was certainly more interesting than any other he had ever known. Then, even before Pike spoke, he saw a possible solution to the whole affair and he became so intrigued with its possibilities he only half-heard the man who stood so challengingly before him.

"No, Mister Smith," Pike was saying, "I refuse to fall into every ambush you set for me. I did not get where I am because I was asleep in my tent all the time. I *know* there is a storm hereabouts. I want full information on that storm, and I want to be kept fully supplied with further information as long as it presents the slightest hazard to this community. If you do not co-operate in the fullest, I will request another meteorologist from Tuamani at once and you may consider yourself discharged. I don't think I need to point out that my report on the reasons for your dismissal will hardly be favorable to you."

Pike rocked back on his heels, then settled into parade rest again. Adam took a deep breath. So the old saw was true and necessity was the mother of invention. You found yourself walking down a path and, if you ever expected to reach the end of it, you had to follow that path regardless of twists and turns. In this case it seemed that no harm could be done and life on Nikki could attain a more peaceful air if you were just willing to make a very slight compromise with your integrity. Maybe, he thought, your father was right when he said that you were often too stubborn. It could be called controlled compromise to give Pike what he wanted, and then in a few days it would all be over. And there was no reason to involve that damned newsman in this jam . . . yet. He might have a wife and kids to support.

"All right, sir," Adam said slowly. "There is a storm. But it doesn't amount to much . . . which is the reason

I didn't bother to tell you about it . . . not because I wanted to deceive you or put you on a spot. If it did amount to anything I would have informed you at once. I'm sorry as can be about the confusion. It looks like I was wrong."

Adam was profoundly shocked at how easily the words came to him. Could it be, he wondered, that I am a natural-born liar? And Pike was visibly relieved. It was so easy.

"If the storm is so small, how come you bothered to inform Tuamani about it?" Pike asked.

Adam searched desperately for a plausible explanation. The newsman and his family, if there was one, would have to share his fate. There would have to be *some* elements of truth to support this tottering structure.

"I think I can explain that, sir. Last night when I was fooling around . . . I mean when I was making a plot of the storm . . . a newsman, I think he said his name was Hanover, dropped by the office. It's very possible he made something of it. . . . Yes, I'm sure he must have."

"Hanover? How could he . . . ? I shall have a very serious talk with him at once."

"I really think the less said about this to anyone, the better, sir. You know how people exaggerate. It honestly doesn't amount to a thing and . . . well, I doubt if it will come anywhere near Nikki."

"You're right," Pike snapped. "See that you keep your own mouth shut. In the meantime I want a report on the situation every two hours."

"It wouldn't be practical, sir. I don't have enough reports myself to follow a storm that closely."

"Can't Tuamani help? They have plenty of ships and planes."

This invention could get out of hand, Adam thought, unless I think fast.

"No, sir. You see this storm is to the south of us . . . where there isn't much of anybody. It's . . . well, it's moving very slowly and I should say the chances are very good that in a few days it will disappear altogether."

"How can a storm disappear?"

Pike had his storm. Now Adam saw to his horror that he wanted to play with it.

"It dissipates. It loses force when the pressure pattern begins to equalize. This one will very likely just . . . well, sort of blow itself out down in the so-called Roaring Forties. That's a long way from here."

This was unbelievable! Adam Smith was not only talking like a magpie, which he had sworn not to do, but what he was saying was worse than untrue because it was a lie based upon a hastily assembled collection of scientific facts which were fortunately, or perhaps unfortunately, very solid and true.

Adam stared at the floor. He was confused now, and he found it suddenly difficult to remember that Lazy Ethel did *not* exist. Well, he would get rid of it in a hurry, a process which was beginning to appear much more difficult than its creation. Pike's earliest opinions were very nearly right, Adam thought frantically. I do make the weather!

"How often can you give me the situation?" Pike was asking with the most solemn determination.

Adam hesitated. Invention on top of invention! And it would have to be reasonably believable. He was going to be a very busy man! "Once a day," he said uncertainly.

"Is that all?"

"Yes. There's a lot of work involved. Really, Governor . . . it doesn't amount to a thing. Er . . ."

"We both have our work cut out for us," Pike said with a grim smile. "In the meantime Tuamani demands some satisfaction. You will file a report immediately through regular channels, and along with your technical mishmash you will clearly indicate that you personally did not consider the storm severe enough either to notify me or alarm them. Do you understand me thoroughly, Smith?"

"Yessir, I'm sure I can handle that. And could I suggest again that we keep this more or less quiet, Governor? No use to get people all excited."

"Right. We'll keep it plenty quiet. Maximum security on this. You will prepare two charts. One chart for me, which you'll bring to this office yourself, and your usual chart brought up by that teletype girl. She knows too much already. Took the teletype from Tuamani. I've already cautioned her and will do so again."

"I doubt if she's the type to start rumors," Adam said.

Pike frowned at him. "All women start rumors. They live, eat, and breathe rumors. Very poor security risks as history has often proven. This has got to remain a secret between you and me."

"It certainly has," Adam said with a sigh of relief.

"Get going. Do a good job for me on this and I'll forget our past misunderstandings. I'm that way, Smith."

"Yessir!"

When Adam left the porch and emerged into the brilliant sunlight he glanced up at the sky and was rather surprised not to see telltale streaks of high cirrus clouds which might foretell a storm. There was, of course, nothing of the sort aloft; only the normal little build-ups of fluffy cumulus which always accompanied trades. He paused for a moment to study the now slowly drifting cumulus and found them strangely reassuring. For they promised that he had not entirely lost his wits and that the session with Pike had only been like something out of a meteorological nightmare in which he, Adam Smith, was magically empowered with the ability to create a holocaust. Well, now, in the sunlight, with the very real streets and buildings of Pistol Two about him, it was possible to return to reality and even smile about this little deception.

Moving down the street in his easy, loose-limbed fashion, Adam began to relax. Smiling inwardly, he supposed that there were certain elements of risk involved, but at the worst he could only lose his job, which he had come very near doing anyway. Lazy Ethel! The name itself gave the explanation for its performance. He would place its center to the south in accordance with his lie, and he would allow it to move very slowly toward the east and the open Pacific, until after a few days he would report it as no longer worthy of anyone's attention. But he would have to watch Tuamani. They were far enough away to prevent any exact check on his analysis. But if they sent airplanes to investigate, that might be a very different matter. Their immediate curiosity would have to be satisfied. Just how was still a problem, but there was no reason, as long as Pike was willing to have two charts made, why Tuamani should make any special effort to confirm Lazy Ethel. Not for a few days, anyway.

Again he was surprised at this new and unusual way his mind seemed compelled to work. Maybe, he mused, I am a frustrated criminal at heart! Certainly I am scheming and plotting like one, finding ways to cover my tracks if I should be questioned, fabricating alibis, even planning methods of escape when the deed is done! But what harm? Adam supposed that occasionally the most honest bank tellers surrendered to impulse and stuffed a few thousand dollars in their pockets just to see what it felt like. What harm if they replaced every penny of it after a few minutes, or at least before the daily accounting was done? It could be an exhilarating lift in an otherwise dull day; a tiny episode which could momentarily enliven a job as prosaic as a meteorologist's.

He caught himself. What kind of thinking was this? You are going off your rocker! It was said that some people just could not stand the isolation of a Pacific atoll, yet those people were neurotics who had a record of instability wherever they landed. And most certainly no one had ever accused Adam Smith of instability. On the contrary, your record in college and at Continental Airlines was of such solidness and dependability several people had, in an offhand way, suggested that you break out and live a little.

What happened if the bank teller failed to return the money in time? Suppose, on that particular day, someone chose to do the accounting at an earlier hour, or the vault locks stuck in a closed position? One chance in a million. Just as there was here. And anyway, for all you know, there may very well be a storm to the south. It was, when you came right down to it, almost a certainty. Because the Roaring Forties would not be the Roaring Forties without some kind of disturbance. That's where the name came from. Sailors in the old windjammers running down their easting in the forty-degree latitude had reason to curse that area of the Pacific. For the needs of Lazy Ethel it was not overly important that the Roaring Forties were a long way south of Nikki atoll. Lazy Ethel was an errant spawn of the Forties. She just happened to wander a little far north of the usual track. She could wander right back again . . . after a decent time.

Then if she came from so far, how did you manage to learn of Lazy Ethel? Tuamani would know what Pike would never admit; that storms were not located by a pain in the shoulder. Their extent and nature and probable track were plotted from a series of reports on barometric pressure, temperature, and wind velocity. It was unlikely, in fact nearly impossible, that a single man on a lonely atoll would be able to obtain such information. Yet it had happened. The typhoon which completely devastated Wake Island in 1954 arrived without any official warning whatsoever. And there were not only trained meteorologists on the island at the time, but a vast system of aircraft and ships to supplement and aid their observations. No one had known in advance about that storm. It was very conceivable, then, that Adam Smith would be the only person who knew about Lazy Ethel. How? Stopping in the middle of the street between the teletype shack and his own office, Adam was again surprised at the ease with which he found the answer. One more slight invention. Just a little one, but it had to work.

He turned and went into the teletype office.

9

Adam was disappointed not to find Margaret in the tele-type office. Instead, the other girl who occasionally came for his charts and who, Adam vaguely recalled, was known as Smilie or Sunnie, looked up from a movie maga-zine and said, "Good morning. What can I do you for?"

Adam waited uneasily. Margaret obviously knew about Lazy Ethel, but what about this girl? And would it really make any difference if she did know? There were so many things to be considered, he thought. Quickly, very much too quickly it seemed, the possible reaction of everyone on Nikki had to be anticipated.

"Cat got your tongue?" Sunnie Mandel asked.

"I want to send a message."

"Why not? We got umpteen thousand bucks' worth of equipment and nobody's using it."

She rose from her desk and moved slowly toward Adam. He saw with alarm that her movements were openly inviting, as if she had been waiting breathlessly for his arrival. And then he was sorry for her. She was so frail, so flat in every respect, and now her walk became a pitifully grotesque imitation of any movie star. He wondered that he had never noticed it before.

Looking up at him she said, "I wish more people would come in here with messages. It gets awful lonesome. When Margaret's gone I get babbling to myself . . . like some female hermit who is fabulously rich, has all her money in old tin cans . . . and won't talk to the outside world."

"Where is Margaret?"

"Gone to Aubrey for a haircut. But don't broadcast it. You aren't s'posed to get haircuts on government time. Only coffee breaks. Like I was saying to Margaret last night, it don't make any special difference *where* you're working for the government, the rules and regulations are always the same. There is the kind of rule that is printed down and the kind they put on bulletin boards which everybody has got to initial to prove they read, but those regulations are just made up by people who have to pass the time and they don't mean a thing once you know your way around. No matter where it is, it isn't like private industry with capitalists in gray flannel suits thinking up things for people not to do. You work for the government and you got no worries so long as you live by the regulations which are *not* written down. This produces what I call massive ennui."

"Those are pretty big words," Adam said, still trying

to decide if he should give this girl his message or wait for Margaret's return.

"I like to play around with big words," Sunnie said. "You can therefore better express what's on your mind. The idea when you work for the government, and I should know, is to do exactly what you're told and absolutely, positively, do not do one little thing more. Because if you do, you're liable to upset somebody's applecart who is up above your category and who is trying very hard not to do one single thing more than they were told to do. It's a chain reaction and it goes right on up to the President. Nobody hardly ever gets fired for not doing their job right. They get transferred to another agency if their boss has enough influence and energy, or maybe they might be dropped a category if they're low on seniority anyway, but they do not get the can. You get the can when you peel the mildew off your brain and start getting ideas how maybe you could do your job quicker and maybe better. Do I make myself clear?"

"You certainly do," Adam answered with a smile. Peter Hildebrandt was wrong. You got around and talked to a lot of people, or rather they talked to you. Peter should have tagged along on this morning, for example.

"So Margaret won't really get the can because she's having her hair cut on government time. She will, though, if she thinks up some new way of sending a teletype message that maybe goes quicker or don't use so many words."

"My message is very brief."

Sunnie looked into his eyes and sighed. She said, "From you, what else? Look, Silent Sam, I don't care how many words you put in a message. My job is to punch those keys until I hit EOM, which means end of message. The character who thought up that abbreviation was probably fired just for doing it. And while we're on the subject do you mind if I mention one little thing before I let you out of my clutches?"

"I guess not."

Sunnie laughed. "You couldn't stop me, anyway. Nobody can once I get started. Anyway, I'd just like to go on record that you are the darnedest pebble kicker I ever ran into. There's a certain girl on this lousy little island who wastes a lot of time, including the government's, thinking about you. So why don't you break down and give her the time of day once in a while? Just so you won't be scared to death, the girl isn't me. Now what's your message and where's it going?"

"To Tuamani," Adam said hesitantly. "To the meteorological office."

"That's MET around here. TUA dash MET. Cuckoo, isn't it?"

"If you have a pencil handy I'll write it out; then you can more or less put it in your own style."

"Oh no," Sunnie said, handing him a pad of forms. "I'm part of the massive ennui. Remember? Your words. I send." She tapped her head. "Monkey see. Monkey do. I won't go up a single category if I think."

Twisting his mouth thoughtfully, Adam slowly printed out the words which had come to his mind in the street. As he did so, he found himself wondering again about the temptations of bank tellers and it seemed certain to him now that there was no possible retreat.

He handed the pad to Sunnie Mandel and watched her eyes carefully as she read it aloud.

LAZY ETHEL ANALYSIS BASED ON INCOMPLETE RADIO INFORMATION OBTAINED JAPANESE FISHING BOAT VICINITY PERIOD REGRET DID NOT CONSIDER SOURCE SUFFICIENTLY

RELIABLE FILE FORMAL WARNING OR NOTIFY GOVERNOR
PIKE UNTIL SITUATION CLARIFIED PERIOD WILL ADVISE IF
FURTHER DEVELOPMENT PERIOD

SMITH

Sunnie looked up at him and shrugged her shoulders.

"I suppose I would be wasting my time if I asked you who Lazy Ethel was?"

"Yeah," Adam said. "You would."

"You slay me."

She turned to a teletype machine and sat down before it. Adam experienced a strange, almost triumphant, sensation throughout his body as her fingers began to play over the keys. He whistled when he went out the door.

"*Well,* Mister Albright!" Pike said, enunciating the *Mister* with very little more warmth than he had addressed Adam. He prodded his shoulder and winced. As Pike's eyes roved over him, Albright was unable to discover the slightest evidence of approval.

He lit a cigarette and waited, swaying slightly in an attempt to maintain at least the appearance of easy confidence. It was not easy these days, he thought; partly because in Pike's presence he had the damnedest feeling of inferiority and partly because he found the emotion extraordinarily boring. Yet what else except boredom could one expect of the military mind? The whole of Nikki, its population, its very purpose, was boring beyond any sane person's imagination! Who was there on this godforsaken atoll who might discuss literature, at least elementary music, or, say, the ballet? Who read the *New Yorker* or ever heard of Henry James? The migrant clods on Nikki were all devoted to the *Reader's Digest* and the *Saturday Evening Post,* which hardly put them in a way to enjoy the

Saturday Review. Sometimes, like this time, Albright was certain that on the day he signed up with the A.E.C. he had been either drunk or bewitched and had somehow mistaken his application for an income-tax form.

Pike was still looking at him. He said, "Do you always have to wear shorts, Albright?"

"I find them most comfortable in this climate. Is there something wrong with them?"

Albright was convinced that Pike would jolly well have trouble finding anything wrong with his shorts. They were especially designed for his narrow hips by a Madison Avenue tailor and they cost a comparative fortune. During an impromptu style preview of his going-away apparel in Albright's New York apartment, his friends had clapped their hands and exclaimed at their smartness and they had all enthusiastically agreed he looked like a British officer long in the desert. Rather like a Sandhurst man, one of them had said. And, recalling his friends, Albright wished with all his heart that he was back with them, instead of standing like a congenital idiot, awaiting the pleasure of a man whose taste and sense of delicacy must have been nurtured near the rear end of an artillery horse.

"I've always thought shorts took a certain amount of dignity from a man," Pike was saying. "They look more appropriate on Boy Scouts."

"I'm sorry if they offend you, sir."

"Oh, now don't get uppity with me, Albright. It's not that bad. The matter is of no consequence at the moment because the climate is going to change around here, anyway."

"I'm afraid I don't quite follow you."

Pike prodded his shoulder, then moved his thumb experimentally down his arm. He said, "If you would get up a little earlier in the mornings you might be in a better position to follow a lot of things. For instance, I'm sure it's news to you that we're probably in for a hurricane. Do you know what that means?"

"It sounds a bit grim."

Albright stopped swaying. He remembered two hurricanes in New England, one in 1944 while he was still at Yale, and it had been an absolute ball. At least something might relieve the boredom of Nikki.

With a dramatic sweep of his hand, Pike unrolled a map of Nikki and spread it across his desk. "It means," he continued gravely, "that we've got our work cut out for us whether the storm comes or not. Of course, I'm hoping it doesn't come anywhere near us, but we've got to be prepared in advance regardless. Once it heads this way it will be too late. Our job is to anticipate what we might call the enemy's movements, make every possible defense . . . and, if necessary, even make a strategic retreat."

Pike allowed a slight smile to creep across his mouth. God! Albright thought, as Pike beckoned to him and pointed at the map. Hannibal is now going to cross the Alps. Napoleon is at Austerlitz. This man, so starved for action, was going to bombard a hurricane!

"I've got this all figured out," Pike went on. "It's going to take some organization and a lot of work, but we won't be caught sleeping on our arms. We just can't afford to be, or somebody is liable to get hurt."

He pondered the map a moment, and Albright saw that his blue eyes were alive with determination. Standing beside him, dutifully imitating Pike's examination of the map, Albright considered that they would have made a far more picturesque pair if they had been standing on the summit of a hill overlooking troops in full battle.

"Our intelligence, such as it is, informs us the storm will

be most likely to approach from the south. In that case we should move our people somewhere in here . . . to the north side of Nikki so we'll get protection from the southerly reef and also the lagoon itself."

"I see," Albright said as solemnly as he could manage.

"The situation is complicated by the fact that we are dealing with civilians and so we must take every precaution to prevent panic. The only way I know is to maintain absolute secrecy. Our people must not know *why* they are being moved until the fact is accomplished. Once safely encamped on the north side, we can explain matters and prepare for the worst."

"Are you suggesting, sir, that we move everyone on Nikki bag and baggage to the north side?"

"No. Not bag and baggage. Their personal effects must be left behind. We will only take every available tarpaulin for use as shelters . . . our workmen can rig up some kind of tents for the children at least . . . and we'll require at least three days' provisions . . . plus some means of cooking."

"How about the natives across the channel?"

"They'll have to go, too, whether they want to or not. I don't want to be responsible for the loss of a single life . . . or even any injury if we can help it. Doc Case will have to take his medical supplies along, of course."

Slowly, almost as if one of his regular attacks of mess-hall nausea had overcome him, Albright began to appreciate the magnitude of Pike's enterprise. Much more quickly he envisioned a mass of detail exploding in his face, all tedious, all involving endless argument, evasion, and lack of sleep.

"General," he said, "there are an awful lot of people here. To just pick them up and arrange for a mass exodus will be a tremendous undertaking."

"It's got to be done. What's more, we're pressed for time."

"When is the storm supposed to arrive?"

"I don't know exactly. It's maneuvering to the south right now."

"Are you basing this information on that Smith chap?"

"Yes."

"You seem to have renewed your faith in him."

"I have not for a moment done so. Believe me, I am keeping a wary eye on our Mr. Smith. But his prediction has practically been confirmed by Tuamani and, what's more, I've received a few signals of my own."

Pike poked his thumb into his shoulder and, to Albright's astonishment, winked at him. Then he said, "I doubt if even our Mr. Smith would fumble a situation as serious as this. If the storm is coming our way he'll tell me with no *if*'s, *and*'s, or *but*'s about it."

"When do you want to start all this?" Albright asked. He tried to hide the misery in his voice.

"Now. Right now. You will begin by commandeering every boat, launch and canoe on the island. I want them at the wharf manned and ready to load at noon. Earlier if you can make it. This is logistics, Albright. Allow an hour to cross the lagoon and an hour after we get there to settle down. Sergeant Doolan and his men will stand by during the loading and patrol here until the last boat is ready to leave. We don't want any looting. The boss laborer will be in charge of loading the tarpaulins. Messhall personnel will prepare three days' rations . . . there doesn't have to be anything fancy . . . and see that those are loaded. You'd better arrange to contact Chief Tanni on the other side and have him get all his people set. They'll have to bring their own rations. Oh . . . those girls in the teletype shack should also be assigned to the last boat. I want to keep communication with Tuamani right up to the last minute."

Pike shot his arm forward and glanced at his wrist watch. He frowned. "It's almost nine-thirty now so you'll have to get cracking. Oh . . . don't forget light. We'll want illumination of some kind. See that electrician fellow. He may have some kind of a stand-by generator . . . one of those little gasoline-powered jobs that are portable. If not, have him make do with something. . . . Maybe he can round up some emergency pressure lamps. I know damn well there aren't any flashlight batteries available . . . and another thing. Absolutely no whisky or spirits of any kind are to be taken except for medicinal use by Doc Case if he says he wants some. We don't want this thing to turn into a brawl. Remember there will be all kinds of types mixed close together under campaign conditions . . . kids and everything. We'll have enough trouble as it is."

Overwhelmed with the trouble he could see, Albright sought momentary consolation in the ceiling. The attempt was a failure, for he saw in the plywood above him only signals of vast confusion and acute discomfort, in which he, Livingston Albright, who preferred to do his camping out amid the better restaurants of New York, was pinioned in the exact center. He could distinctly taste the rancid flavor of woe in his mouth when he found the will to speak again.

"Governor," he began apologetically. "If I start stirring up this hornet's nest, people are going to start asking questions. They are going to want to know what it's all about. The preparations can hardly remain a secret. What am I supposed to tell them?"

"Say as little as you can, although naturally there will be inquiries. Tell them . . . I have it! You tell them this is merely a drill which we always intended to hold anyway . . . at least twice during our stay. A hurricane drill. . . . Nothing more. They should regard it as a relief from their routine duties. . . . An outing, if they please. There is no reason for them not to regard it as sort of a holiday. Let the children think they're going on the biggest picnic of their lives. A real adventure! I want to be very certain they aren't frightened."

"Supposing some of the people refuse to go. Maybe they don't care for picnics."

"Ah!" said Pike as if he had discovered a large and poisonous spider moving across the map of Nikki. "You have a point there which I missed. I just can't get used to dealing with civilians. It's so damn unhandy and this is a perfect example. We'll have to use some persuasion if there should be any firm objections . . . which I very much doubt there will be if you present this thing properly. Put it this way if you have to. Those who refuse to go will find themselves outcasts. The mess hall and all the food will be locked up. There won't be any light and the water-evaporation plant will be shut down. They will be a lot more comfortable with us. Make them understand that thoroughly. Then if there are many holdouts, send them to me. Now get on with it."

"Yessir," Albright said, walking hopelessly toward the doorway. He could see himself challenged by that brute of a man, Barney Dunbar, who headed the carpenter shop. Or worse yet, Mrs. Walsacki or any one of her chattering group would want to know exactly what the children were going to be fed. And when.

"One more thing," Pike called after him. "Smith is going to come here with the latest on Lazy Ethel at noon . . . says he can't follow it any closer. We may postpone, but you proceed anyway unless you get a written cancellation from me."

"Lazy Ethel, did you say?"

"Yes. That's the name of the hurricane."

Albright arched his eyebrows, then shook his head sadly. He was suddenly filled with a mighty weariness.

"Who thought up that name?" he asked.

"Our Mr. Smith."

"So? I hardly thought him capable of such imagination. Sounds like a fat whore."

"She might be just that," Pike said grimly.

Pike was alone for only a moment. He was making a list of the vital papers he should take with him when he heard Sue-Anne's voice. He looked up and saw her posed in the doorway. In spite of his preoccupation he noticed that she was unusually well groomed for so early in the morning. Her hair was combed and, though she wore only a negligee, her face was carefully made up. He thought that, considering the ordeal of the night before, she looked quite beautiful. He waited for her to complain of a hangover.

"Zebulon," she said, "I thought that man was coming to fix the plumbing."

"You misunderstood me, Precious. He wasn't really coming."

"That's what I thought you said, but it didn't make sense."

"A lot of things don't make sense around here. Including the fact that you're going on a picnic."

"A picnic? Now really, Zebulon! You know I don't like picnics. All that sand in my food."

"You won't like this one at all. I want you to pack a few things . . . the regimental bracelet I gave you at

Knox, your pearl earrings and that photo of you and me with Mark Clark. Take anything else you think is valuable, but nothing more than you can slip in a handbag."

"What kind of a picnic is this? Zebulon, you've been working too hard."

She advanced toward him and walked around his desk until she could clasp his head in her arms. She pressed it against her bosom and said, "I'm sorry about last night, Zeb. I don't know what gets into me. Forgive me . . . forgive ol' Sue-Anne. I let you down."

"You're forgiven, Precious. How are your feet?"

"All right, thanks to you. Did you find my shoes?"

"I didn't look for them. I don't think we need to worry about little things like shoes this morning."

"Are they finally going to shoot the bomb? What is all this picnic business?"

"Never mind right now. Just be all set to go by noon. Wear as much clothing as you can. It might be chilly."

"Here? In this godawful . . . ?"

"Yes. Here. Now run along. I'm up to my ears in work."

Sue-Anne released him and backed away. She patted his cheek, and when she smiled he thought how magnificent she could be when she felt like it. A real soldier. No prying questions. Just appreciation of the need for orders . . . and obedience.

"Of course, Zebulon," she said. "I'll be ready. You just send up a flare when you want me."

She strolled into the hallway, moving with such grace that Pike in one blazing instant of desire thought of abandoning everything on the desk and lifting her off her feet. He would carry her laughing down the hallway and on this fateful morning they would be together again.

At the door she turned to smile at him. "I really am sorry about last night," she said.

She was gone before he could quite raise himself from behind the desk.

By ten-thirty Adam had his regular map prepared and was waiting for Margaret to call for it. It was a true map, monotonously similar to those he had drawn for weeks. Based on his own observations and the routine sheaf of teletype clips which came in from Tuamani every morning, he had again plotted a mild low-pressure trough to the west of Oa Titia atoll and an occluded front some five hundred miles east of Tuamani. The occluded front was practically stationary, shifting back and forth only a few miles each day, and since it was very near the doldrums area its presumed movements could be as much influenced by cumulative errors in reporting and plotting as any true activity. It was extremely unlikely that it would ever have the slightest effect on the weather at Nikki.

Over the rest of the area covered by his chart, there was nothing remarkable. Nikki lay almost in the middle of a large and easy high-pressure ridge, which the lines of barometric pressure defined more or less in the shape of an egg.

Now, regarding the map with some distaste, Adam knew that for the next few days at least, the winds would be light, the temperature and humidity about normal for the season, and there would very probably be the usual tropical rain squalls during the nights. There was not the slightest evidence of any Lazy Ethel or even a remotely comparative storm. So be it.

His map would not have been considered as wholly accurate or even entirely reliable by an airline operating within the United States itself. None of them ever had been, since they were drawn upon the information offered from a bare minimum of reporting stations. Adam estimated that for the same area in the States he would know the pressure, dew point, temperature, the wind direction and force prevailing at no fewer than fifty stations. Here, he was obliged to rely on only seven stations, Tuamani, Oa Titia, Trigger, the explosion site, a chartered motor vessel two hundred miles to the northwest of Trigger, a Coast Guard cutter two hundred miles to the east of Tuamani, and his own observations on Nikki. These reports had been occasionally supplemented by advice from aircraft and regular merchant ships which came close enough to the area, but Adam had little faith in it. It was almost always incomplete and usually so old by the time it was sent on to Nikki as to render it useless. Later, when Operation Zeus approached explosion date, Adam understood that a considerable number of Navy ships and Air Force planes would be employed to gather weather data and check particularly on the movements of the upper winds. He sincerely hoped so. The winds above thirty thousand feet would govern both the spread and radioactive fallout of Zeus. If they set the damnable thing off while relying on only those scanty reports now available, he believed they would be taking a terrible chance.

Beneath the regular map Adam had spread a blank form ready for the following day. Underneath the form he had concealed Pike's special map which he would personally deliver at noon. He had drawn it with care and considerable forethought. Lighting his pipe he smiled when he recalled how easily he had contrived to place the center of Lazy Ethel just far enough to the southwest of Nikki so that Pike's neuritis would receive full satisfaction. Yet it was not close enough to make anyone, least of all Pike, ask why the climate on Nikki was not being affected.

On a separate paper he had tentatively sketched in the future of Lazy Ethel. Tomorrow morning he would show her as moving well to the southeast of Nikki and on the following morning she would begin to dissipate an obviously safe distance to the east. By the next day he would explain to Pike that Lazy Ethel had completely vanished off his map. As for Tuamani, if they kept their interest and became overly curious, he could say that no further reports had been intercepted from tuna boats and apparently any disturbance had blown itself out. Pike would have had enough excitement to satisfy him and perhaps he would leave Adam Smith alone. A harmless deception at the worst—and, he mused, well deserved.

Now if Margaret would only come. He blew smoke at the clock on the wall and saw that she was already five minutes late.

He was rolling up the map for Margaret when he heard the screen door slam behind him. He turned around on his stool to smile and was instantly disappointed. His visitor was Hanover.

"Well," Hanover said, wiping the ever-present perspiration from the pouches under his eyes. "Well, good morning to you, Abe Lincoln, and what's with the Union Army?"

Hanover's fingers trembled as he lit a cigarette and sauntered from the door to Adam's drawing board. Leaning on the board he said, "I hope you don't mind me calling you Abe. You're a dead ringer, you know."

"I've been kidded about it before. I wish the resemblance went a lot further."

"Good answer. Now I also hope you don't mind if I ask a couple more questions. To begin with, friend, what's new?"

"Nothing that I know."

"Is that so?"

Adam did not like the tone of Hanover's voice. It suggested that they were old friends who met on every morning and perhaps, just now, shared a secret. The way his eyes widened in mock surprise left little doubt that he knew about Lazy Ethel and had been the person who had informed Tuamani of its existence. Adam took his time snapping the rubber bands around the rolled map. This Hanover, unless carefully diverted, could be a banana peel beneath a well-planned walk. He would be the janitor who accidentally fell against the switch and closed the bank vault just as the teller decided to return the money. He could make a lot of trouble.

Adam managed with some difficulty to return Hanover's fixed smile.

"Just the same old thing around here. If anything turns up, I'll let you know."

"Sure you will, friend. You've got my interests at heart. You've thought it all out how I've been going crazy trying to get some kind of a story out of this hunk of coral and you're lying awake nights trying to think up something for me to write about. I want you to know how much I appreciate your efforts. Have a cigarette."

"I just use this," Adam said, tapping his pipe. "Now I'd like to ask *you* a question. Have you got a family?"

"No." Hanover's eyes became questioning and then solemn. "No . . . Is it that bad?"

Adam sighed unhappily. This was, he thought, all he needed.

"Now look here, Abe," Hanover was saying. "Be a good guy. I have to make a living just like you do. How about briefing me on what's going on? I want it from the original. In my business we call it from an informed source . . . or an authoritative spokesman. I'll use either one if you don't want your name mentioned. What's going on?"

"What *is* going on?"

"You know, friend," Hanover said easily, "you missed your calling. You should have been an actor. Right now your eyes are as innocent as a pugilist accused of taking a fall. Don't just sit there and tell me you of all people don't know what's going on."

Adam shrugged his shoulders. The gesture helped him to ignore the sudden queasy feeling in his stomach.

"What have you been doing for the last hour?" Hanover asked.

"My work. Drawing up the daily map."

"Sure, you have. Then *of course* you wouldn't know why all hell has broken loose on this paradise of the Pacific. You wouldn't know that our idyllic little Polynesian refuge has been suddenly turned inside out . . . and when I say *out*, I mean just that. You wouldn't know why our dear General Pike has selected this particular morning for a so-called hurricane drill?"

Adam bit hard into his pipestem. It was already lit, but he reached for a match anyway. When he struck it and applied the flame to his already hot pipe, the resulting cloud of smoke almost smothered Hanover. As Adam had hoped, he moved back from the drawing board. Behind his smoke screen Adam sought frantically to collect his thoughts and find an answer which might subdue his fears.

"A hurricane drill?" he asked.

"Yes, friend Abe. Only I happen to know it's not a drill. All this stuff Albright is passing out about our moving the whole shebang over to the north side of the island . . . just one big happy family on a picnic to end all picnics, is ridiculous. You might have drills—maybe you line up four landing craft, two speedboats, and a barge along the wharf to make things look right and give whoever is responsible for the practice—but you don't start actually loading them with the essential needs of mankind . . . food, shelter, and light. You may go through the motions, but you don't actually start closing down the normal facilities, and what's more you don't post marines around with real bullets in their guns, or stir up your simple-minded neighbors across the channel until they don't know whether to consult with their priest or a witch doctor. I've been through plenty of lifeboat drills in my time. I know the form, and I know when you're just supposed to go to your station and stand there and look at the boat and when it's for real and the ship is on its way to the bottom. Now come on, Abe. Give! I know about Lazy Ethel. Give with the details. Let me get my story off while there's still time and I'll leave you alone."

Adam barely managed to sit placidly and puff on his pipe. Holy mackerel, he thought, what have I done? And what has Pike done? To cover his confusion he pinched at the bridge of his nose, making a face as he did so. For a moment he wondered whether it was Pike or himself who had gone mad.

"Come on, Abe. Unroll that map and show it to me. Give me the straight dope and I'll get the hell out of here."

Then he said with an honest sincerity which appalled Adam, "I know you're plenty busy even if you don't act like it, and I realize you're going to be a lot busier. If I have a chance I intend to do a piece on you and the discovery of Lazy Ethel. How bad is it, now, really? Tell me, Abe. My life insurance is paid up. I can take it."

"I wouldn't worry," Adam said, hearing his own voice as if it came from a total stranger. "I just wouldn't bother about the whole thing."

"You mean it's that rough? I remember Wake Island. Will it sweep clean across Nikki like the one did there?"

Adam shook his head. There must be some way out of this, or should he confess now? And if he did, would Hanover believe him? He said, "I . . . I doubt it very much."

"Then why all the preparations? I went to see Pike. He claimed he was too busy to talk to me. For once, I believed him."

"Look," Adam said hesitantly. He was about to tell Hanover the full truth, yet he could not for the life of him find an easy or convincing way to begin. He would sound just as he had before Pike, confused and determined to hide something. "Look," he began again. "I don't know what steps Pike has taken . . . he's sort of excitable, you know . . . but I doubt if there's much chance this storm will come anywhere near us. Pike is probably just getting things ready in case there should be a change."

"He's doing more than getting things ready. He's going. Departure is set up for noon. Christ, if I only had a decent camera!"

"I can almost guarantee you any departure will be canceled," Adam said heavily.

Hanover seemed not to hear him.

"When is Lazy Ethel supposed to hit? When will we see the first indications? It's a funny thing, but when I came over here I looked up at the sky and it sure seemed to have a funny color to me. Weird."

"The color of the sky is now perfectly normal," Adam said firmly. "I can't just say when you might see any indications."

"What's the difference between a typhoon and a hurricane?"

"None, really," Adam answered with a momentary sense of relief. It was so much easier to talk about the theories of weather than it was to create it. And far less involved.

"Both hurricanes and typhoons are cyclonic in nature, although as a general rule a typhoon covers a much larger area. The difference is really in terminology. The word *typhoon* is customarily used to describe cyclonic storms in the Western Pacific. The word *hurricane* is normally used in the Carribean and Atlantic area to describe similar disturbances. I don't know just how or why both terms are used. In the southern hemisphere the winds revolve clockwise . . ."

"Aren't typhoons usually accompanied by a tidal wave?" Hanover interrupted. "For instance, couldn't one follow Lazy Ethel and sweep Nikki clean?"

"Both types of disturbance are frequently followed by a definite rise in the level of the sea along coastal projections or islands, but really . . ."

Adam was shocked to see that Hanover was taking notes. How far could this thing go? He had to stop it right now! There was probably a severe penalty for inventing storms although he could not remember any mention of one in his entire study of air-mass analysis. Did they send you to prison for drawing storms which did not exist? Or did they, when a government project was concerned, shoot you for treason? That girl in the teletype office was absolutely right. It did not pay to think when you worked for the government. Nor anywhere else when you were guilty of thinking this way.

"How hard will the wind blow?" Hanover pressed.

"There's something I want to explain to you . . ."

Adam paused while a truck roared down the street. He looked out the window and was horrified to see it piled high with what were obviously food supplies from the warehouse. The driver and the two men who hung on near the tailgate had a peculiarly grim look about them. Now, looking down the street, he saw that it was alive with activity. Another truck was maneuvering down by the equipment park and a jeep, racing along at high speed, raised a cloud of coral dust near the Marine headquarters. Nikki was usually very quiet at this hour.

Adam was about to start the explanation which he now knew almost by heart, how Lazy Ethel would soon pass harmlessly out of existence, when Margaret came through the screen door. She said in a way that he thought was all too bright for the moment, "Hi. Is the map ready? Oh, hi, Mr. Hanover."

Hanover said, "Hi. You all ready for the big picnic?"

"Sure. But Sunnie and I are bound to miss some of the fun. We're assigned to the last boat."

"Then chivalry is dead on Nikki," Hanover said. "I always thought it was women and children first."

Adam wanted to hide under his drawing board when Margaret replied that the children were getting ready to go any minute. "But it seems we're supposed to stay around with the teletypes."

"That's sensible," Hanover said. "Much to my surprise, Pike seems to be handling this thing right."

"Of course, it's just a drill," Margaret said with a long look at Adam. Once more he put down a desire to crawl under the drawing board. Her expression was a strange mixture of sympathy and what he thought might almost be resentment, as if he should have told her about Lazy Ethel on the wharf. He was amazed when he remembered that just last evening, hardly fifteen hours ago, he had never heard of Lazy Ethel himself. Then he remembered staring down at the whirlpools in the channel after Margaret had left the wharf, and he knew when this troublesome beast had first been conceived. He was going to have to kill it in a hurry.

"Naturally," Hanover was saying to Margaret, "a hurricane drill is the most natural thing in the world around these parts. As far as I can find out after a brief conversation with a man named Terry Mack who lives on the other side of the channel, there hasn't been a storm here since about 1915. He thinks we've all gone crazy and made some fairly pointed remarks about the emotional antics of Americans in general."

"I'm late," Margaret said, looking at the roll of paper beside Adam's hand. "Can I take the map?"

Adam handed it to her and as he did so he wished that Hanover would go away so that he could talk to Margaret alone. He wanted to begin by telling her all about Lazy Ethel from the very beginning. Perhaps, having had as much contact with Pike as any of the lesser mortals on Nikki, she might understand why he had been compelled to create it. And if she did, then that would be a very satisfactory thing in spite of the ultimate disaster which now seemed certain. She had been right when she said that heads would roll. My own first of all, he thought.

"Would you come back here for a minute after you've delivered the map?" Adam said to Margaret.

"Sure. If Pike doesn't think up something else for me to do."

"I'll just walk up that way with you," Hanover said, opening the door for Margaret. Then he said, "Thanks, Abe. I'll be back later, too."

"Yeah," Adam answered without the slightest invitation in his voice.

Another truck roared past as they went out the door. Beyond them Adam saw Carlos Raveza sitting on a piece of machinery in the back of the truck. He grinned when he saw Adam, shouted something unintelligible and threw him a careless salute. He looked, Adam thought, all too much like a brave recruit hurrying off to war.

He turned slowly around on his stool and placed his hands over his eyes. He had to think, and he had to think fast. Now he became increasingly aware of the noise outside his office, and he found it almost impossible to concentrate. How could he have got himself into such a jam? What had begun as a harmless fancy seemed to have expanded like a thunderhead until it had become a monstrous thing. It was rapidly threatening to take charge. "I am sitting on a personal Zeus," he murmured.

He opened his fingers far enough so that he could peek between them at the street. It was now well populated. Those people who did not appear to be carrying something, or bound on some urgent mission, were standing in groups talking earnestly. Adam could guess what they were talking about. How many others besides Hanover, he wondered, had made up their minds this was not a drill?

He saw Margaret walking briskly toward Pike's office. Hanover was still beside her. Damn him! Why couldn't he find his stories somewhere else?

He closed his fingers again, blotting out the sight of the street. He yearned for darkness, silence, complete isolation. He must make one last desperate attempt to find an immediate and honorable end for Lazy Ethel. But the bank vault was closed. It had been slammed shut, way ahead of time! How can I get the money back where it belongs? God help me! What have I done? His hands slipped down and around his neck in an involuntary gesture, and he bent his head low.

10

On the opposite side of the channel, Chief Tanni leaned against a coconut palm and alternately pondered both the white beach which formed the nearest lip of the lagoon, and the sky. The beach he knew well; almost every granule of coral on it had at one time or another known the weight of his bare feet. It reminded him now of the pearling season when there were always excitement and activity enough to rouse the laziest of his people. Those were the good times on Nikki, and Tanni found it saddening to think that his status as chief forbade him true participation in the pearling. Ahwei! It was not always so.

He could see himself before he was elected chief, that

would be five years ago, and the vision pleased him. He was not so fat then, and during the season he had departed from the same beach every day, bound for the pearling grounds near the center of the lagoon. It was a voyage of nearly ten kilometers to the center of the sparkling blue water; and when the wind was faithful they made it in a very short time . . . twenty canoes when the price of pearl was low and only a few divers from the other islands considered it worth while to come to Nikki. As many as seventy canoes when the price was high. Ahwei! They would spend the entire day diving and surfacing and diving again in the water, which was neither too cool nor too warm, shouting to each other across the wavelets and laughing at jokes spewed out along with the water from their mouths. Then, Tanni remembered wistfully, he had thought nothing of diving twenty meters, even twenty-five meters if the bottom looked promising through the glass in his water box. And there were others who were so driven by a mixture of greed and pride that they sometimes dared to dive even farther into the blue lagoon. The results were not always so happy, Tanni recalled. For the bodies of those who had been either too brave or foolhardy, were often carried ashore twisting in agony, or sometimes as limp as a needlefish. Then the priest would come, or one of the Mormon elders. And the young body would never slip beneath the surface of the lagoon again.

But almost always the return to the village was a happy and triumphant affair. When the lowering sun robbed the depths of workable light, then the divers' lungs were sore from the special laboring, anyway. So the canoes would start back laden with shell. And if the wind was just right, there would be a race to arrive on the beach first, and if the wind had dropped dead, then the paddles would flash red in the afternoon sun and there would still be a race.

And the beach, Tanni thought, would sound and appear almost exactly as it did now.

He looked down at his people, knowing every one of them down to the last child screaming its delight, and he saw that they were almost finished with their preparations. Every canoe in the village had been dragged to the edge of the water, even a few which had not been used for years and so were cracked with dryness and leaked, and there were others which had been left awash and were soggy with neglect. Now in a spasm of activity, broken outriggers had been repaired, and a great exchange of paddles had taken place so that even those who had not used their canoes for a long time were properly equipped. Amid much hilarity, both Fat Sue and Yip Kee, who were merchants and had never been in a canoe in their lives, were instructed in the proper ways to handle the craft Tanni himself had lent them. In return they were bringing along a generous assortment of the precious cans from their shelves, both agreeing that when the storm came they would lose all anyway and they might as well use this opportunity to create good will. Tanni saw M. DeLage helping his native wife load their canoe, which had an ancient outboard motor attached to the stern. And since M. DeLage could not paddle any better than the two Chinese, Tanni hoped the motor worked better than his wireless, which after almost the full morning's nursing had failed to establish even momentary contact with Papeete or anywhere else over the horizon.

Evaluating the situation on the beach, Tanni estimated that all would be ready for departure long before the time set by the Americans. His people were working together. . . . The Mormons and the Catholics were assisting each other as if there had never been the slightest division of interests. Terry Mack was, as usual, running about from group to group, chattering like a monkey and making a nuisance of himself, but generally the people were too busy to pay him much attention. . . . Which was good, because the little Melanesian who didn't belong on Nikki anyway and never could, had been the first to bring news of the storm from across the channel. He had been running about ever since on his spindly legs, foretelling the most awful debacle. It was good that his words were not swallowed entirely for there was not going to be any debacle, which was the French word Terry Mack had used over and over again. There was going to be a storm, but not a debacle if the people across the channel, who were very clever to have known of the storm so far in advance, had done the rest of their thinking properly. Tanni was not so sure about that.

He studied the sky for a long time. Ahwei. Yes, the Americans were clever although how they could have known that a storm was on its way before the sky itself showed a certain milkiness, was beyond his understanding. They were clever, too, in denying that any real storm was approaching, which, of course, was an untruth, but if they preferred to start that way Tanni could not see any harm done. Long before the Americans were ready to leave their own settlement, Tanni's people would rendezvous beneath the low scrub which dotted the land on the north side of the lagoon and would have their cooking fires ready. They had been told to settle down and wait at that place which Tanni knew very well since he had often explored there in his youth. Now he thought of it without enthusiasm. It was not, he considered, the best place to seek refuge from any storm which

215

might strike Nikki. It was the flattest part of the atoll and the lowest in respect to the sea. The land offered nothing except the scrub and a few mounds of coral intermixed with small hummocks of sand. None of these elevations were higher than a man's head.

Still enrapt in the sky, Tanni tried to remember the last big storm which had passed across Nikki. But he was only six years old when that had occurred and he found it impossible to recall anything except a vision of his mother singing to him. Thinking back, he was not at all sure the memory did not reflect some other occasion. He had always been under the impression that all storms approached Nikki from the north. Yet whether his belief originated from remembered fact or simply echoed opinions he might have long ago heard from his elders, he could not be sure. He had confirmed his vague opinion by talking with Huahenga's mother and the uncle of Apakura, who were the oldest people on Nikki. Both had shaken their heads dubiously and said that the north side of Nikki was the wrong place to go. They agreed that much more favorable protection would be found on the south side, where there was a fifty-meter hill if things became really bad.

Tanni rubbed his eyes because staring so long at the sky had made them begin to water. And he was getting a headache, whether from his observation of the sky or the argument within himself, he did not know. If the Americans had learned of the storm so far in advance, he finally decided, then they must know what they were doing. If they said the storm would come from the south, then it would come from the south in spite of Huahenga's mother and Apakura's uncle, who were old and addled anyway. The Americans were modern. They had machinery and they knew. Look how, in so short a time, they had built a village far more comfortable than Nikki. Ahwei!

Pushing himself away from the coconut palm, Tanni strolled slowly down toward the beach. There was no longer any reason to look at the sky, for of its present nature, at least, he was very certain.

As they passed the post office, Margaret told Hanover she would have to leave him and see if there was any mail for the Governor's house. When he said she would be wasting her time because the mail plane hadn't come and probably wouldn't under the circumstances and why shouldn't they stop in the store and he would buy her a Coke, she said she had to make sure about the mail anyway.

Leaving Hanover, she went into the post office and found that it was closed. So, too, was Aubrey Tinsman's beauty salon. She was surprised because less than an hour before Aubrey had given her a haircut. Now he had left a sign on his door, GONE TO PICNIC! She waited a moment, not wanting to rejoin Hanover. All the way from Adam's office he had tried to persuade her to show him the map and it was getting to be a bore refusing him. Hanover had also proven himself to be a fanny pincher, perhaps still in the embryonic stage, but there was no other logical explanation for stumbling twice and reaching to her hip for support . . . not when the street was perfectly smooth coral. Fanny pinching, Margaret thought with a wry smile, was not necessarily confined to older men or, for that matter, to any special time of the day. Hanover should know better.

When she went out into the street he was still waiting for her. "Just like I told you, wasn't it?" he asked.

"Yes. It was closed."

"Everything is closed except I still think we can get that Coke."

"No. Thanks very much," Margaret said, starting out for Pike's house with a firm step. She added, "See you at the picnic."

But obviously Hanover had not chosen to hear her. "About that map," he said, again falling into step beside her. "I don't see how you could possibly get in any trouble if you just let me have a peek at it."

"It isn't a question of my getting into any trouble. I'm just a messenger girl, Mr. Hanover. Why don't you ask Pike if you want to see it?"

"I imagine he's pretty busy right now with all this going on."

He nodded at a group of laborers who were nailing temporary battens across the windows of the water-evaporation plant. He said, "A good newsman picks his time if he possibly can and sees people when they're not up to their necks in something else. So for the last time, how about just a peek?"

"*No*," Margaret said decisively.

Hanover sighed. "Have it your way, girl. I know what's on the map anyway. Abe Lincoln told me."

"Oh? He did?"

"Regular Gettysburg Address on the nature of hurricanes. He's a smart fellow, but a very poor actor."

They reached the intersection where the narrower road from Pike's house joined the main street. Without slowing her stride Margaret turned into it. Hanover stopped, reached out, and seized her wrist. "You and Abe are making a mistake. It never pays to hide things from the press. We can be very helpful people."

"I said I'm just a messenger girl!" Margaret twisted

her arm until her wrist was free and quickly walked away.

Her anger was replaced by complete surprise when she entered Pike's office and he smiled broadly at her. "Good morning to you again, young lady!" he said cheerily.

Not certain she had heard him accurately, Margaret advanced until she could place the map on his desk. She saw that it was littered with papers, some of which were prominently labeled SECRET and others RESTRICTED. A small hand compass and a many-bladed knife had been placed just behind the sign which bore his name, and a pair of binoculars held down a sheaf of papers on one side.

"Good morning to you again, sir," Margaret said hesitantly. "There wasn't any mail."

"Of course not," Pike boomed without the slightest sign of disappointment. "And a good thing, too! We've got enough going on around here without getting lost in a lot of paperwork. *Well!*" he went on, still smiling, "all packed to go on the picnic?"

"I was told I would go in the last boat so I thought I had plenty of time."

"Better get your gear together. I may move the departure up a half-hour or so. No sense in waiting until the stable is on fire before you move the horse. Ho, ho!"

As Pike chuckled to himself, Margaret studied his face in wonder. What in the world had gotten into General Zebulon Pike? He was acting as if he were really going on a picnic and one which he would thoroughly enjoy. His eyes, normally cold and always, she remembered, a little uncertain as if his pride had somehow just been wounded, were now fairly snapping with anticipation. Now, of all things, he carelessly tossed the rolled-up map aside and smiled again at her.

"Here's a message I want sent off right away," he said, ripping a sheet of paper from his note pad. "There may be one or two more, but I doubt it. Better read it to make sure you don't have any trouble putting it on the teletype. My neuritis is giving me the very devil and I'm afraid my penmanship isn't quite up to par."

Margaret read the message which was written in Pike's careful, almost Shakespearean hand. It was perfectly legible, quite beautiful visually, she thought. If Pike apologized for his writing, she mused, he should try to read mine. The message was for Tuamani.

Situation Pistol Two well in hand. All possible measures being taken protect personnel and government property. Classified documents secured. For your information have assumed emergency authority placing Marine detachment under my direct command. We are ready for Lazy Ethel.
Pike.

"It's quite clear," Margaret said. "Anything else, sir?"

"No. Just get it out right away."

Before Margaret started toward the door Pike winked at her. "Better take along some warm clothes," he said. "You just happen to be one of the very few people who knows this isn't a drill. No sense in catching cold."

He looked at her and his voice took on a tender, protective note. "Not a little afraid, are you?"

"No, sir."

"Good. Brave girl. It won't be so bad. Everyone will be taken care of."

When she reached the main street again, Margaret looked carefully down its length to make sure Hanover was not waiting for her. But he was not to be seen. Instead, the street was now almost deserted except where it terminated down by the wharf. There she could see a considerable crowd of people. She had not realized so many lived in Pistol Two, probably, she thought, because they had quickly dispersed after their arrival and had never all been assembled in one place again. As she approached the communications shack she saw that many of the people were already in the boats. Those still waiting to board were laden down with packages and clothes, and the mothers were having a busy time corralling the children.

In spite of herself, Margaret knew a sense of pleasurable excitement. At the very least Lazy Ethel was going to be inconvenient and she supposed that it could be dangerous; but just now with the sun shining and the leisurely, almost festive air with which the people milled about the wharf, it was hard to believe the gathering represented anything more than a picnic. Albright, whom she could see striding anxiously about in the best tradition of a social director, seemed to be the only harassed person on the wharf. Just like the Beloit J.C.C.'s, she thought, only on a considerably larger scale.

She entered the communications shack and found Sunnie Mandel engrossed, as usual, in a movie magazine. Margaret had never been able to understand how her supply of movie magazines seemed so inexhaustible. Until one day Sunnie had explained she read each one several times in the belief that careful study would enable her to write for them. "The people who write this stuff have it made," she had explained. "They get paid for yakking with the stars. Imagine!"

Now she did not look up from her magazine, but did acknowledge Margaret's entrance with a throaty hello.

"Hi," Margaret answered and went directly to the number one teletype machine. As she sat down before it and clipped Pike's message to the scanning board she said, "It looks like we're about on our way. Have you done any packing?"

"Unh-uh. They won't let you take enough to make it worth while. I'll be satisfied with a toothbrush."

"We'd better take something to keep us warm, anyway."

"I suppose."

There was a long pause while Margaret's fingers tripped over the teletype keys. She waited for Tuamani's stand-by acknowledgment, then sent Pike's message.

When she had finished, Sunnie said, "Our hero was in this morning."

"Who?"

"Silent Sam, the weatherman. Only he's not so silent lately. We almost had a conversation."

"Fine," Margaret said. "I think he needs someone to talk to."

"He does indeed. Say, what's with him?"

"How do you mean?"

"What's with him? He acts like he's been in the cookie jar . . . like he's sick in the head from something he et."

"I don't understand you, Sunnie."

"We-yell. . . ." Sunnie closed the movie magazine and, doubling her fists, placed them beneath her chin. She leaned forward on her elbows and stared thoughtfully across the street at the weather office. "Well, maybe I know something I shouldn't. For my money, anyway, it just doesn't figure. This is all aside from the fact he's madly in love with you."

"Oh now, come on, Sunnie. You're not making sense."

"I am. But he isn't. My twisted little mind has been working overtime and what it comes up with scares me."

Margaret sighed. There were times when Sunnie Mandel could be anything but a delightful companion. She was often given to long periods of brooding and the most merciless self-analysis. It came, she freely admitted, from wanting a man so badly she sometimes caught herself shivering all over at the mere sight of a likely male. Margaret wondered if she would ever suffer the same affliction. Maybe a few more years of government work would do it. The Ree-Jay Club always had room for new members.

"Get this," Sunnie said. "Out of a clear blue sky this morning comes a message from Tuamani asking about a storm. They don't know a thing about it, see, and we are supposed to cue them. Okay. But, before that, is there any message from us to anybody about said storm? There is not. So how did they find out about it in the first place? They have a crystal ball, maybe?"

Sunnie furrowed her brow and placed a fingernail between her teeth. She was about to start gnawing on the nail when Margaret said sharply, "Stop that!"

It was a habit they were both in league to break and Sunnie lowered her hand in shame.

"So what happens?" she went on. "A little later, Silent Sam comes in here and he's got a message he wants to send to Tuamani. It says he got the dope about the storm from a Jap fishing boat. So okay. I send it. Now what bothers me is how did Silent Sam hear from this fishing boat? He has a special radio in his room, maybe, which speaks Japanese?"

"I don't see where it really makes any difference."

"It does to me and I'll tell you why in a minute. Or did you receive some click from a fishing boat . . . maybe when I was gone to the biffie?"

"No. I didn't."

"All right, then. Neither did I. Those machines have been silent as a busted-down organ all morning. There wasn't anything yesterday afternoon or last night either. We didn't hear from any boat even if it were possible for them to get on the circuit, which it isn't . . . but I do smell something fishy."

Margaret was touching up her lips before the mirror which hung over the number one machine. She paused now, wondering what strange avenue Sunnie's mind would venture along next.

"You know what I think?" Sunnie said.

"No, I don't know what you think. Frankly, I'm never quite sure."

Margaret knew she was vaguely annoyed and she could not understand why she should be just now. Sunnie was merely chattering along in her standard style. Perhaps, she considered, I am actually a little nervous about going to see Adam Smith without an official reason. But that was silly. Well, anyway, her lips were now all right.

"I think there isn't any storm," Sunnie said flatly.

"What in the world would give you that idea?"

"I think somebody threw a curve at Tuamani just for kicks and they fell for the gag. Now, who would do a thing like that is the next thing I ask myself. And the answer comes through right away clear as if it clicked off number one machine. Silent Sam, it says. Who else?"

"That imagination of yours!" Margaret said, wondering again why she felt so uneasy. "Why would he do a thing like that?"

"That, I can't answer. But like I told you he wasn't himself when he came in here. He was nervous as a witch on Hallowe'en. When he sent that message to Tuamani he was covering for himself."

"I'll tell you what I'll do," Margaret said, trying very firmly to put down her misgivings. "I'm going across to see him right now, anyway, and I'll just mention the fact you don't think there is a real storm. Maybe for once he'll laugh right out loud. Or he would if there was anything funny about a storm."

"Don't!" Sunnie said hastily.

"Why not? He deserves a laugh."

"Just don't. Please. It wouldn't be smart. Especially for you. Men are funny. They don't like suspicious women and he might blame my thoughts on you. I want him to like you."

"I thought you said he was madly in love with me?"

"A figure of speech. That comes later. Now don't go louse anything up. Please."

Because of her tennis shoes, Margaret made no sound as she entered Adam's office. She allowed the door to close very softly behind her and stood waiting for a moment in silence. Adam was bent over his drawing board, his back to her, and at first she thought he was deeply engrossed in his work. Then she saw that his eyes were closed and there was only a blank piece of paper beneath his elbows. His shoulders sagged and his whole body had somehow taken on a posture of utter dejection. She wondered if his work with the storm had kept him up all night.

"Are you just taking a nap?" she said finally. Hanover was right. He did look like Abe Lincoln, and she thought it very strange that she had never really noticed the resemblance before. Only now he looked like a very weary Lincoln, somewhat like the portraits she remembered in her schoolbooks.

He stood looking down at her in silence for so long Margaret began to be uncomfortable; then very suddenly she decided she would wait for him to speak first if it took all day.

"Thanks for coming back," he said at last. "I wanted to apologize for making such a fool of myself on the wharf last night."

"You already did that. Forgiven."

"I like you."

Margaret swallowed hard. When Adam Smith did speak he certainly didn't beat around the bush. "Well . . . good," she said.

There followed another silence, and again Margaret was determined he should do the talking. She stood motionless, her hands clasped behind her, looking up at him almost defiantly. She was no longer uncomfortable.

"There's something I want to tell you," he began. "It isn't easy and, for a little time at least, you will be the only person besides myself who knows it. I want to tell you because someday I would like to see you again . . . maybe under better circumstances. I . . . well, I just never before met anyone who . . . well . . . I want you to believe me now when I try to explain how I feel about you . . . because maybe later on you won't believe me. I'm making an awful bungle of this."

"You are a little vague," she said. For some reason she wanted him to tell her again that he liked her in just the same way he had done before. It should have been embarrassing, but it just wasn't. Yet he was deeply troubled and before he spoke again she knew what he was going to say.

"I've made an even bigger fool of myself. I invented a storm which doesn't exist and I named it Lazy Ethel. The reasons why I did this thing are so childish and complicated there's no sense in trying to explain, but I certainly never dreamed it would cause such an uproar and inconvenience so many people. I just underestimated Pike's craving for action, and what with one thing and another it's a cinch I won't be around here very long. I wanted you to know the truth before I went up and told Pike. Then maybe someday . . . when you come back to the States, I could find you, somehow . . . and when I told you again you'd believe that business about my liking you."

His eyes were so miserable Margaret wanted to reach up and caress them. She would believe Adam Smith, all right. Anywhere.

"I guess that's all I have to say. You can go now."

"What . . . do you think Pike will do?"

"Can me, for sure. Then call the whole thing off. I just wish he hadn't been so hasty or I could have stopped him."

"You'll break his heart. I never saw a man so full of enthusiasm for a project. He's a changed man, too. It's all right up his alley. You've done him more good than harm."

"I doubt if he'll look at it quite that way. I'm sorry. I'm very, very sorry about this whole mess."

"Pike is going to be a lot sorrier. I've got a hunch he has to prove himself. He has the bit in his teeth and he's going to hate dropping it. Isn't there some other way? Couldn't you just let him have his fun?"

"I tried that and it's already out of hand. I still have to live with myself."

He went quickly to his drawing board and after a moment's hesitation scribbled a name and address on a piece of paper. He turned back to Margaret and handed it to her. "Here. Please keep this and write me a card when you get home. It's my brother's address and it will be forwarded to me. I'm not just sure where I'll be after this."

Margaret folded the paper and placed it in her pocket.

The silence between them was broken by the sound of the engines in the landing craft. As she listened they roared to full power, then gradually diminished. When it was quiet again, she said, "Anyway, they'll have a fine boat ride at government expense."

Adam went quickly to the door.

"That must only be the first load. I've got to stop the rest. I'd better go see Pike right now."

"Good luck."

"So long . . . Margaret. Thanks for taking my folly the way you have."

She did not leave the weather office immediately. Instead she climbed on Adam's stool. Through the screen window she could see him hurrying up the deserted street toward Pike's house. He looked so very much alone. And she thought, if anyone knew what it was like to feel alone in a hostile world, she did. So she tried very hard to think of some way to help Adam Smith.

11

There were forty-five people in the first landing craft to leave the wharf at Pistol Two. As it cleared the channel and entered the calm expanse of the lagoon, the passengers settled down as comfortably as they could manage in the confined space. For many it was their first real view of the lagoon, so the novelty of its clear depths held them entranced for several miles. The children were especially excited, and it was all the mothers could do to keep them from falling overboard as they clambered up and down the high-sided craft and fought for vantage points. There was no complaining, most of the passengers having accepted without question Albright's explanation that it was only a drill. There was even, as Pike had hoped, a festive air about the expedition. This atmosphere would have been easier for all of them to maintain if the diesel engines had made less racket. Because of this noise the majority of the passengers were obliged to settle down and wait in thoughtful silence.

The only place in the craft where it was possible to carry on wholly intelligible conversation was in the bow. When the channel entrance and the buildings of Pistol Two had sunk beneath the horizon, several passengers gathered there who were not attached to any particular family group. So it was that Peter Hildebrandt found a comfortable seat on a box of canned peas which he almost immediately surrendered to Crystal Blum, who ran the laundry.

"Don't thank me," Peter said with a little bow. "I am in your debt for doing such a nice job on my shirts."

"Oh, Mr. Hildebrandt!" Crystal said with a delighted giggle, "you are a true gentleman!"

"The old scoundrel will sully your honor if you give him the chance," Dr. Case said. "I wouldn't trust him."

Dr. Keim, the astronomer, stood looking aft. He rubbed sunburn lotion into his bright-red nose and said, "Look. You can still see the top of the control tower. Just the top of it is sticking up . . . right there. In case any of you are interested there is perfect proof the world is round. Our visibility is much less than you think it is from this height. Not much more than three miles."

"We're out of sight of the land," Aubrey Tinsman said. "I shall pretend I'm cruising on my yacht."

Turning to Carlos Raveza, who had been assigned to the first boat on the theory he would have time to set up his portable light plant, Aubrey said, "Steward, you may bring my bouillon now."

"For a certainty this is absolute foolishness," Carlos Raveza answered. "If we are going to have a drill, why not just go for a boat ride and then when it has been proved no one knows what they are doing . . . we can return to our quarters like sensible people. I have no want to spend the night on some deserted beach. There will be mosquitoes."

"I didn't think there were any mosquitoes on Nikki," Crystal Blum said.

"Pike banished them by directive," Dr. Case said.

"There will be mosquitoes. There will be mosquitoes wherever I go," Carlos sighed. "It is a curse of my family. If there was not so much as a single mosquito before, then there will be swarms of them now. I am one of those people. When I left Tampico forever the mosquitoes soon starved."

Peter Hildebrandt was struck by a thought which suddenly robbed him of further enjoyment on the voyage. He had been brooding on the disposal problem which must attend the dislocation of so many people. Viewing the situation with the confidence and detachment of an experienced professional, he was thus not greatly concerned until he remembered something he was certain no one else had remembered. "Pardon me for bringing up such a delicate subject, but did anyone see any toilet paper put aboard?"

There was a long and embarrassed silence while the entire group surveyed the collection of boxes which now served as seats.

"What about cigarettes?" Aubrey Tinsman said with genuine alarm. "I only brought one pack and it's nearly finished."

"Beer," Carlos Raveza growled. "I don't see any beer. What kind of a picnic is this?"

Dr. Keim was still looking back at the fast-sinking control tower. It had nearly disappeared now, and the two other landing craft following in their distant wake were the only prominent objects on the horizon. "Maybe all that stuff is in the other boats," he said without any real hope in his voice. "If it isn't, then this is a very poorly organized drill."

"What about blankets?" Crystal Blum asked. "We ought to have something to sit on. It isn't very comfortable just sitting on sand. I went on a vacation once at Virginia Beach and—"

"Or sleeping on it," Dr. Case interrupted sourly.

"What do you mean sleeping on it?"

"We are obviously supposed to spend the night or Mr. Raveza would not have been invited to bring along his lighting plant."

"Have no fear," Carlos said. "I will never get it to work. There is no possibility. We will have to go back then."

"Is this trip really necessary?" Aubrey said. Then his attention was captured by a line of dark objects stretching across the cobalt blue of the water ahead. "Look! Cannibals! White man, go no farther!"

Hearing the sound of engines, Tanni looked back over his shoulder and saw the landing craft of the Americans approaching. Instinctively he quickened the rhythm of his paddling although he knew very well that even his enormous arms were little better than useless in a race against machinery. He glanced at his wife and his two children, who sat smiling in his own canoe, and then he looked thoughtfully at the long line of his people's canoes spread out on each side of him. Ahwei! This was good! The people were singing and laughing and joking as if it were Bastille Day. The other men, now aware of the overtaking power craft, were paddling as if a fortune in pearl waited for them only a few meters ahead. The canoes lifted to their efforts and small white wavelets appeared beneath their bows. The paddlers began to shout, urging each other to greater speed, and then they began a chant which Tanni had not heard for a long time. The sound of it, rising rapidly stroke by stroke, caused a tingling of pleasure along the skin of Tanni's bare arms; and though he knew his children had never heard him sing so before, and would wonder what had come over their father, he joined in the chanting. He allowed his heavy voice full expression, not caring for the frowns of the Mormon elders in the nearest canoe. Farther along the line he was delighted to hear the unmistakable voice of Huahenga, penetrating even at a distance. And it was not, he thought with strange satisfaction, a rhythm or a melody she had ever sung in church. There were no formal words to the chant for not even Huahenga's mother was likely to remember them, but the rhythm and proper joyousness soared up from the breasts of all the singers and Tanni found it more deeply moving than anything the elders had ever offered. "Alli, alli, yay! . . . Alli, alli, yay! Ah*wei!*"

Then, without intention, Tanni fell silent. The joy left his face and the tingling subsided beneath his skin. For the chanting had brought him a vision of the lagoon which was so different from what he could see now. He wanted to groan instead of sing. He saw the lagoon as it had once been, as his grandfather and great-grandfather had described it, in voices which even in the telling became vigorous again. The lagoon and the sea around Nikki were dotted by a thousand canoes. This same chant echoed and re-echoed across the lagoon and was carried far over the horizon when the young men paddled and sailed the six hundred kilometers to Tuamani for war. There were villages situated around the entire coral circlet of Nikki, and there was even a large settlement near the very place they were headed now. Ahwei! There was no longer any trace of it, nor of the others. The people of Nikki had vanished, or nearly so. Outsiders had begun to frequent Nikki in his great-grandfather's youth. They appeared more frequently and were welcomed in his grandfather's time, and his father had seen the true beginning of the end. The people died because the outsiders brought disease they could not fight with their clubs or spears. The people died because the old customs upon which they relied were pronounced evil, and this had a way of killing the desire to live. And so, in time, many more of the people simply expired.

Tanni looked over the pitiful fleet about him. There were no more than twenty canoes or, perhaps, twenty-five, and there were less than a hundred people in them. Which was all of the people in the village of Nikki.

He glanced behind him again at the snarling landing craft. They were almost upon the line of canoes and in a few moments they would pass. What were these outsiders bringing? Why had they felt the need to come to Nikki? Why had they left their own villages and traveled so many kilometers only to leave again and vanish as surely and completely as his ancestors? According to Terry Mack they would cause an explosion, not on Nikki, but near Tuamani or Oa Titia, and this would kill all the fishes and the birds which had survived a hundred storms. They were not doing this unexplainable thing on Nikki, because they did not wish to kill people—not even the few on Nikki. Then why, if they did not wish to kill people, did they go to so much trouble about the whole affair? Certainly not just to kill the fishes and the birds, for it was said they would not even touch their dead bodies. Then why?

Tanni felt his headache returning, and just as the first landing craft came abreast of his canoe he decided the hurt between his ears came from utterly useless thinking. He looked up and saw heads appearing like bleached coconuts along the sides of the landing craft. The owners of the heads were shouting and waving, and a few of them were taking his picture with their cameras. Tanni saw very distinctly that they were agreeable and most friendly. Certainly they did not appear to be the kind of people who would devote so much effort to the killing of fishes and birds. He found himself wondering if they would soon begin to vanish like his own people. Or had it already begun? Were there atolls where they had come from, once heavily populated and now almost deserted? Had they, too, somehow lost the desire to live? Ahwei! My head!

Tanni paused long enough to raise his paddle and acknowledge their waving. He saw with approval that his people in the other canoes were doing the same thing. Almost at once their delighted shouts of greeting were drowned out by the exhaust from the engines. The landing craft passed swiftly through the line of canoes, leaving them bouncing wildly in their wakes.

The singing had ceased in the canoes, and for a moment there was only the fast-diminishing roar of the engines. Then, before it was entirely quiet in the lagoon, Tanni raised his voice in the chant again. Looking at the sky, he thought that the sooner they reached land again, the better. So in spite of the terrible ache in his head he gave his voice all the lustiness within him. The others soon joined in the singing and paddled as industriously as before.

Tanni did not know why his skin failed to tingle again or why the chant seemed to have lost zest. Now it seemed to have taken on a melancholy tone. Perhaps it was because the big American craft had left them behind so easily, or perhaps it was because of the color of the sky.

Adam did not bother to knock before he entered Pike's office, so he was neither surprised nor disappointed when he was greeted with a heavy frown.

"Where is the real chart?" Pike asked, looking with disapproval at Adam's empty hands.

"You have the real chart," Adam said firmly. "I sent it up with Miss Trumpey at the regular time."

"Now come on, Smith. There's no storm on that chart. I checked just to make sure."

"No, there is not any storm on it or anywhere else, Governor. There just *isn't* any storm, sir. Lazy Ethel simply does not exist and it never did. You've got to believe me and put a stop to all this nonsense immediately!"

"Nonsense, is it?"

Pike pushed back his chair and stood up. His eyes never left Adam as he slowly circled around his desk. "Just what kind of a shenanigan are you up to now, Mr. Smith? I was under the impression you were all straightened out. I thought you had taken a brace and were going to play honest ball with me."

"I straightened myself out and I am being honest. I know you're going to fire me and I don't blame you, but you have got to believe me. *There is no such thing as Lazy Ethel!* There never was and it is extremely unlikely there ever will be. I dreamed it up just like I told you the last time I was here. Then I lied because it seemed to be easier going along with you than arguing. You aren't an easy man to talk to, Governor."

Pike studied him in silence. After a moment he turned abruptly away and walked over to the flag standard. He remained with his back to Adam, looking alternately at the flag and the line of palm trees beyond the window for a long time.

At last he turned around and Adam was instantly sorry for him. He was like a man who had collided with a tree in the dark. His face bore a crumpled look, as if he were totally incapable of mastering the disappointment and honest bewilderment which fought for supremacy within him. When he spoke his voice was flat and so subdued Adam was not at all certain the sound came from Pike at all.

"You mean this, Smith? You confess that you have deliberately tricked me? This isn't a new deception? There isn't any Lazy Ethel?"

"No, sir. I'm sorry. I really am *very* sorry. I didn't set out to trick you. It just worked that way."

"What would make you do a thing like that?"

"I don't know. I've tried to think it out, but I didn't come up with any very satisfactory answers."

There was another long silence while Pike stared at his boots. Finally he said, "You are discharged, of course."

"You have every right to feel the way you do, sir."

"I won't go into the fact that you have betrayed a trust. Perhaps it's better things turned out the way they have . . . now. God knows what you might have done when explosion date comes around."

Pike returned to his desk, crossing the room very slowly as if the shock of Adam's revelation had somehow brought a stiffness to his joints. "There will be some severance papers for you to sign," he muttered, and now he so deliberately avoided any recognition of Adam's existence he might have been standing out in the road. "I will arrange for transportation to Tuamani for you as quickly as possible. In the meantime I want a full written report from you on this whole matter."

Pike looked directly at Adam, and the hurt in his eyes was such that Adam decided that under no circumstances would he mention Pike's heckling, but would only blame himself. "You realize, of course," Pike said quietly, "that you have succeeded in making me look like a complete damned fool?"

"I'm sorry, sir."

"You will go to your quarters and remain there until further notice. I do not like to use the word *arrest*, but you should realize I have the authority to use it."

Adam turned, grateful that, at least, the whole thing was over. He wondered if there was some gymnastic feat whereby he could kick himself.

Pike called after him, but now there was neither antagonism nor any indication of a military order in his voice.

"Smith. If you are as sorry as you claim to be, then there is one thing you can do for me. I have no intention of striking a bargain with you, but if you will at least try to co-operate, perhaps I can modify some of the opinions which must be in my own report. Our people have been sent off with the impression they are doing a drill . . . fortunately. I don't see where it will have any bearing on this case if that impression is allowed to remain. It will not help their morale if they learn the full details of this unfortunate incident. On the other hand, it will help me considerably if they don't. Therefore I will appreciate it if the matter remains between you and me. We'll think up some logical reason for your departure and that will be the end of it. Is that all right with you?"

"Yessir," Adam said quickly. "I'll be only too happy to keep my mouth shut."

"Good day, Mister Smith."

When Adam had left, Pike spent a long time aligning the pencils behind the little sign which bore his name. Once they were exactly end to end, he carefully restacked a small pile of paper clips until they were also perfectly set one upon the other. And when there no longer remained any convenient preoccupation for his hands, they automatically came together in his comfortable isosceles triangle, the apex of which he employed to support his chin. He sat immobile in his chair, his eyes closed tightly, his mind composing innumerable teletypes for Tuamani, all designed to explain away one Lazy Ethel. None of his compositions offered a reasonable excuse for his action in closing down Pistol Two and sending the entire population over ten miles across the lagoon. None of the messages, forming and re-forming in his mind, suggested that a responsible and, most of all, stable personality was in charge on Nikki atoll.

Gradually, Pike saw the ingredients of a personal disaster creeping across the clutter of teletypes in his thoughts, and he knew only too well that he was poorly armed against high-echelon censure. Whether Adam Smith had originally intended to bring about his final defeat was beside the point. There were nuances of peril of which he could not possibly have been aware.

For example, Smith could not have known of the backstage maneuvering which had brought Zebulon Pike to Nikki in the first place. It had been a very close thing indeed, and there were several times when it had seemed only wistful hoping that the job could be won. Pike knew of at least five retired general officers, three of them with most distinguished war records, who were even now cursing over their peony gardens and protesting to the highest authorities that in the selection of Zebulon Pike, the most flagrant favoritism had been shown. Which was true enough. There was, of course, nothing crooked about it, although the words *scandalous, outrageous, criminal, fantastic,* and *God-damned shame* had all been uttered by the disappointed candidates and their respective families. It was largely a case of nostalgia which had prompted Pike's old polo teammate, "Owlhead" Wheeler, to recommend him. And since "Owlhead" had served through many years of staff assignments, he knew his way around Washington much better than he had ever learned to hit a near-side forward shot, despite his remarkable ability to revolve his head. He had pointed out to the selection board that highly decorated war heroes were ever reluctant to forget their prerogatives. They might be dashing, but they also reveled in friction and trouble. Examination of Pike's record easily proved to the most doubting that none of these things need be feared in his case. He was, one member of the board remarked, as obscure as a titmouse.

Once the Korean war had limped to conclusion, the surplus of formerly high-ranking army officers became appalling. Pike could not imagine where they had all come from and, of course, there was the Navy, too. Every peaceful retreat in the United States suddenly blossomed with discreet signs identifying the modest house behind it as the final residence of General Blank or Admiral Blank or Colonel Dash or Commander Dash. The countryside sprouted with these men puttering in their gardens, raising dogs which did not require too much food, donning tweed coats when they escaped long enough to go for the mail, and serving on as many local committees as they could possibly infiltrate. On the whole they tried to participate as actively as they could in every local enterprise. And they conducted themselves with notable dignity, perhaps too much, Pike thought. They were almost fiercely determined to be good citizens.

It was not easy. The sudden loneliness, for one thing, was chilling. An elderly stranger, hale and handsome to look at, perhaps, but still perforce a stranger, settled amid a community which had grown up together. However small or large, the population was bound to each other by a million invisible ties of background and circumstance. All of these had been established while the military man served out his active life elsewhere; occupied, and at the same time almost totally isolated, in what might just as well have been another world. It was a rare officer who found it either possible or desirable to retire in the vicinity of an Army post or a Naval base. They went out into their native land as children, hopefully, willingly; convinced that at last they would reap some kind of reward. Except for those very fortunate few who had married rich wives, the results were far from spectacular. They soon discovered that their pensions left no provision for that occasional bottle of Scotch which might make entertainment of their new neighbors an easier and more congenial affair. They found it almost impossible to understand or participate in conversations with the younger men who were engaged in the fast-changing business of making a living. Having always known that their own basic needs would be provided for, talking to businessmen of their own age was not much easier. If they were also retired, then those harness-worn men preferred to recall the era in which they had served as executives in some corporation, a world of secretaries, contracts, conventions, and tolerated conniving. They were not even slightly interested in the maneuvering of battalions or who commanded what battleship, unless the tale involved actual combat; and even then it had to be something they remembered reading about in the newspapers. Worst of all, there were those whom Pike and his fellow officers thought of as professional taxpayers. They secretly, and sometimes not so secretly, resented the very existence of any retired military man. They resented his meager pension as if they had just reached into their wallets and paid it directly, and they had a great deal to say about how, by God, no one had ever offered to take care of them from the cradle to the grave. This was the cruelest rebuff of all.

So cruel, in fact, many retired military men set forth once more into the world and tried almost desperately to mitigate their status. Unprepared, they sold real estate or at least tried to; they sold insurance and automobiles, ran motels or gun clubs. There were admirals who had not so long before commanded five thousand sailors and a flotilla of ships, who were now themselves quite familiar with the business end of a mop. There were generals and colonels responsible for the lives of many thousands of their fellow Americans and millions of dollars' worth of material, who became hopelessly lost between the lines of a simple lease. And frequently their wives sold Christmas cards.

There was another category of retired military man who moved in a more rarefied environment. Pike knew that it was unlikely he could join them and so had never given them much thought. For they were specialists of a kind, not mere soldiers or sailors, and their change-over to civilian life had brought them even greater benefits. These men were welcomed and highly paid by large corporations who employed them as "Advisors," or frequently and more specifically, "Advisors to the President." It surprised no one that those firms were heavily engaged in production for or services to the Armed Forces. Or they would like to be. In recent years some Air Force officers had not even found it worth while to await their retirement. They simply resigned, exchanged their uniforms for well-tailored suits, and joined whatever airline or aircraft manufacturer had offered the most enticing bid for their services. Pike did not resent their good fortune. He realized that the large majority were highly trained technicians, as well as very personable men. He was even willing to concede that, had they begun their careers in civilian life, they would probably have done better. Most certainly they were not just old "war horses" . . . especially the kind who had never been very near a war.

So it was not going to be easy . . . this explaining away of Lazy Ethel. There were men on Tuamani who remembered the circumstances of Pike's selection, and at the very least a few of them would begin to wonder if the original objectors were not right. The slightest inefficiency within the vast framework of the A.E.C. met with the most searching appraisal. The whole project, of which Zeus was only a minor adventure, was so vulnerable to criticism, the slightest foul-up shook everyone from top to bottom. Pike and his superiors on Tuamani were well aware that the breath-taking budget of their Commission was nearly impossible to justify no matter how the sabers clanged around the world. As a consequence, the general feeling within the colossus, and particularly among those directly charged with its confused destiny, was that the less said publicly about it the better.

Yes, indeed, Pike thought. A cog like himself, who might even momentarily attract the spotlight, would be sacrificed instantly. He was at once haunted by three dismal visions, each originating in such a catastrophe. There would be the loss of his twenty-thousand annual pay. There would follow the hopeless prospect of trying to live on his pension, for there was not a dime saved in any bank. And Sue-Anne would seek permanent escape from her sorrows via the bottle. Lovely. And damn that weatherman to hell forever!

Besieged with his thoughts and visions, Pike leaned far back in his chair, clasped his hands behind his head, and broke wind. He was honestly embarrassed when Albright entered his office almost simultaneously. He at once pretended to be engrossed in his papers.

"Your barge awaits, sir," Albright said, swaying somewhat less than usual. "The last landing craft left twenty minutes ago and I think things are pretty well in hand. Everyone reasonably happy and all accounted for except yourself, Mrs. Pike, our weather wizard, and two marines I thought best to hold for the last boat. I presumed you intended that we should all ride along with you?"

"Yes," Pike answered vaguely. "Very good, Albright." Then he fell silent. How the hell was he going to explain this thing even to a nitwit like Albright? Finally he said, "You didn't have any particular trouble?"

"Rather to my surprise, I did not. How goes our affair with Lazy Ethel?"

"The situation has changed somewhat. Did you say there are still two marines here?"

"Yessir. Sergeant Doolan and one of his men. Peterson, I think his name is."

"Tell Doolan I want him to come up here and stand

by the porch for possible assignment. Something special may turn up."

"Yessir."

"You'd better leave the other marine here too. Because of certain new developments, er . . . which I haven't time to explain just now, I'm going to change the setup a bit."

Pike prodded his shoulder with a gesture that had already become habit. Dammit, his neuritis was *still* with him. Amazing, he thought, the power of the human mind. Only it seemed the mind could change much more quickly than the symptoms it generated in the body. Nursing his shoulder, he said, "I'm sure you'll be needed at the camp, so you take off right now and you might as well take Mrs. Pike with you. When you get there have a good look around and see if we've omitted anything essential. Then send the boat back for me with any requests."

"What about Smith? Do I take him along?"

"No. He'd better remain here for the time being. I don't think he feels very well."

"Maybe he's been worrying too much about Lazy Ethel. I wish you'd give me the latest poop, sir. I'm naturally interested, and when I get over to the north side I'll have to answer a lot of questions."

"As far as our people are concerned this is still a drill. Let's leave it at that for just now."

Pike knew he was procrastinating and he could see that his indecision was suspect in Albright's eyes, but he was still fishing for some kind of escape. It seemed that every damned road he turned down was barricaded.

"They'll all be wanting to know when they can come back," Albright said.

"Avoid a direct answer to that question."

"Then you just want me to stall?"

"Yes. Just stall them off for a while. Organize a baseball game or something. I'll be along and straighten things out later. But don't let anyone start back until you receive word from me."

"Don't stall too long yourself, sir. Lazy Ethel may suddenly find some energy."

"Ho! Ho!" Pike forced a chuckle and wished that Albright would get the hell out of his office and fetch Sue-Anne, and they would both leave him in peace so he could do some thinking. "Ho! Ho! Don't you worry about old Zeb Pike. I'll clear out long before the advance patrol shows up. You'll find Mrs. Pike on the side porch or possibly in her room. Just give her a call. She's all ready to go."

Albright hesitated. He seemed about to speak, then apparently changed his mind. Pike thought with a strange sadness that his attempt at an about-face was the clumsiest he had ever observed. And the shorts only made matters worse. Also his actions would have been easier to stomach if Albright had not chosen to speak out a crisp and very British "Right!" as he marched away.

To prevent what he knew might become a flood of self-recrimination, Pike stood up. He gathered the papers marked SECRET and CLASSIFIED and began placing them back in the safe.

Adam had no exact idea how long he had lain on his bunk, simply shifting one of his long legs from time to time, mostly just staring at the unpainted rafters above him. He tried unsuccessfully to sleep, anything to pass the time, and then decided that he might as well get his packing done.

When he finally sat up and yawned he wondered if

he actually had slept, for certainly a considerable time had passed. The room was much darker than when he had entered it, as dark as if it were nearly evening. He glanced at his watch and found that it was only three-thirty. . . . There was still a lot of this endless day remaining. Then he looked sleepily out his window and saw that the sky was overcast, a heavy layer of stratus from the look of things, and he thought, Well, it's going to rain and for once I won't have to listen to Pike grousing about his movie.

He reached under his bunk and hauled out his duffel bag and, after it, his small and much-battered suitcase. He crossed the room to his bureau and was about to pull out the top drawer when he saw that two pocket books had been set pyramid fashion on top of the bureau. On top of the books was an envelope, and around it someone had wrapped a piece of white paper. He could not imagine why he had missed the odd arrangement except that, when he had entered the room after leaving Pike, he was not noticing much of anything. And when he stretched out on the bed he had been facing the other way.

He removed the paper from the envelope and unfolded it. Inside he recognized the bold scribble of his roommate.

Adam—

Sorry missed you in haste of departure. Everybody in a big flap about not holding the boat up. Will see you later at picnic. Young lady in teletype asked to leave enclosed for you. Congratulations! You are apparently making some progress there.

Peter

He let the paper fall to the floor and quickly opened the envelope. It contained another note which was clipped to a long sheet of yellow teletype paper. He moved quickly to the window for better light and read eagerly.

Dear Adam,
Thought you might like to have this sheet as a souvenir. It came through our copy machine after you went to put your head on a Pike. It doesn't make sense to me, but then I'm not half-bright about these things anyway. But I *will* write to you. Good luck.

Hastily,
Margaret Trumpey

P.S. You certainly cooked up quite a storm!!

Smiling sadly, Adam read the note through twice. Then he removed it from the teletype sheet and folded it carefully. He placed it in his pocket and began, without any real interest, to study the lines of gibberish on the teletype sheet. It was merely an exchange of messages between the other stations which were a part of Operation Zeus; they had automatically been recorded throughout the entire teletype circuit. At first it distressed him to think of himself as the instigator of all these words which clicked so magically through the atmosphere; then as the symbols and abbreviations translated themselves in his mind, his fingers pressed harder on the paper.

Each message was separated by a blank space to avoid any possibility of confusion. He did not study the time of each transmission until he sat down bewildered on his bunk and read the entire series through a second time. The first message was from the northernmost atoll concerned with Zeus, Oa Titia. It was consigned to Tuamani.

OA-TUA

RE OBSERVATION FROM PISTOL TWO BELIEVE LOCATION IN ERROR POSSIBLY DUE FAULTY TRANSMISSION PERIOD WE LO-

CATE CENTER LAZY ETHEL APPROX ONE HUNDRED MILES
SOUTHEAST OF TRIGGER PERIOD MOVING SOUTH SOUTHEAST
APPROX 20 KNOTS PERIOD CONFIRM PERIOD EOM

Then Tuamani had followed a few minutes later with
an inquiry to the barren bit of coral upon which Zeus
would actually be exploded. Adam knew that two very
lonely men would be making weather observations there
until only a few hours before the actual event.

TUA-TRIGGER
ADVISE YOU HAVE ANY DOPE ON LAZY ETHEL QUESTION
MARK EOM

Their answer, Adam thought, was brief and certainly
to the point.

TRIGGER-TUA
NEGATIVE PERIOD EOM

Tuamani was not so easily satisfied. The time of their
next message was only a few minutes later.

TUA-TRIGGER
ADVISE PRESENT WEATHER YOUR STATION PERIOD EOM

Adam saw that the reply had not been sent for more
than thirty minutes.

TRIGGER-TUA
OVERCAST PERIOD LOWER BROKEN STRATUS PERIOD LITE
RAIN PERIOD VISIBILITY TEN PERIOD CEILING 5000 PERIOD
TEMP 68 PERIOD DEW POINT 65 PERIOD WIND WEST TWENTY
WITH GUSTS TO THIRTY PERIOD BAROMETER 29 POINT 90
PERIOD FALLING SLOWLY PERIOD WHAT'S THIS ALL ABOUT
QUESTION MARK EOM

Adam could all too easily imagine the confusion on both Tuamani and Trigger.

TUA-TRIGGER
DUNNO PERIOD IF OA TITIA ANALYSIS CORRECT LAZY ETHEL IS TO THE SOUTH OF YOU PERIOD EOM

TRIGGER-TUA
WHO IS LAZY ETHEL QUESTION MARK EOM

Adam groaned inwardly. Then he thought, It must surely have been some wag on Tuamani who sent the next transmission.

TUA-TRIGGER
YOU'LL FIND OUT PERIOD CONTINUE SENDING YOUR COMPLETE WEATHER EVERY HOUR THAT IS IF YOU ARE ABLE PERIOD EOM

Trigger's reply was characteristically brief.

TRIGGER-TUA
WILDO PERIOD EOM

After a month's tour of duty on the explosion site, Adam concluded, the two men had probably lost the art of conversation both with each other and with the outside world.

He wished they had more to say, for . . . just a minute! Just an all-fired whopping damned minute!

Clutching the paper, Adam jumped to his feet. He went quickly to the window and examined it once more. Just an all-fired Jumpin' Judas minute! What was this? Oa Titia did not deny the existence of Lazy Ethel! They said, or at least that's the way it looked . . . they

250

claimed there *was* a storm and Oa Titia had almost as big a meteorological staff as Tuamani itself. They were only protesting its *location!* Could they have just talked themselves into it? Like Pike? Hell, no! They were technicians on Oa Titia and they knew what they were doing. Then there had to be a storm *somewhere* and they had just assumed it was Lazy Ethel. Their information was doubtless obtained from far more reliable sources than Adam Smith's imaginary fishing boat!

Hardly trusting his eyes, he quickly reviewed what Trigger had to say. Trigger was only a hundred and fifty miles from Nikki. If any real storm was to the south of it, then that distance could easily be halved, or it might put such a disturbance in a direct line to the west.

Glancing again at his watch he found that Trigger's reply with "present weather" was already more than four hours old. Rain? Trigger had been deliberately chosen because it was known to be the driest bit of vacant land in the hemisphere. Overcast, lower broken clouds . . . meaningless. But the wind! West at twenty knots . . . Gusts to *thirty!* He could not recall reading a single report from Trigger with a wind of over ten knots. And it was always from the east in accordance with the trades. It could be, then, that Trigger was feeling the effects of a storm's topside, presuming that a clockwise revolving air mass was to the south of them. The barometer was not especially low at the time the message was sent, but they had reported it as falling.

Adam looked out the window. So? Nikki was also overcast and the layer of clouds appeared to be thickening. Could it be that some genie had decided to give birth to a real Lazy Ethel?

He studied the line of palm trees which bordered Peter's new dump and the airstrip. They were nearly motionless. Only an occasional movement of a frond revealed that they were not painted against the sky. Adam cursed himself for thinking that the very air itself now appeared to be heavy and unusually oppressive. "Oh, cut it out!" he said aloud. "You are worse than Pike!"

But he could no longer tolerate the confines of his room. He hitched up his pants and walked thoughtfully down the corridor to the entrance of his quarters. He stepped outside and saw that Pistol Two was totally deserted. Cautioning himself that he must not allow his imagination to complicate his life again, he looked up at the sky. It was unrewarding. A vacuous, completely inanimate cloud mass blanketed all he could see. Now it did not even appear as if there might be rain. Yet visual observation, Adam knew only too well, was about as reliable as Pike's neuritis. He had to reassure himself. He had to be sure that he was not going mad.

He started to walk slowly toward his office. To hell with Pike and his confinement to quarters. He was not a soldier. He was not even an employee any longer. I am a nothing, he thought. But there was a triangle and a T square on his drawing board which he had a perfect right to pack since he had paid for them himself. During the first part of his walk he refused to admit that he really wanted a look at his recording barometer. It just might be very interesting. Holy mackerel! Suppose . . .

By the time he was halfway down the empty street, he was running.

12

Adam's recording barometer was placed on the spare desk in his office. It was enclosed in a glass case which he removed every eight days to wind the mechanism. The device itself consisted of a clock-driven metal drum around which he secured a strip of paper each time he wound the spring. Vertical lines on the paper divided it into segments of eight days, and it was further marked with parallel horizontal lines representing the divisions of atmospheric pressure. As the drum turned, a scribe filled with red ink recorded the rise and fall of pressure on the paper. The scribe was activated by sensitive metal bellows and so the result was a fine line of red ink tracing the pressure changes. Since the day segments were further divided into hourly intervals, a very accurate history of the atmospheric pressure on Nikki was constantly visible.

The instrument expressed the pressure in inches of mercury, the red line rising or falling accordingly. On Nikki, Adam had never seen any erratic movement of the line. Ever since his arrival it had maintained a remarkably constant pattern, the line undulating in easy wavelets, rising slowly through the day and descending gradually toward evening. This formula had become so monotonous that Adam had occasionally wondered if the barometer was working properly. The peaks of the red line rarely exceeded thirty and three-tenths inches of mercury, and the valleys had never descended below twenty-nine and nine-tenths inches. These readings were normal companions to fine weather in any part of the world.

Now Adam stood aghast before the glass box. The last time he had looked at it was just before he went to see Pike. He saw that the red line had not departed from its habitually innocuous tracing until about an hour after he had left. Then it had begun a gradual descent, leveling off for approximately another hour at twenty-nine and nine-tenths inches of mercury.

The line's behavior during the next two hours caused him to emit a low whistle, the tone matching the descent of the line as if he were reading measures of music. For two successive hours the red line had plunged almost straight down, until now it terminated at an even twenty-nine inches! And apparently it was still descending! The lowest pressure Adam ever remembered hearing or even reading about was twenty-eight and three-tenths. That pressure had produced winds of one hundred and thirty miles an hour. . . . Supposedly the last recording before the anemometer itself was destroyed.

Wherever its center might be, and it could be very

near, this storm was evidently not going to be any Lazy Ethel! It was going to be a beast, even if the scribe failed to descend another millimeter.

Adam quickly removed the glass cover from the instrument, and peeled off the paper graph. He wrapped a fresh paper around the drum, replaced the glass cover with hands that were far from steady, and started for the door. Then he paused very briefly for a last glance at the barometer. He was not at all sure he would see it or his office again.

He ran down the street, his long legs striking far out in front of him. By the time he reached Pike's house he was gasping for air and wet with perspiration. He labored up the steps and saw Doolan and one of his marines playing acey-deucy on the magazine table. Neither of the marines bothered to acknowledge his arrival with more than a grunt. They turned back to their cards as he crossed the porch.

It was dark in Pike's office, so dark that Adam was at first uncertain if the figure seated behind the desk was actually the man he sought. The voice reassured him.

"What's on your mind now, Mister Smith?"

"Governor, you've got to listen to me!"

"I thought I told you to stay in your quarters."

"Will you please turn on a light? I've got something to show you. It's extremely important."

"I couldn't turn on a light if I wanted to. The generating plant is shut down and you of all people ought to know why."

Adam fumbled for a moment with the strip of graph paper he had removed from the barometer drum.

"I don't know how I'm going to explain this to you, sir, but there *is* a storm. I have the proof right here. Please, haven't you got a flashlight or something?"

255

"No, I do not have a flashlight. At least one that works. And the reason that I haven't is because you are not the only idiot on Nikki. We even have our dishonest idiots. Now will you go back to your quarters like a reasonable man and wait until I send for you? Even a man in my position is entitled to some privacy."

Pike's voice came out of the gloom in patiently measured tones as if he were convinced he was dealing with a lunatic. There was also a distinct note of weariness, almost an appeal for understanding, which Adam had certainly never heard before. It was only with the greatest effort that he kept his own voice as calm.

"Governor . . . please. I *know* . . . I admit you have every reason to think I am out of my head. But there *is* a storm! You've just got to believe me. There is one hell of a blow coming and you've just got to do something about it right this minute."

"I believe you," Pike answered with such unctuous patience that Adam wanted to jump around his desk and haul him out of his chair. "I do indeed. If you say there's a storm, then of course there is one. That ends it. Now will you go . . . quietly?"

"No, I will not go. Not until you get those people off the north side of Nikki. I don't know for sure just where this storm is, but I'm convinced it's between us and Trigger, which would bring it in from the north. Those people just couldn't be in a worse position."

"I see. Where do you recommend I ask them to move? Up or down? We are short of both submarines and balloons."

Pike allowed a very taut ho-ho to escape his lips.

"Please, sir. This is a very serious business."

"You are absolutely right."

"If my guess is right, we haven't much time. Those people should be moved down to the south side of Nikki as fast as possible. They should be sent to the highest available ground and stay there. It may mean their lives, sir . . . not to mention our own. This has all been practically confirmed by other stations and even by Tuamani."

"Good old Tuamani," Pike said. "They also confirmed Lazy Ethel. Very agreeable people."

Adam could contain himself no longer. "For Christ's sake, Governor! Will you listen to me with an open mind!"

Then even in the darkness he saw Pike's fingers form themselves into their triangle. "Will you have the good sense to look at *this!*"

He placed the graph paper before the shadowy figure in the chair and after a frantic search through his pockets found his matches. He struck one, and the flare revealed not only the paper but Pike's cold appraisal of Adam's violently shaking hand.

"Just what is this gibberish?" Pike asked. "I'm afraid I am not much interested in stock-market trends at the moment."

"Our barometer readings for the past four hours."

Trying to control his finger, Adam managed to guide it along the red line. "See how it took a dive? Normal . . . that is, standard pressure, is twenty-nine and ninety-two hundredths inches. When I took this off the recorder just a few minutes ago it was already down to twenty-nine. A typhoon like the one that wiped out Wake Island probably didn't go much lower."

The match burned Adam's fingers before Pike spoke again. He had hardly glanced at the paper. "Look here, Smith," he said finally. "You have been under great strain . . . just why, I don't know. Perhaps I am the one to blame for it. Now, young man, I want to help you in any way I can, but if you think I am going to be taken twice for the damned fool and ask our people to move ten miles across a lagoon in the middle of the night, which it would be by the time we got there, you're very much mistaken. I don't want to be any more severe than necessary, but if you persist in annoying me and don't leave this office at once in a quiet and peaceful manner, I shall be forced to call on Sergeant Doolan for assistance."

"Governor! Dammit! *There is a storm!* Won't you recognize scientific fact? This is *not* something I invented! Throw me in irons! Shoot me! Do anything you want, but for the love of God get those people down to the south side of Nikki! *Now!* If you don't you may well be a murderer!"

Adam had not realized that in his anxiety he was shouting. And he was pounding his fist so hard on the desk all of the pencils and paper clips jumped from their positions. Then from the gloom he heard Pike's voice cut through his own and it was the high cry of a professional drill master.

"Sergeant Doolan! On the double!"

"You can't possibly realize what a wind force like this can do . . ."

Adam was not able to finish before he felt Doolan's hand seize his arm.

"Yessir?" Doolan said.

Pike was standing up now and he said coldly, "Sergeant, Mister Smith is unwell. Could you hear him shouting at me from your post on the porch?"

"Yessir."

"Mister Smith is having trouble with hallucinations. You will bear witness that his shouting was violent and of a threatening nature."

Doolan hesitated and glanced unhappily at Adam. "Well . . . it didn't sound too friendly."

"You heard him accuse me of being a murderer?"

"I did not say that!" Adam protested. "I said that if you didn't move those people . . ."

"I think you've said quite enough. Sergeant, for Mister Smith's own protection I think it best that he be placed in protective custody. You will take him to his quarters and see that he remains there until further orders."

"Yessir."

"Dismissed."

As the pressure of Doolan's hand tightened on his arm, Adam jerked away. He faced the dim figure of Pike. He was thoroughly angry now. Pike just had to listen.

"You can't do this to me. I'm a civilian! I demand . . ."

"This island has been declared in a state of emergency for several hours. Under those conditions I have full authority to perform my duty as I see it. Take him away, Sergeant."

As Doolan shoved him toward the door, Adam yelled over his shoulder, "But what about the storm? Sir, this is madness!"

"It certainly is. You will bear witness, Sergeant."

There was no arguing with Doolan. Though he was a good foot shorter than Adam, the Marines had taught him well. He was an expert at escorting a man to a destination which might not be of his own choosing. He did say, "Sorry, fella," as he propelled Adam across the porch and down to the road.

Pike watched them through the window, then returned to his desk and sat down again. Was there anything else that could go wrong? Now he was saddled with a madman, or at least a man who was suffering such mental tribulations he was as much a problem as a squalling baby. It was going to be difficult taking Smith over to the north side when the boat returned. He would undoubtedly start yelling again, accusing everybody of all kinds of things, and at the very least it would be extremely embarrassing. But he couldn't be left behind either. Left alone he might cut his wrists, hang himself, or some such messy thing . . . and Tuamani would send down investigators on top of investigators. Technically he was still a government responsibility and his family could bring all kinds of charges. The thing could snowball and might even become another *Jeanette* inquiry. A whole Congressional Committee had been called on that little episode, and even the best advocates of the United States Navy couldn't save the reputation of the *Jeanette's* commanding officer. Pike recalled, with sorrow, that the *Jeanette* affair had also concerned antagonism between a civilian and a military man. Moreover the civilian, whose name Pike tried desperately to recall, had been assigned to that expedition as weatherman. Personal persecution was alleged and damn near proven, even though both parties involved had lost their lives before the inquiry was held. It made no difference that the affair took place on a ship locked in Arctic ice. It was a U.S. government ship and it could just as well have been Nikki.

Pike rose from his chair and began circling his desk very slowly. All right, what could be done with Smith? God, what a thorn! A complete pain in the neck ever since the first day he became noticeable, which would be the very first night on Nikki. Which would be the time he more or less said the movie was not going to be rained out, and it was.

Reviewing that incident with distaste, Pike recalled that he had said a few sharp words on the matter, intended more to express his disappointment than anything else. Had it begun then? Had Smith nursed those statements, allowing them to ferment in an already troubled brain until everything said to him was taken amiss? If so, Pike was sorry, very sorry, he mused, for people in mental distress deserved sympathy and understanding. Yes . . . every person involved in a project like Zeus should be cleared through psychologists *before* they were hired. Then their presence would not present a lot of problems to operational personnel who had enough troubles without delving into motivations and kindred mysterious manifestations they were not trained to recognize. Much less, offer any cure.

He sat on the edge of his desk and picked up the strip of graphed paper Adam had left. He studied the red line. Here was a perfect example of what a tortured mind could produce. A trained medic would know exactly how to handle it. How to sympathize and satisfy. Smith was a "Section 8." The army had once issued a complete manual on the treatment of psychos. He should have read it more carefully. His own attempts at agreement had obviously been all wrong, for he had only succeeded in making Smith become more violent. Pike did remember reading that the first step in the pacification of any demented personality, whether suffering from shell shock or otherwise, was agreement. All right. At first he had deliberately agreed there was a storm. And what happened? More nonsense.

He was about to crumple the strip of paper and throw it into the wastebasket when he thought better of it. No. It should be kept. If there was ever an inquiry, particularly one which might somehow try to advance the proposition that he was a fiend incarnate and had devoted his entire time on Nikki to the persecution of a single innocent civilian, then this reflected the unhappy scrawling of a sick mind possessed by one Smith! What tortures he must suffer, having now apparently convinced himself there really was a Lazy Ethel. The name alone could hardly have been conceived in a totally normal mind. Perhaps he might feel a little better if he had something to eat. That, thought Pike, is the very least I can do.

Then he went to the window and leaned through it until he could survey the length of the porch. As he had hoped, one of Doolan's marines sat with his feet propped up on the magazine table. He appeared to be dozing.

"Marine?"

Peterson jumped to his feet. He made one quick pass at his sleepy eyes before his heels clicked to attention.

"Yessir!"

"Any sign of my boat yet?"

"No, sir."

"It's still a little early although how you could observe it with your eyes closed is beyond me."

"Sorry, sir."

Pike held the keys out to him.

"One of these fits the mess-hall kitchen. I want you to go down there and scrounge up a sandwich or two. There ought to be plenty of things lying around. Take them down to Mister Smith's quarters with my compliments. I believe he's in Building C. If you like, make a sandwich for yourself and Doolan, too."

"Yessir. Thank you very much, sir."

Peterson reached for the keys and stepped back.

"You don't happen to have a workable flashlight, do you?"

"Not with me, sir. But I think Doolan has a couple stashed down to our own quarters."

"Bring them back with you. If my boat is late we might need them."

"Yessir."

"Oh . . . and check around the kitchen for some candles. I recall several birthday cakes since we've been here. The cook just might keep them handy . . . or they could be in the bakeshop."

"Yessir."

"On your way."

To Pike's immense satisfaction, Peterson saluted smartly and executed a perfectly timed about-face. As he marched off the porch Pike shook his head with approval. There were a few left. Yes . . . a very few real soldiers left here and there. Even in the Marines.

He looked up at the heavy sky and his momentary pleasure was destroyed. Poor Smith, indeed. Poor Zeb Pike! Because of the tricks played by his own mind, his shoulder was throbbing unmercifully. And he still had to find some explanation for all the trouble with Lazy Ethel!

After considerable persuasion Doolan allowed Adam to stop by his office long enough to pick up his barometer. Nestling the instrument tenderly in his arms, stepping as lightly as he could so the scribe would not be shaken, Adam carried it to his quarters. He placed it gently on the writing table between his own bunk and Peter Hildebrandt's. Then with Doolan leaning casually against the door jamb, bored almost beyond his richly developed capacity for boredom, the two waited in the gathering darkness.

Adam paced miserably back and forth between Doolan and the window. He halted frequently to peer at the glass box. When he had taken it from his office the scribe had descended to twenty-eight and ninety-five hundredths inches. Now it was down to twenty-eight ninety. Adam saw that it was still slipping downward.

When he paused in his pacing and remained absolutely

motionless, listening carefully, he could hear the faint ticking of the clock mechanism which turned the drum. It was so still outside the window. The palm fronds were now dead.

"You hear that?" he said to Doolan. "That's your time running out. And mine, too. Everybody's."

"I don't hear nothin'," Doolan answered with an obliging smile that said if Adam wanted to hear things it was all right with him as long as he didn't start any trouble.

"Listen!" Adam said, waggling his finger at the glass box. "Just listen . . . that's all I ask you."

"I *am* listenin'. You tryin' to tell me you got some time bomb or somethin' there?"

"In a way you might say it is. And the fuse is getting awfully short."

"I wish you wouldn't talk that way, Smith. I almost believe you. You'll have me buckin' for Section Eight if you don't shut up."

"You'd better believe me unless you want to get blown to kingdom come. And everybody on this island with you."

"It don't look like no bomb to me and in case it's any never mind to you I sweated out a whole course in demolition at Camp Pendleton."

"This isn't the same kind of demolition, Doolan. It's going to be total and complete. It might even be as big as Zeus. Maybe bigger."

"Sure. All alone you're going to do better than the U.S. Government who only has to throw a couple of billion bucks around trying."

"I'm not going to do it. God is."

"Oh, brother!"

Doolan shook his head sadly and folded his arms across his chest. Then he sighed and said aloud to himself, "What did I ever do to deserve this?"

Looking at Adam he asked not unkindly, "How do you feel?"

"Terrible."

"Sure you do. Why don't you just calm down and hit your sack for a while? You'll feel better all around when you wake up."

"You think I can sleep with the end of the world coming? Practically right here?"

"Keep on and you'll have me singing Judgment Day right along with you. My aunt from Carolina used to sing it all the damned day long, so I even know the words. Please. Will you lie down?"

Adam had not the slightest intention of lying down. Somehow, some way, he must reach the northern side of Nikki and talk to the people there. Especially one Margaret Trumpey. But there was no getting past Doolan unless he could be convinced. Looking at him now, his face a mask of studied indifference, Adam knew it was not going to be an easy task.

"Doolan. Come here a minute."

"Unh-uh. You stay there, and I stay here."

"Why do you think I'm under arrest?"

"Now look. I don't want to hurt your feelings."

"You think I'm crazy, don't you?"

"Well . . ." Doolan's voice trailed off in embarrassment.

"Do you?"

"Well . . . like Pike said, maybe you ain't been feeling too good. You admitted that yourself. Just now."

"I didn't mean it that way, Doolan. I feel fine . . . physically and mentally."

Adam spoke slowly and distinctly as if he were talking to a very small child. "I'm only deeply concerned about a terrible storm I am sure is coming. This little instrument foretells a storm, do you understand that? I know how to read it. Pike doesn't. The people who went on the so-called picnic are going to be in very great danger if someone doesn't tell them to move to the south side of the island . . . and even then I can't guarantee their safety. I want to warn those people and get them moving while there's still time. Look out the window, Doolan. Have you ever seen it so dark at this hour? If you don't believe me or this instrument, look at that sky. Have you ever seen it look like that before?"

"It looks like we're probably going to have some rain. Too bad. It'll spoil the picnic."

"You bet we're going to have some rain. Tons of it. So much you won't be able to see the end of your nose. And there's a damn good chance the sea will sweep right over Nikki. Are you listening to me, Doolan? If you've got an ounce of heart for those people out there, if you've got half a mind of your own, you'll let me talk to them. I won't try to escape. You can go right along with me if you want. May God strike me dead this minute, Doolan, if I'm not telling you the truth."

There was a long silence. Doolan puckered his brow. He shifted his weight from one foot to the other, and his gun belt squeaked with the movement. He compressed his lips tightly, then blew air through the crease that was his mouth.

"Look at the instrument, Doolan. It's gone down some more. I didn't cause it to do that. You've been right here. You've seen for yourself, I haven't touched it. The *storm* is moving that scribe."

"Pike says you stay here. What you want to do? Get me busted? I like these stripes."

"They won't show up so well on your dead body floating in water."

"Aw, come off it."

He was making progress, Adam thought. Not much, but a little. Doolan was shifting uneasily from one foot to the other now. There was, unless he was being too optimistic, Adam decided, the slightest suggestion of fear in his eyes.

"Doolan, listen to this. If you'll go with me to the north side and a storm *doesn't* come, I'll swear I came up behind you and hit you on the head and escaped. We'll stage things so it looks like you went beyond the call of duty and recaptured me. You'll probably get a medal."

"You don't sneak up behind no good marine and cold-conk him. Especially not a sergeant."

"Then I'll run away from you. I'll run slowly so you can't miss. You can shoot me down deader than a mackerel. How much more can I offer than that?"

Doolan lit a cigarette. He filled his lungs and exhaled with such force the smoke went straight out from his mouth. He repeated the process immediately. "It would look phoney," he said finally. "Besides, I don't want to shoot you or nobody else."

"Doolan. You just heard me stake my life on this. No matter what you think, I'm not that crazy. I'll stay in front of you every minute of the time. All I want to do is talk to those people! Look at that sky, Doolan. It's getting darker and darker. We won't be able to see each other pretty soon!"

Doolan rubbed the end of his nose violently. "How would we get there? There ain't no boats."

"I don't know. There must be a canoe or something that will float in the native village. If there isn't, we'll have to do it the hard way and hike it around the beach."

"You mean swim that channel?"

"Yes, I do. And I'm not much of a swimmer, either. That's how much I believe in this thing. If I drown, you can just say I ran away and committed suicide by jump-

ing in the channel. The main thing is we've got to get
going right now."

"Nuts."

Doolan again drew heavily on his cigarette. He closed
his eyes for a moment and said through the smoke, "This
whole operation is nuts."

"You're an intelligent man, Doolan. You didn't get to
be a Marine sergeant for nothing. You can read an instrument, and especially this one, as well as I can. The
least you can do is take a look . . . just to satisfy yourself I'm not talking entirely through my hat. Come on.
What you'll see on this instrument now is something you
can tell your grandchildren about. You'll be looking at
history . . . certainly the beginning of one of the biggest storms in history. Go ahead. Look! I'll stand way over
at this end of the room if you still don't trust me! I
couldn't possibly get within three feet of you!"

Slowly, so slowly Adam hoped he was not just imagin-
ing the movement, Doolan rolled his shoulder about the
door jamb and looked at the glass box on the table. Adam
held his breath as Doolan's hand slipped down to his hol-
ster. Then he placed his weight on both feet and faced
the table. Adam waited in agonized silence as Doolan
took a single hesitant step into the room. He halted, his
head cocked suspiciously to one side, looking at Adam
and then at the glass box. Another step toward the table.
Another. Adam was sure that, if in the next moment he
spoke, Doolan would certainly retreat.

Another step and Doolan bent down, placing his powerful hands on his knees. His eyes were level with the instrument.

"I can hear it ticking all right," he whispered.

"Sure you can. Look at that red line. The paper is

268

marked off in hours. See how the line goes down."

Doolan studied the interior of the glass box as if it contained a snake. His underlip shot forward and he twisted it around and around. He scratched his forehead and wrinkled his nose. Then his eyes rolled upward to look at Adam. "It's gone down, all right. I can see that."

"Smart man. Now figure it out for yourself. That's an expensive instrument. *There's something driving that line down and it isn't me!*"

"I don't really see it move."

"Of course you don't. You can't really see the hands of a clock move, either. But if you stood there even half an hour, you'd see the difference."

"Maybe we better take this gadget up to Pike and show it to him."

"I already did that. At least I took the previous paper. That's what our big argument was about. I was yelling at him because he just wouldn't listen. You know Pike. He's a hard-headed man."

"All generals are hard-headed. They got a brass brain."

"You're absolutely right, Doolan. Now can we go while there's maybe still time?"

"I still think we oughta see Pike."

"He'll only stop us, you know that. He'll stop us because, like all generals, he hates to approve anything that isn't his own idea."

"Yeah . . ." Doolan said very slowly. He rose to an erect position and glowered at the sky beyond the window. "Yeah . . . maybe you got somethin' there. It wouldn't be the first time I stuck my neck out."

"Good!" Adam said quietly. "Let's go."

"I'll be right behind you. All the time. And I got every marksmanship medal in the book. Just keep that in mind."

Pike fretted in his office. Now the gloomiest doubts assailed him, as dark as the sky outside his window. He had already envisioned a series of ugly spectacles in which he played a most ignominious role. He had suffered through a preliminary hearing on Tuamani during which he found himself very hard put to account for certain of his decisions; and all too quickly thereafter, he saw himself in Washington, gulping and perspiring before a committee which practically included both houses of Congress. It was an easy mental journey from there to the hard pavement of a used-car lot. He saw himself passing out business cards with the legend ALMOST HONEST JOHN'S SUPER BARGAINS, prominent on the face. His own name was along the bottom not nearly so large. Zebulon Pike—Sales Representative. At least, he thought, the "U.S.A.-Ret." would be neither necessary nor proper.

Ye gods, suppose there really was a storm! Suppose Smith was not crazy at all, but for once in his miserable life had been perfectly sincere. If there was any truth to his story about the barometer he might still be ready for a padded cell and yet, from habit if nothing else, recognize a storm. Oh, no. The case was cut and dried. Pure, unadulterated case of vengeance against imagined injuries. Then why was it so damn dark outside? It was only a little after five. And where *was* everybody? For a terrifying moment he saw himself as entirely alone on Nikki . . . the last man on earth after a number of Zeuses had been exploded. Ye gods, it was Zeb Pike who was about ready for a padded cell!

He wished now that he had not sent Sue-Anne along with Albright. She made very good sense, Sue-Anne. When she was sober, of course. He could have talked this whole thing out with her and she would have settled his mind. She would undoubtedly say the whole business was a tempest in a teapot and what in tarnashin was he worrying about? Forget it, honey, she would say. You're just making a peck of trouble for yourself because you take everything too seriously. She would say you just can't get out of the habit of doing your duty and another man would have sluffed the whole thing off as just one of those things. She would say things like that . . . if she was sober. In the opposite condition she would be more likely to say Zebulon, you bonehead, a trained technician came to you and told you there was going to be a storm and you told him he was crazy. That's just like the time you told one of the world's best armament manufacturers his outfit didn't know how to rifle a gun. It just cost you your only chance at Staff College, that's all. You were still singing the praises of French seventy-fives when the Germans were lining up their eighty-eights, which happened to be very similar to the gun the manufacturer only asked the opportunity to prove. When you were in procurement, and it was a good thing they got you out of there before we lost the war, if a new item didn't come down through channels it was no damn good. Not for your popgun brain, anyway.

Yes, if Sue-Anne was loaded she might say a few things like that.

Brooding on what Sue-Anne might have said, and what she still might have occasion to say, Pike remembered his boat. Where the hell was it? Albright had been lolly-dollying again. And where the hell was that marine? How long did it take to make a sandwich even if you used a bayonet to slice it? And what about those flashlights he was going to bring? Where the hell was everybody!

As if his unspoken demand had a magical power to bring results, he heard footsteps on the porch. The steps approached quickly, and in a moment Peterson snapped to attention before him. His salute was marred by a sandwich in his hand.

"Where the hell have you been?" Pike said, choosing for the moment to ignore the sandwich.

"Looking for Doolan and that other guy, sir."

"What do you mean, looking for them? I told you where they were."

"They ain't there, sir. I looked every place for them, sir. I looked in the quarters you told me and then I looked everywhere else. I even looked down to the wharf."

"And you couldn't find them?" Pike said incredulously.

"No, sir. I didn't see *nobody*. It's kind of scary. Every place is deserted like it was a ghost town or something and most places are locked up. I even looked down to our own quarters thinking maybe Doolan might have gone back there if maybe he forgot something or run out of cigarettes or . . ."

Pike jumped to his feet. "You must be blind, marine. We'll see about this. Did you bring some flashlights?"

"Yessir," Peterson said, reaching into his hip pocket. "I brought two. They were all I could find. One of them, the battery is sort of weak."

Pike reached out and took a flashlight from Peterson's hand.

"Follow me."

"Yessir. Jeez, it's just like we are the last two people in the world out here."

Pike shot a quick frown of disapproval at Peterson and marched out of the office.

By the time they had stomped through the building which contained Adam's room, then doubled back to the

Marine quarters, Pike was yelling Doolan's name with such force his voice echoed and re-echoed between the buildings and along the deserted streets of Pistol Two. With Peterson half-trotting along a few paces behind him, Pike challenged each building as they passed, though most of the windows were crossed with boards and the doors were shut tightly. Now as they returned to the main street, Peterson shivered at the sound of Pike's voice, which was becoming increasingly hoarse and eerie in the gloom.

It was so dark that the oval pattern from Pike's flashlight sweeping the street and the buildings was clearly visible. The blob of light revealed nothing which might suggest that Pistol Two had once been an active settlement. A few drops of rain spattered against their faces, and Pike began to divide his attention between the buildings and the sky. His demands also lost concentration, for he began to call out Smith as often as he called the name of Doolan. Peterson wished he would abandon the search. Somehow it was like yelling in a graveyard.

Pike halted before the weather office. Though it was dark and obviously unoccupied, he called out Smith's name with such authority and assurance Peterson would not have been overly surprised if an answer had come through the screen windows. Pike stalked back to the middle of the street, faced about, and glanced at the building as if its very silence was deliberate. Then suddenly he tilted his head to one side and pointed a cautioning finger at Peterson. "Listen!" he said furtively. "Do you hear what I hear?"

Peterson listened obediently, turning his head in imitation of Pike's. He did not at this moment want to hear anything unless it was the comforting growl of Doolan's voice.

"It's in there," Pike said, taking a step toward the communications shack.

"Sounds like a typewriter," Peterson said.

Pike crossed the street quickly and, rising on his toes, peered through the screen window. Immediately afterward he moved around to the door. "It's one of the teletypes. Somebody left the damned thing on."

He tried the door. It was locked. "We'll have to kick it in," he said to Peterson.

Pike's frustration seemed to find outlet on the door. He kicked at it so viciously Peterson had little chance to assist him before the door collapsed. Pike charged through the splintered wood and directed his flashlight at the teletype machines. The last one in the line continued to click busily. Then it stopped very suddenly.

Pike approached it warily. How could the machine function if the main power supply was off? As he had ordered! That idiot chief electrician! If he had disobeyed orders he would have to do some fancy answering. Or was he so dumb he had just gone off to the picnic and forgotten about the one thing he was presumably on Nikki to attend?

While Peterson watched, Pike's flashlight swept the office. It came to rest on the cord of the overhead light. He reached out suspiciously and jerked the cord. The light flashed on and both men blinked at the illumination.

"Well, I'll be damned!" Pike said.

"Sure is nice to see some light, sir . . . that is, after stumbling around with flashlights for so long."

"That idiot's idiot!" Pike said. "I'll tell you one thing, young man, giving orders to civilians is a waste of breath."

"Yessir," Peterson said, looking out the window. "You want I should go get us some rain gear, sir? It's beginning to come down pretty good."

"Do that. You'll find mine hanging just inside my office door. Bring Mrs. Pike's, too. It's in the hallway."

"Yessir."

"I'll meet you down at the wharf in five minutes. My boat should be along any minute now."

"Yessir."

"On the double."

At the door Peterson turned as if reluctant to travel the street alone. "I guess this will sort of spoil the picnic, sir."

"Yes. I'm afraid it might," Pike said absently. He was staring at the line of teletype machines and almost appeared to have forgotten Peterson. "Keep your eye out for Doolan and Smith," he said.

"I just got a hunch I won't see them, sir," Peterson said forlornly.

When he was gone Pike crossed the room very slowly until he stood in front of the last teletype machine. He leaned forward and saw the end of a message beneath the glass. The signature was Keating. It would be from Tuamani then.

Hesitantly, almost as if he knew the contents of the message, he reached for the end of the yellow paper which had fallen over the back of the machine. Now he saw that there were several messages. The machine had been busy, all right, apparently working ever since the girls had left. The paper reached nearly to the floor behind the machine.

He carefully pulled it upward, then found the knob on the side of the case. He turned it until the last message was above the glass and tore the whole paper off. He moved beneath the light. Much of the printing was unintelligible to him, but there were parts which caused him to pull back the desk chair and sit down.

TUA-TRIGGER
HOW ABOUT YOUR PRESENT WEATHER QUESTION MARK

TRIGGER-TUA
YES MAN PERIOD WE KNOW WHAT YOU MEAN NOW PERIOD PRESENT WEATHER HEAVY RAIN PERIOD VISIBILITY NIL PERIOD WIND SOUTH SIXTY KNOTS GUSTING TO SEVENTY PERIOD LONESOME PERIOD

TUA-TRIGGER
HOW CAN YOU BE LONELY WITH LAZY ETHEL QUESTION MARK BE OF GOOD HEART PERIOD CENTER OF STORM NOW DEFINITELY LOCATED MORE THAN HUNDRED MILES SOUTHEAST YOUR STATION PERIOD YOU ONLY HAVE EDGE PERIOD

TRIGGER-TUA
TAIL END YOU MEAN QUESTION MARK

TUA-TRIGGER
ROGER PERIOD NIKKI WILL GET THE FULL BLAST PERIOD

TRIGGER-TUA
WHEN QUESTION MARK

TUA-TRIGGER
DUNNO FOR CERTAIN PERIOD SOME TIME TONITE PERIOD ALL ATTEMPTS CONTACT PISTOL TWO SINCE 13:00 NEGATIVE PERIOD WE ARE GOING TO SEND BLIND TO THEM AS SOON WE HAVE MORE DOPE PERIOD

TRIGGER-TUA
GLAD TO BE HERE PERIOD

TUA-TRIGGER
CONTINUE TO STAND BY FOR POSSIBLE INTERCEPTION MESSAGE FROM PISTOL TWO PERIOD CIRCUIT MAY BE LOUSED UP PERIOD EOM

TRIGGER-TUA
WILDO PERIOD

There followed an interchange of messages between Tuamani and Oa Titia.

TUA-OA
YOU HEARD ANYTHING FROM PISTOL TWO QUESTION MARK

OA-TUA
NEGATIVE PERIOD

TUA-OA
STAND BY FOR POSSIBILITY PERIOD THEY PROBABLY HAVING
PLENTY TROUBLE ALREADY PERIOD

OA-TUA
WILDO PERIOD

Pike noted that the time of the answer from Oa Titia was fifteen hundred. Over two hours ago. There was a blank space, then several lines of X's interspersed with frequent A-A's as if the machine had developed a speech impediment. Finally he came to a long message which caused him to groan audibly. He saw that it had been sent an hour before and was specifically addressed to himself.

TUA-PISTOL TWO PERIOD URGENT PERIOD PIKE
LAZY ETHEL NOW DEFINITELY LOCATED WITH CENTER AP-
PROXIMATELY SIXTY MILES WEST OF YOU PERIOD SAME
MOVING IN GENERAL EASTERLY DIRECTION AT APPROXI-
MATELY TEN KNOTS PERIOD EXPECT WINDS POSSIBLY EX-
CEEDING ONE HUNDRED PLUS HEAVY RAINS PERIOD

STRONGLY RECOMMEND MOVING ALL PERSONNEL TO ANY
AVAILABLE SHELTER SOUTH SIDE REPEAT SOUTH SIDE NIKKI
ATOLL AT ONCE PERIOD RESCUE SHIPS WITH ALL DISASTER
SUPPLIES ALREADY ENROUTE YOUR ASSISTANCE PERIOD AIR-
PLANES WILL ARRIVE FOR CASUALTY EVACUATION SOON AS
CONDITIONS PERMIT PERIOD YOU AND PISTOL TWO METEOR-
OLOGIST MERIT COMMENDATION FOR BEING ON TOES
PERIOD WITH FEWER FACILITIES YOU SPOTTED LAZY ETHEL
LONG BEFORE ANY OF US PERIOD GOOD LUCK PERIOD

KEATING

There were two more messages, the second of which
had just been transmitted.

TUA-PISTOL TWO URGENT
IF STILL ABLE TO COMMUNICATE ADVISE YOUR LATEST
WEATHER AND DISPERSAL OF PERSONNEL PERIOD

There was, of course, no answer. Where the reply from
Pistol Two should have been, the paper offered only a
blank space to Pike's agonized eyes.

TUA-ALL STATIONS-SPECIAL
ASSUME PISTOL TWO EVACUATED PERIOD HOWEVER ALL
STATIONS ON CIRCUIT WILL STAND BY FOR POSSIBLE MES-
SAGE INTERCEPTION FROM THERE PERIOD CIRCUIT WILL
REMAIN CLOSED TO ALL EXCEPT EMERGENCY TRANSMISSION
UNTIL LAZY ETHEL LEAVES AREA PERIOD

KEATING

For the first time in his life Zebulon Pike looked down
at his strong hands and found himself wishing for a
gun. There was, he thought with a mind that had suddenly become remarkably clear, only one answer. His

West Point ring glistened in the light and he found it a hideous mockery. Other officers who could not live with themselves had found the answer before . . . and, at least, there was some sympathy for their memory. It was the oldest creed of the true soldier in any country, as ancient and time-honored as the Roman Legions. Yes, he could easily borrow the marine's automatic.

He stood up with the definite intention of appropriating Peterson's gun as soon as they met on the wharf. Nor was it fear which caused him to change his mind as he carefully turned out the light and left the communications shack. Zebulon Pike had been laughed at aplenty since the day he was first commissioned a second lieutenant. Zebulon Pike was a paper warrior with a very few friends who had nursed him through a whole blundering career, and he could think of three times when only near miracles had saved him from earlier disgrace. But no one had ever accused him of not being a soldier. This last time for Zeb Pike was not going to be a failure. He was not going to cover for himself. He would get the people of Pistol Two down to the south side of Nikki, behind the hill. He would do so no matter what difficulties were involved.

He marched calmly through the rain, his shoulders well back, his arms swinging in easy cadence. He knew now that he was not parading before others, but before himself, and he marched proudly. When his people were safe, or at least as safe as they possibly could be under the circumstances, then he would get on with the other business. As befitted Zebulon Pike, General, U.S.A.

When he reached the wharf, Peterson was waiting for him. He was standing beneath the eaves of the warehouse huddled in his poncho. Pike forced an easy smile when he saw him.

"Any sign of our boat yet?"

"Yessir. I saw the lights. They should be here in a minute. You want your rain gear, sir?"

"Yes. Thank you very much. Fine night for a picnic, eh, marine? Ho. Ho!"

Compared to the terrain which now confronted them, Adam and Doolan saw that their swim across the channel might rate as the easiest part of their expedition. They had found the native village completely abandoned. A few minutes' search of the beach area confirmed their fast-growing fears that nothing which might be practical for crossing the lagoon had been left behind. They discovered one ancient canoe beneath a copra-drying shed, but it was badly split along the bottom, the outrigger was missing, and there were no paddles. So after only a few minutes' hopeless discussion of its suitability they set off along the beach, following the inside rim of the coral ring which formed Nikki.

The first mile along the beach proved easy going. Then, just as the first drops of rain began to fall, they met the first shocking obstacle. They came upon an inlet which could not be circled because of the heavy entanglement of brush surrounding its entire border. This inlet was much wider than the channel between the native village and Pistol Two.

For the first half-mile they were able to wade across the inlet although they stumbled frequently on the uneven bottom and Adam, who was in the lead, stepped off twice into deep holes and floundered wildly before he could find sure footing again. Soon afterward the floor of the lagoon sank abruptly and they were forced to swim the last part of the inlet. At last they reached a slime-covered ledge of coral which lay only a few inches below the surface. Doolan promptly sat down and cursed Adam with monotonous devotion to the details of his ancestry. When he had exhausted his extensive vocabulary and his words had brought no reaction from Adam other than a mild request that he get on his feet so they could move again, Doolan said grudgingly, "You long-legged son of a bitch, you should have been a marine."

"I'm hardly the type, but thank you anyway," Adam answered and started off sploshing through the shallow water.

It was nearly dark. The lagoon was now a deep gray and indefinite mass on their right hand. The rain obscured any horizon. The land was a featureless blob narrowing to a vanishing point as far ahead as they could see. Its existence as part of a giant circle was not apparent in the half-light and the minor configurations were never recognizable until they actually stumbled upon them.

One inlet followed another. They were able to work their way around a few without entering the lagoon, but the majority required wading at least waist deep and several obliged them to swim. Doolan complained they were making less than a mile an hour and stated with profane conviction that they would never reach the north side of Nikki until the following morning . . . if they ever did. Adam remained silent, pausing only occasionally to glance at the fast-darkening sky.

Eventually they came upon a region of the beach where the undergrowth was impenetrable. They turned inland, away from the lagoon, and toward the sea itself. Here, Adam stubbornly refused to pause for a rest and led Doolan through several hundred yards of brambles and cactus-like undergrowth, which sliced at their clothing and left long, deep cuts on their skin. Finally they were able to turn forward again, and with the last light they moved along the narrow strip of land separating the lagoon and the sea.

They found it easier to avoid the beach itself although the terrain consisted of seemingly endless undulations of coral and sand. They panted up the steep sides of hummocks, often sliding backward in the loose sand, and they staggered clumsily across deep pits filled with sea shells and rotting vegetation. It was more than two hours before they saw a glow of light ahead and knew for certain that they were approaching the north side of Nikki. The rain was still spasmodic and much lighter than Adam had dared hope. He was grateful, too, that as yet there was no definite indication of wind.

They paused for only a moment to look at the light. Doolan moved beside Adam and catching his breath said huskily, "Now *I'll* be a red-haired son of a bitch! We almost got it made."

When the boat snorted up to the wharf Pike was astonished to see Sue-Anne standing in the bow. She was the only passenger. She was wet and he knew that she was angry. When she held out her hand for aid to the wharf, Pike ignored it and jumped down beside her.

"What are you doing back here, Sue-Anne?"

"What am I doin'? I came back for some bourbon, that's what. Who but you would think of slinging a picnic without any liquor? Why, there's not a drop up there, as if it wasn't the dullest place I evah been, anyway. What are we supposed to be doing? Working for our Eagle Scout badge?"

"Shut up."

Pike said it quietly, yet very firmly. Then he turned aft to the boat operator. "Shove off," he said. "Get us back to the north side at full speed. Give her everything you've got!"

Peterson slid reluctantly into the boat. "Sir? What about Doolan and that Smith fella? We just leave them here?"

"I'm sure they've gone already. We have a lot more people to worry about."

The operator gunned his engines and the boat slid swiftly away from the dock. Pike turned to Sue-Anne and held out a raincoat. She regarded both the coat and her husband in stunned disbelief.

"Zebulon Pike," she said finally. "You gone right out of your mind?"

"Maybe I found that I had one."

"You told me to shut up," she said accusingly.

"I did. Put this raincoat on."

She hesitated; then without taking her eyes from him she moved into the coat. Something in his manner and his eyes caused her voice to soften.

"What's wrong, Zebulon? What's come over you?"

"Lazy Ethel."

"Who?"

"Lazy Ethel. It's the name of a storm. It's coming this way fast and it isn't going to be any picnic. Because of me you'll all be lucky to get out with your lives."

"What have you got to do with a storm? *You* haven't had a drink, have you, Zebulon? If so, I'll never forgive . . ."

"No. I haven't been drinking although I might just as well have been. I've been blind enough and stupid enough to qualify for a lot of things."

His voice trailed off while he took her hand and held it thoughtfully. Then he said, "I wouldn't admit it to myself, but I've known what you've thought of me all these years. And you were right. You married the dumbest soldier in the American Army."

"Zebulon . . . I don't know you just now! You're tired. You're in trouble."

"I'm not a bit tired."

He turned aft and yelled at the boat operator. "Can't you make this thing go any faster?"

The operator shook his head. Pike gently placed his arm around Sue-Anne. Looking at the black lagoon, he said, "I'm sorry, Precious. This night isn't going to be much fun for anybody . . . especially not for you."

13

Those who were encamped on the north side of Nikki passed the early part of the afternoon with little complaint or discomfort. The children, shepherded with varying degrees of success by their mothers, found endless, screeching pleasure in their exploration of the sand hummocks. Barney Dunbar and a group of laborers seasoned by years of employment on government projects, and long accustomed to completely incomprehensible deviation from the specific tasks they had been hired to perform, took the opportunity to sleep. Many of them snored with gusto in spite of the squadrons of sand fleas which circled and chandelled about their upturned faces.

Albright was everywhere, mincing and swaying and

mashing potatoes with his voice, and yet showing surprising concern for the welfare of his charges. When Aubrey Tinsman decided to go for a swim and cut his foot on a jagged piece of coral and was nearly reduced to tears as a result, Albright acted as a crutch so that he could limp to Dr. Case for treatment. Not long afterward Mrs. Walsacki came to him and complained that something should be done about allotting separate relief areas for the men and the women. She had just been surprised by Miguel, the bartender, as she squatted behind one of the low bushes which topped the sand hummocks. She was more angry than embarrassed. Albright sought out Peter Hildebrandt, who at once took the project to his heart. Refusing all outside aid and advice, he erected two remarkably efficient shelters of tarpaulin and sticks.

Albright was less successful in the latter part of the day, shortly after his return from seeing Pike. He knew then that the picnic would continue through at least a part of the night and something had to be done about light. After an extensive search, he found Carlos Raveza slumbering peacefully beneath a bush. A small bird was perched on the rising and falling mound of his stomach. It flew away as Albright approached.

"Wake up, if you please, Mr. Raveza. We're going to need some light eventually."

Carlos opened his eyes, rolled over on his side and regarded Albright with ill-concealed distaste.

"So? Then you have come to the wrong person."

"You're the chief electrician, aren't you, old boy?"

"Yes. But I am not an old boy. I am like a young boy, you might say, in especially when I am dreaming in the manner which you just stop. You broke the film just as it reaches the most interesting part, where the young lady compares me favorably to an Altura bull. I do not like you for this."

" 'Let there be light.' . . . Then you can go back to your dreaming."

Discouraged by the total lack of interest in Carlos' face, Albright reminded himself that perhaps Pike was a more patient man than he had thought.

"You do not comprehend," Carlos said with a mighty yawn. "It is true that I am in charge of light . . . along with the help of God. But I am not mechanic. The machine which makes the light is small and obstinate. It is a gasoline engine and it is complicated. It does not function at all. When someone fixes the machine, then it will make sense for me to hook up the wires. It will not make any sense to do such a thing until the machine works. Even you will understand that it is depressing to look at wires which are dead and lamps which are also dead. So until the machine is fixed, please go away and leave me alone. I would like to close my eyes and say ah this is where I came in. Adios."

It was almost dark before Albright found one of the mechanics and persuaded him to tinker with the portable light plant. In fact, Albright's chief problem in the encampment was the peripatetic tendencies of his flock. They were constantly going off in the two directions which the narrow strip of land afforded, and they were particularly attracted to the area occupied by Tanni and his people. Knowing that Pike would be anything but enthusiastic about fraternization between the two groups, Albright did what he could to keep them apart. Dr. Case proved to be the most consistent offender, having found, as he described it, a soul mate in Terry Mack.

"We share a common lack of respect for authority,"

he explained after Albright had persuaded him back to his own area for the third time. "That little fellow is a jewel. When he discovered I was a doctor he laughed right in my face. He said to me, 'Well now, blimey, if you haven't got all the earmarks of a doctor. You got yourself a low tone of voice which is supposed to make sick people feel a little sicker than they are, which is your bread and butter. The voice says if you'll listen to me carefully for ten shillin's' worth you'll enjoy whatever is wrong with you much more because you done all you could by just callin' the doctor. The voice says take this pill or that pill and choke it down and the sound of my voice all soothin' and the like, you can either spend ten bob more and get sicker, or be satisfied with what you spent and get well.' "

The last time Albright retrieved Dr. Case he told him about Terry Mack's eye.

"I asked him if he had ever had any treatment for it," Case explained, "and I'm going to think about his answer for a long time. 'No, m'lad,' he said to me. 'Because I don't really miss it so much as you think. When I want to see something I turn my good eye at it and when I don't I turn my head just a little the other way. Convenient, huh? And there's a plenty of things I don't want to see, m'lad. This way I don't have to close both eyes to avoid such things like most people do when they are sad or in trouble. The main reason we got eyes, anyway, is to keep us from stumbling into things or falling down. The real things, the things that count, you see inside yourself and you don't need no eyes at all for it. The blindest man in the world can see something ugly, or if he's of a mind, he can see all kinds of beauty, too.' "

"Please," Albright said without having heard a word. "Please stay over here with us. That's all I ask, Doctor."

There was no marked change in the atmosphere of either encampment until the first droplets of rain fell. Then, as it grew darker and the people were drawn together, those of Pistol Two began to complain. The children cried more frequently and fought out their pettishness in small, unorganized wars which the mothers could not stop. The laborers, slept out, and almost as restless as the children, demanded to know what the hell this was all about. Were they going to spend the whole night in this lousy place which smelled of dead fish? And what about some chow? Why not just take the boats and go back to Pistol Two and gear up the mess hall and at least get something in their bellies before everybody got soaking wet?

Albright temporarily dissuaded them by pointing out the tarpaulins they had brought. If they would just rig those between the boats and perhaps fasten the ends as far up the beach as they could, then everyone would be more comfortable until word came to return.

By the time the portable generator putted to life and Carlos Raveza had managed to connect a line which carried two bare lamps, it was obvious that further amenities would be required to pacify Albright's charges. The rain was creating real anger, and several of the men were muttering that they didn't like the look of things one damned bit. So this was only supposed to be a drill? Well, the weather was sure co-operating. How come Nature knew about it? Pike's name was mentioned with increasing frequency, and since the references were far from complimentary Albright thought it just as well Sue-Anne had demanded transportation back to Pistol Two. The situation further deteriorated when the two pressure camp stoves refused to work in spite of the best efforts of Mrs. Riley, her husband, and various volunteer experts from all departments. They were obliged to imitate the natives, and after a great deal of milling about over the hummocks they found enough suitable wood to build a small fire. As many as could push through the crowd around it stood in angry silence, only forsaking their places when the pungent smoke became unbearable.

At last when the rain steadied to more than isolated showers, a delegation of six men led by Barney Dunbar approached Albright. He found it extremely difficult to maintain a casual air as they gathered before him, and his uneasiness compelled him to sway even more than was his habit.

Barney Dunbar cleared his throat ominously and, placing his gnarled hands on his hips, said, "Look here, Mr. Albright. We been talkin' this thing over and we don't like what we see. You told us this was a drill and, well, we could make it sort of a picnic if we want. . . . Well, we had enough drill and picnic, too. Our kids are hungry and they'll be up past their bedtime pretty soon. And our wives don't like this sittin' around on the wet sand and we don't care much for it neither. So our idea is to get out of here now and go back where we belong."

"I cannot authorize you to leave until I receive word from the Governor," Albright said, wishing that, for this occasion at least, he was not wearing shorts. Laboring people, those who worked with their hands, were necessary creatures, of course, but, after all, emancipation was for politicians. How could you understand what such people were thinking really, and mightn't they consider shorts as a possible object of ridicule? And wasn't ridicule of those in power an early warning of revolution? Hearing the faint rumble of tumbrels rolling in his direction, Albright added, "I'm dreadfully sorry, really, but we must remain here."

"We just ain't goin' to, Albright. We talked it all out and we're loadin' up our families and takin' the boats. In other words, we're goin' home and Pike can yell all he wants. He can't fire us all."

"I forbid you to go near those boats," Albright said with as much assurance as he could muster. "Really, gentlemen, I must ask you to co-operate."

"You ain't forbiddin' anything. Not that it would do any good, anyway. We got our rights and we're goin'. We done all the co-operatin' we're about to do for one day."

The original delegation had now been augmented by most of the male population of Pistol Two. They formed a gradually closing circle about Albright, and he searched frantically for at least a few sympathetic faces. At the edge of the crowd he saw two marines. Both were avoiding his eyes.

"I should be most reluctant to request aid from the marines," Albright said. "I hope you realize I can do it?"

"Them marines are nice boys and smart ones, too. They won't give us no trouble."

Oh dear God, Albright thought, where is Pike? I did not sign up for martyrdom. Pacifying peasants is not my forte.

"Well . . ." he said uncertainly. "I suppose . . ."

Whatever he had in mind to say Albright gratefully left unfinished. For all attention was suddenly diverted from him when two disheveled men stumbled out of the night and pushed their way through the crowd of people. Albright saw they were Sgt. Doolan and Adam Smith. Perhaps Doolan could do something with the rabble.

When they reached the center of the circle Adam hardly glanced at Albright before he turned to face the people. He held up his hands, and he was so tall that when he stepped quickly on top of a small sand hummock all could easily see him.

"Can I have your attention, please!" he began. "Please . . . Everybody . . . Listen to me! This is very important!"

As Adam waited in the dim light from the two small bulbs, he heard several uncomplimentary remarks about his appearance. His pants were nearly in shreds and there were several cuts on his face. And he seemed very near exhaustion. *"Listen to me, please!"* Adam begged, and such was the appeal in his eyes that their talking subsided momentarily until there was only the sputtering of the light plant to compete with his voice.

"You must believe what I am going to tell you, even though you have every reason to do some wondering . . . about . . . well, about what you've been asked to do. I'm not much at speech making as you can see . . . or hear, I mean. Now what I want you to believe is that your trip up here was not a drill. There was a mix-up which was my fault to begin with. . . ."

Knowing he was doing a very poor job expressing himself, Adam paused a moment to collect his thoughts. Now everyone in the encampment was coming toward him, even those who had held a favorable position beneath the tarpaulins. He was about to begin again when he saw Margaret Trumpey standing near the outer fringe of the crowd. She was looking up at him, and once more the sequence of what he wanted to say fled from his mind. He wiped the rain from his face while he sought words which would impress and yet not alarm the faces around him. He knew his silence was already overlong and was not doing his cause any good, and he was startled when he heard a man say, "What's this guy up to? Looks like he's off his rocker to me."

"No, it is definitely not a drill," Adam said desperately. "There is a real storm coming and it will hit Nikki very soon . . . maybe in a few hours. . . . I can't be sure about that part. But I am sure the winds will be very strong, probably of hurricane force . . . and so you've got to leave right now and go down to the south end of the island, where there is some high ground and you'll have better shelter. You've just got to believe me when I say this could be a matter of life and death for all of you!"

"Just a minute," Barney Dunbar called out. "What's going on around here? First they make us come up here to the north side, and now you're telling us to go down to the south side. I'll tell you right out I don't think much of takin' my family all around the lagoon after dark just to get wet."

"How did *you* get here?" another man demanded.

"I walked. And it wasn't because I enjoy hiking."

"How come you didn't ride up here in the boats with us? You're the weatherman, aren't you?"

"Yes, I am. And I know what I'm talking about. There's a very good chance the sea could cover this whole part of Nikki because the storm will approach from the northwest. On the south side you'll at least get some protection."

Adam turned to Albright and said, "Please. Can't you help me? They should start out in the boats right now."

Those who were within the inner ring of the crowd listened attentively to Albright's answer.

"Indeed I will not. I just finished telling them they must remain here. Those are Pike's orders."

"To hell with Pike! I know what I am talking about."

"Neither your manner nor your appearance would suggest that you do. Furthermore, I'm having quite enough trouble without your meddling. Sergeant Doolan! Will you please escort Mr. Smith to a less conspicuous place."

"I been escortin' him for the past two hours. I think he means what he says."

"That may very well be true, Sergeant. But Governor Pike is the authority here. Until he arrives we are his representatives. Furthermore, I can personally vouch for the fact that Mr. Smith is very likely to disagree with anything Governor Pike might say."

From the middle of the circle a woman's voice came through the rain. "He looks cuckoo to me. I'm not going to put my children through anything more. I want to go home."

A murmur of approval passed through the crowd. Then another woman yelled at Adam and there was a hint of hysteria in her voice. "If you're telling the truth why weren't we told about this here real storm? What do they mean by sending us up here?"

A man called out, "Where is Pike, anyways? How come he isn't here and hasn't been here? Somebody ought to be in real authority around here and I right now nominate Barney Dunbar."

"We got to have some kind of a leader!" another man said. "You can't do anything right unless somebody says so and so is so!"

Another man said, "Maybe we ought to elect some kind of a committee!"

"The hell with all that! Let's go home and get dried out!"

"I could use a drink!"

A woman's voice cut through the others. "Where's

Pike's wife, I'd like to know? I saw her leaving in one of the boats before it got dark. Are they hiding someplace?"

"I second the motion for Barney Dunbar!"

"It's gettin' so you can't trust nobody!"

Adam spread his long arms wide. "*Please! Everybody!* You haven't got time to debate this thing. You must leave right now and you can't go back to your homes. It may be just as bad there as it will be here."

A man said, "I can't figure out just what for, but you and Pike must be in cahoots about something. I still want to know why you had to hike it up here?"

"Yeah! And how come Doolan is with you? The only thing I believe that you've said is that there's been some kind of a mix-up. It looks like you're the one who's mixed up, mister!"

Now the noise from the crowd became more than a murmur. The sound multiplied upon itself until the puttering of the light plant dissolved within it. Adam searched the upturned faces anxiously. For the first time he could feel wind on his face. And though it was still feeble, its strength was increasing. The wind was coming, as he knew it must, from the north. Not too far away to the westward, then, swirled the center of Lazy Ethel.

Again he held up his hands and achieved a measure of attention.

"Maybe you'll believe me if I explain something more to you! It is not Pike's fault you're here, but mine. I deliberately gave him the wrong information . . . never mind why now. He thought he was doing the best thing for you. What I did is unforgivable, I know. I deserve whatever punishment you think up for me. The reason I had to hike here was because Pike not only fired me, but put me under arrest. I am still under arrest, which is why Sergeant Doolan is with me. He knows, too, there is a real storm coming. Ask him how he saw the barometer falling. And *believe* me . . . *please,* for your own sakes and the sake of your families, believe me and go down to the south side right now!"

A stunned silence fell upon the crowd. Again Adam searched their faces. Only one held his attention and it gave him even less comfort than the others. For it was Hanover, the press representative, and he was smiling as if this was exactly what he had been waiting for. Adam looked beyond him and found Margaret Trumpey again. The girl called Sunnie now stood beside her and they were both obviously puzzled. Margaret alone seemed half-convinced, and after a moment he thought he saw her smile.

Then a man called out from the side of the crowd and his voice was heavy with mistrust.

"Looks to me like we been lied to. If that's so, somebody ought to get hung for it!"

"Maybe we could begin with a little tar and featherin' party," another voice called out. "That is, when we get to where there's some tar and feathers."

"I've had enough of this! Let's dump him in the lagoon and hold his head down 'til he gives us the truth!" his companion yelled.

"Shut up!" Dr. Case challenged.

"Nobody's goin' to make me shut up if things are as bad as he says they are. All of us got a right to know what this is all about!"

Beyond the ring of light, somewhere under the tarpaulins, a child began to cry. As if the sound separately inspired each person, the crowd began pressing in more closely around Adam. He watched them hopelessly, appalled at his inability to make his words take effect. Knowing himself, he should have foreseen this. He should have taken time to prepare a speech that would convince, and not just rush blindly at them with a mixed-up relation of mix-ups. But I have never been a speech maker, he thought unhappily. I have never been able to say exactly what should be said, even standing alone with a girl on a wharf.

"*Please!* . . ." he began again, but Hanover's voice rode over his own with chilling assurance. Turning his back to Adam, Hanover faced the crowd and said, "You people have every right to question the behavior of this man. And Pike, too! Why they both deliberately chose to conceal the fact there is a storm coming, I don't know, but I guarantee you, both men have known about it since last night. They even knew its name . . . Lazy Ethel. I think we ought to go back to Pistol Two, find Pike, and make him tell us the best place to go. It looks to me like they outsmarted themselves and now they're trying to cover each other. As a result we're going to get it in the neck!"

"Stay away from those boats!" Albright called to three men who were moving out from the crowd. "You must have some organization or . . ."

A laborer pushed Albright aside before he could finish. The man was nearly as tall as Adam when he stood before him. He was at least fifty pounds heavier and for a moment he merely stood quietly, flexing his fingers into fists. Adam was very sure that in a moment the man was going to take a swing at him, and he saw approval in the faces of the crowd. They waited, glancing at each other and working their mouths in anticipation. Maybe if I just let him hit me and do nothing, they'll believe me, Adam thought. That is, if I can just stay on my feet.

The man stooped slightly and took another step up

the sand hummock. He looked back over his shoulder at the crowd as if seeking their support, and as he turned he was suddenly shoved aside. Adam saw that Margaret Trumpey had made her way around the back of the crowd and now stood where the man had been. A laugh of appreciation came from the faces as she usurped his place. She returned the man's glare with a smile and said, "You won't accomplish anything that way, big boy."

Then she spoke to the crowd and Adam marveled at the clarity and confidence in her voice. "I know a lot of you, but for those whom I haven't met, my name is Margaret Trumpey. I work in the radioteletype shack. That's why I feel I have a right to speak now. It is true there have been a series of communications about this storm. It is also true that some of them have been conflicting. But if a man comes to you as Adam Smith has done and openly confesses what perhaps might have been a serious mistake, then we should believe him. Surely you can all see that to come here under the circumstances, and fight to get here in the way he has done . . . then he must be perfectly sincere. Adam has the kind of courage I think we're going to need. I believe him. If he says we should go to the south side of Nikki, then I believe we should leave immediately. Think about it for just a moment, won't you? Think quietly and soundly. And don't be influenced by men who do not know what they are saying."

She glanced at Adam, then turned back to the crowd. "Take a good look at Adam Smith and you'll believe him . . . as I do. Take a good look at a man who was not afraid to come here and tell us he had made a mistake. Ask yourselves if you would have had the courage to do the same thing."

Now a confused babble spread over the dim mosaic of faces. The solidity of the ring was broken as they turned to each other and clustered in groups and argued among themselves. There were those who wanted to stay and those who wanted to return to Pistol Two, and Adam observed with new hope that many were agreeing to leave for the south side. He tried to ignore the few who were still obsessed with the idea of throwing him into the lagoon before anything else was attempted. To Margaret, who had moved nearer to him, he said, "Thanks for doing what I couldn't seem to do."

The rain had plastered her hair against her head; and as she stood watching the crowd Adam wanted to tell her that as far as he was concerned she was the most beautiful drowned rat he had ever seen, but he decided to keep his silence. Drowned rat, no matter how beautiful, didn't seem to be the best term to explain the way he felt about Margaret. He hoped he would have a chance later to think of something more complimentary.

There was still no indication that the crowd would reach any unanimous opinion when a rhythmic chanting came through the rain and darkness. The singing came from the vicinity of the native encampment, and even at a distance the voices were loud enough to be heard over the light plant. At first the chanting was ignored; then gradually the people in the crowd began to listen and their own conversation lost intensity. Finally their talking lapsed altogether and they listened in uneasy silence. When they were quiet a voice rang out across the lagoon. Both Albright and Dr. Case instantly recognized the derisive tones of Terry Mack.

"Cheerio, Yanks! Chief says to tell you we're leavin' whether ye likes it or no. This place ain't fit . . ."

The rest of what Terry Mack yelled was lost in a

burst of chanting. Those who turned and sought him in the darkness of the lagoon saw only the occasional glint of a wet paddle reflecting the light. In a moment even the reflections were gone and then the chanting diminished rapidly.

"Come back here! I insist you come back here!" Albright called desolately.

"That's enough for me!" a man in the crowd said firmly, and Adam saw that it was Pete Walsacki.

He took his wife's hand and they ushered their two children toward the black forms of the landing craft. Now only a few were still insisting that something should be done about Adam Smith. A splinter group moved back to huddle beneath the tarpaulins and debate the wisdom of complying with Albright's pleas. The majority began to drift like frightened sheep toward the boats.

With an angry glance at Margaret and Adam, Albright left the hummock and, running to the beach, tried to head off the people. Doolan stood solidly on the hummock ignoring his frustrated cries for assistance. "I got my money on you, Smith," he growled at Adam. "I hope you aren't as nuts as some people think."

Alone, Albright was soon overwhelmed by the sheer mass of people from Pistol Two. Finally, in defeat, he dropped his hands to his sides and let the crowd flow past his dejected figure.

The movement of the crowd was anything but an orderly procession. Herd instinct seemed to lead most of them toward one boat while the others were left nearly unoccupied. Finally a few of the landing-craft operators took their positions and started their engines. Many of the people, still apprehensive and undecided, lingered near the tarpaulins or merely stood along the beach in hopeless silence. Adam saw that, in spite of the Walsackis' example, these were mostly the people with families. Now it appeared certain that unless someone held the boat operators, who were gunning their engines anxiously, a good many people could be easily left behind. And the wind, Adam thought, the wind is no longer a breeze. Whatever influence Albright might have had upon the crowd was now obviously gone. Someone had to take command before it was too late.

It came as a shock to Adam when he suddenly realized that even as a Boy Scout he had always stood in the rear rank. In fact he had never in his life led others anywhere, and the vision of himself trying to order so many people about and see to their safety, was even more terrifying than his conception of what Lazy Ethel might do to Nikki. Why couldn't he be the hero and do something besides standing like a shivering dunce, a hapless mute, while the people waited . . . and Margaret waited? Yet he seemed as rooted to the hummock as if the sand reached to his waist. And he could only think that a coward survived in spite of himself.

He glanced miserably at Doolan, who appeared so completely in charge of himself, and he tried to smile at Margaret before he took his first hesitant step toward the beach. He would probably make a botch of it, but someone, even he, Adam Smith, the young man who vastly preferred to keep his peace, must co-ordinate this now hopeless exodus. Some of the people were already beginning to shove others around as they sought favorable positions in the boats. It was becoming all too obvious that real panic could be fired by a single thoughtless personality.

"I'm going to try and make them go about this sensibly," he said with all the determination he could drag from the depths of his being.

As he left the hummock a landing craft roared out of the darkness and hit the beach with a crunch. Adam saw Pike leap over the side and land ankle-deep in the water. And in spite of his experience with the man, Adam was vastly relieved. For the Pike he could see now was not the Pike he had known. Even at a distance the effect of his arrival was easily apparent. He began at once to move quickly and confidently among the people, directing and encouraging, smiling as Adam had never seen him smile before, and his solid orders rang out crisply across the beach. And best of all, he was explaining that they were bound for the south side of Nikki.

Doolan had gone to him at once and under Pike's commands was posting his four marines before each landing craft. In a few minutes they were counting off the people as they mounted the ramps, and they assisted the women and children as if it was a job they had done every day of their enlistment. While Adam watched, what had threatened to become a dangerous rout was transformed into an orderly retreat.

"I guess we might as well go, too," he said as Margaret came up beside him.

Walking slowly toward the boats, Adam felt the wind on the back of his neck, and he saw that the wavelets fringing the beach were now alive with energy and even beginning to hiss. It could well be too late, he thought, and the passage across the lagoon was certain to be an uncomfortable affair. Yet there was Pike. Pike the bigot, the hard-headed slave to red tape and official decree. There was Pike, the silly and dogmatic bully-boy with his infuriating manner, somehow as transformed as the scene around him. He seemed to know instinctively what was required to get these people on their way safely and speedily and he was getting what was needed. I could never have done so, Adam thought sadly. I am the little man, not Pike. I am a very little man who lost his head and twisted the tail of a tiger. Now it is Pike, of all people, who must slay him.

When Pike saw Adam, he shouted a final order at the operator of the first loaded boat and quickly marched up the beach. Adam instinctively squared his shoulders as he approached. "Here comes my appointment with the firing squad," he said to Margaret as casually as he could manage. "You'd better leave. It isn't always smart to be seen in unpopular company."

"I'm staying right here."

Pike halted before them and stood like a dripping pillar in the rain while he surveyed Adam. His shirt was soaked and the bristles of his gray hair lay flat and wet on his head. Water streamed from the end of his broad nose and dribbled down his hard-set jaw. His eyes, like the man, were new to Adam. Even in the dim light he could see they had lost their cold calculation and were now deeply troubled, which somehow had the effect of making them friendly and warm.

"Smith," he said slowly, "I owe you an apology. A message came through from Tuamani. Your Lazy Ethel is very much alive."

As Pike wiped his face, Adam said nothing for there was nothing to say. He could only guess how difficult it must have been for Pike to come to him, so he glanced up the beach at the tarpaulins, which were beginning to shake in the wind. He had to raise his voice slightly when he finally spoke. "Sir, I wish I'd never heard of Lazy Ethel."

"It would help if I knew how long it will last."

"I can't be sure of that, sir, with what little information I have. But I can make a good guess. The wind is just beginning to come from the north. It will continue to increase until the eye of the storm passes. If we are directly in line with the eye, then it will be calm for a while . . . possibly as much as several hours. Then it will come on again from the south and blow until it's all over. We'll know when that will be without any question . . . that is, if we're still around."

"We will be," Pike said firmly. "When we get down to the south side will you explain that to our people? I think it will be better coming from you."

"Yessir. I will."

"If the wind is eventually going to come from the south, aren't we taking a risk going to the south side?"

"Yes. But I don't see how it can be helped. Our chances of the eye passing directly over Nikki are pretty slim if the storm is not too big in area. The wind itself can't hurt us too much if we stay away from Pistol Two. It's sea water over the whole atoll that we need to worry about most, and the only high ground is to the south. I'm very glad we're leaving."

"And I'm very glad you came to Nikki," Pike said, turning back to the beach.

Striding toward the boats he passed Carlos Raveza, who was ambling through the sand as if he was employed in a leisurely exploration for sea shells.

"I thought I told you to cut off the main power," Pike said so mildly that Carlos turned to him and smiled trustingly.

"It is true. You did."

"I suppose you have some explanation?"

"That I have . . . if you will trouble to listen."

"I'm listening to a lot of things."

"Very good. I did not turn off the power because I like to eat. My belly is always of importance to me. To turn off the power completely was not an order I think you fully think out."

"Why?"

"There are many tons of fresh meat in the freezers. If I turn off the power the meat will spoil, which would be a sin. I was not even a little certain you think of such a thing."

"Thanks. I did not."

"Details," Carlos said, spreading his fat hands to catch the rain. "Leave the details to others and you will sleep as I do."

Sixty-odd miles to the northwest of Nikki, the eye of Lazy Ethel swirled clockwise about itself and moved ponderously through the Pacific night. The air mass which embraced the eye was also circular in form and thus extended in all directions. Near the eye the winds were the most powerful, diminishing gradually toward the outer circumference until the very edge of the mass was merely a full gale. No living thing could see this cyclopean giant, for the albatross and the frigate birds had long ago fled to regions where the membranes in their skin told them it was safe to rest. Even the fishes— the ono, the dolphin, the shark, and the bonito—had left the surface of the sea and dived to colder layers of water which provided almost nothing in the way of food, but offered a less troubled world. The mammals, whales and porpoises, imitated their descent, sounding deeply and remaining below for such periods as their lungs would permit. Even the invertebrates of the sea, the plankton, the tiny purple and silver marine organisms, and the jelly blobs of sub-life descended, driven downward by the fresh-water pollution of their element. For such was the volume and solidity of the rain, the sky seemed to become one with the sea.

Thus over two hundred square miles of the Pacific Ocean was left to the mercies of Lazy Ethel. The surface was a strident pandemonium of sound and furious movement. Even the subterranean depths lost peace. All of this cataclysm moved slowly upon Nikki atoll and sent emissaries forward to warn of its power.

As the landing craft rolled across the black lagoon, the warnings became evident to every person who had lived on Pistol Two. They no longer argued or displayed any resentment against a second crossing of the lagoon. They huddled quietly together in the bottoms of their craft, and the children, sensing the growing fear in their parents, were so afraid only small mewing sounds escaped them.

In a very little time, before the landing craft had wallowed halfway across the lagoon, the wind created formidable waves which frequently threatened to capsize the ungainly vessels. The rain spewed diagonally out of the cloud base, rattling against the metal skin of the landing craft and stinging the faces of those who were foolish enough to turn toward it. The wind swallowed the sound of the engines.

The landing craft moved together in loose formation, and even their bright running lights became frequently invisible. In the lead boat, Sue-Anne shared half of her raincoat with Dr. Case. They had both given up trying to light a cigarette and were looking aft where Pike stood exposed to the full fury of the wind and the rain. He had planted himself on the engine hatch and, peering ahead, gave occasional sharp orders to the helmsman. Somehow he managed to remove all anxiety from his voice and appeared entirely at ease and confident. Dr. Case said, "That's quite a man you have there. I'm beginning to think I've misjudged him."

Sue-Anne shifted her position slightly and pulled her wet skirt down over her knees. Then after a moment she said, "No, you haven't, Doctor. I don't know who that man is, but it isn't my husband."

"He's certainly making the best of what looks to me like a sticky situation."

"You wait. He'll pull a boo-boo yet."

"Mrs. Pike. Because I have a rather nasty disposition myself, I can't help but admire the way you refuse to be convinced."

"Twenty-seven years of experience. You don't change all that in a few hours."

"Is it possible that he's never had a chance to show himself before?"

"Yes . . . I suppose it's possible. But don't be surprised if sooner or later we all don't have to swim for our lives. Say, how badly do I have to be injured before I can apply for some of your medicinal whisky?"

"In your case . . . upon the point of death."

"I like you, Doctor," she said very simply. Then huddling against him she stared thoughtfully at her husband for a long time.

Crossing the lagoon took over an hour, and as the last landing craft reached the south shore the native canoes appeared one by one from the night. They were abandoned immediately, and the paddlers herded their families to the place where Pike stood beckoning with his flashlight. His voice rang out so strongly most of the three-hundred-odd people who now surrounded him could distinctly hear his words in spite of the wind and rain.

"Attention, please! All of you! We should be relatively safe here even if a trifle uncomfortable. Listen to me carefully and for your own sakes do exactly as I say! Is that interpreter here? If so, sing out, please!"

"Right, Guv'nor!" Terry Mack called, and there was a new respect in his voice.

"Are all your canoes here?"

"Right, sir!"

"Good. Advise your chief to have all his people stay closely with us. We will feed and take care of them. Now all of you, that's everybody . . . will follow me around to the south side of this hill. It is of the utmost importance we all stay together. Anyone who wanders off is asking for trouble. We will remain on the south side until the wind shifts. That may be several hours from now. When I give the order we will move around to the north side and remain there until this storm has definitely passed. For your encouragement, assistance is already en route from Tuamani. So we have nothing to be afraid of as long as we keep our heads. Right now, all of you men go back to the boats and pick up everything you can carry—especially boxes of provisions. When we are settled down on the south side of the hill, feel free to come to me with any suggestions, or if you need further help. The main thing is to keep calm, dig a little foxhole for yourselves in the sand if you want when the real wind comes, and remember it won't last forever. Now keep your children close to you and follow me!"

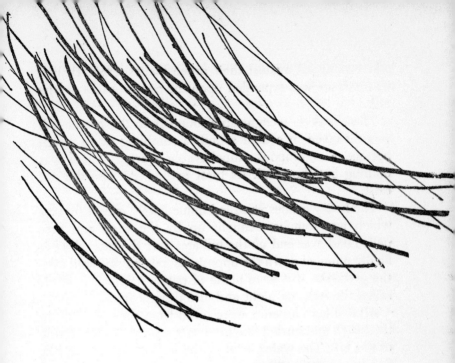

14

According to Adam's watch Lazy Ethel did not seize Nikki fully within its grasp until nearly midnight. It was the last chance he had to look at his watch, for the true wind did not increase gradually as he had supposed, but seemed to explode and reach its maximum within a very few minutes. It was as if something in the void beyond the lagoon had raised a vast curtain and a penetrating cold was released. Adam was certain the temperature dropped fifteen degrees in as many minutes. Yet to the others, clutching like terrified insects at the safety of their earth, the change in temperature went unnoticed. For even their imagination could not conceive of the wind which pounded against their prone bodies, even though its full force was expended upon the opposite side of the hill.

There was no recognizable sound from the people. All was dissolved in a dual sound; a rumbling moan which became a continuous, unbelievable roaring. There was nothing but the wind. Its blast existed. All else did not exist.

The heavy canoes vanished immediately except for one which was somehow caught up by the wind and propelled end over end up the hill and over the top, where it finally plunged down the opposite slope and skittered over the people as if it were made of papier-mâché. Finally it sailed through the night and also disappeared.

All five landing craft were lifted from their perches on the beach and hurled like toy boats against the north side of the hill. The water level in the lagoon rose more than five feet. Yet to Sue-Anne and Pike and Tanni and Carlos Raveza, and Peter Hildebrandt and Terry Mack and Sgt. Doolan, and Sunnie Mandel and Albright, all of this was invisible. Like all the others of Pistol Two and the natives of Nikki, they lay face down in the sand, squirming against it as they sought even more protection, and trying desperately to breathe. There was only the wind, all pervading, stunning every sensibility except the primary urge for survival.

Adam lay in a common pit beside Margaret Trumpey. Their heads were buried in their arms to form a barrier against the stinging wet sand. They breathed in quick gasps, half through their nostrils and half through their mouths. They could not open their eyes nor could they even attempt to speak. Only the occasional movement of their bodies assured the presence of the other. They lay shivering in this position until three-thirty in the morning, when the wind eased. Then Adam turned his head, covered his nose with his cupped hand so he could still breathe, and spoke to Margaret.

"Are you all right?"

"Yes."

"I've been doing a lot of thinking."

"So have I. Some praying, too. When I wasn't doing either one, a tune kept going through my head. Do you know *The Sorcerer's Apprentice?*"

"I think I heard it when I was a kid."

"It reminded me of you and Lazy Ethel."

"Yeah. . . ."

He listened to the wind for a moment, assuring himself that it was actually subsiding. He wiggled as close to Margaret as he could, until their heads were almost together.

"Margaret?"

"Yes?"

"Maybe this isn't the best time to tell you, but I'd never get up the nerve anywhere else. . . . I was thinking it would be a lot easier if you didn't have to write to me."

"Is there any chance Pike will let you keep your job?"

"It isn't that . . . and it doesn't really matter. If I do go home though, I was sort of . . . well, maybe you would consider going with me."

"Is that a firm invitation?"

"Yes. It is."

"You have more nerve than you think. You don't know much about me."

"I know enough."

"I can't cook."

"Learn."

"I'm nearly thirty and . . . well, I don't know anything about making love either."

"Learn."

"You'd be getting what lots of men didn't seem to want. I'm almost a fully qualified reject."

"Will you?"

She was silent for a moment; then she said okay very softly.

Adam was trying to wipe the sand from his lips so he could bend across the pit and kiss her when he heard Pike calling. He looked up and saw him a yard away, crouched in the sand.

"The wind is dropping, Smith! Do you think it's time we moved around to the other side of the hill?"

"Yes, sir. I do."

Pike rose stiffly, keeping his back to the wind. He switched on his flashlight and Adam saw that he was smiling. "You'll have to admit," he said, "my neuritis is pretty accurate."

"I'd like to hook it up to an instrument," Adam answered.

As the wind moderated rapidly, Pike moved among his people like a solicitous shepherd. When he had gathered them all together he asked Adam to explain about the eye of the storm, and how the wind might soon return from the opposite direction. Then he led his people around to the lagoon side of the hill, where he ordered the ration boxes opened.

They ate in relative peace. Now the rain had ceased, and for some five minutes a hole appeared in the overcast through which the stars were visible. The phenomenon inspired Chief Tanni's Mormon elders so that they called upon Huahenga to lead a song of gratitude. As her great voice rose from the sand, all of the people joined with her, though those from Pistol Two did not have the faintest idea as to the exact meaning of her words. It made little difference. The two groups were now hopelessly inter-mixed, and the wife of Barney Dunbar was astonished to find herself happily clutching the wet hand of Apakura.

It was just after the singing when the stars again disappeared and Sue-Anne came to Pike. He was standing a little apart from the others and she said, "Zebulon, I want to have a word with you."

He was staring at the blackness of the lagoon and frequently rubbed at his tired eyes. For the first time in twenty-seven years Sue-Anne saw that his shoulders were slumped.

"Yes, Precious?" he said absently.

She was silent for a moment while she thought about the exhaustion in his voice. "I want to tell you something before the wind comes again."

"Maybe it won't."

"I want you to know I think you've done a damn good job."

"I'm afraid that isn't so. We're just lucky no one has been hurt . . . so far."

"I haven't been a very good soldier, Zeb. I've been the fathead. Given the breaks, I think you could be a general in anybody's army. I won't promise anything because I'm a lot weaker than you are . . . but I'm going to try very hard never to get drunk on you again."

Even as he reached for her hand Pike knew that his respite was ended. For the wind swirled around the hill and came upon the back of his neck and it was already picking up sand.

"All right, everybody!" Pike called. "Let's start digging in again!"

He squeezed Sue-Anne's wrist so hard the charm bracelets left small indentations in her skin. He said, "Thanks." Then he walked quickly toward the people and ordered the heavy ration boxes to be buried as quickly as possible.

There was very little rain with the second wind and it was somewhat warmer. Yet, if anything, its strength seemed greater. Here, on the lagoon side, the hill sloped more gradually, which allowed freedom to the wind and so may have accounted for its seeming increase in fury. And the people, both those of Nikki and Pistol Two, were nearly exhausted from the drubbing upon the exposed parts of their bodies by the wind. And while they had survived the original blasting without any obvious dangers, now a new peril terrified those who opened their eyes long enough to observe it.

Each of the landing craft had carried a full fifty-gallon drum of diesel oil. The new wind snatched these from the overturned craft, hurling them up and along the hill, dropping them and picking them up again as if they were small tin cans. One landed on Hanover's leg and broke it below the knee. His screams for immediate attention were lost in the wind. Another rolled over the entire Walsacki family, who were huddled in a common pit. Miraculously, they suffered only bruises. The same drum finally came to rest against Huahenga's protruding rump, and later it took three men to extricate her from beneath it. Another drum, tumbling end over end, barely touching its edges as it leaped through the people, cut a deep gash in the back of Albright's head and he was unconscious for several minutes. Yip Kee, the Chinese merchant, had failed to dig far enough into the sand. The wind plucked him upward and carried him straight across the slope of the hill until it plastered him helplessly against a scrub bush. His entire body was covered with bruises and cuts, and he was both blind and speechless until long after dawn.

Only then did the wind subside, very slowly, as if reluctant to abandon its playthings. And in the dawn, which arrived without the encouragement of normal light, the people on the hill picked themselves up from their ordeal singly, and in groups of two or three.

As their enterprise returned, they looked down upon the lagoon which they had known as a blue and delightfully clear body of water. Now it was the color of chocolate and littered with debris. What remained of the wind lashed the surface into foaming whitecaps which pounded voraciously on what was left of the beach.

In many places the beach was gone. From their elevation the people could see where the ocean completely covered the flatter portions of the atoll, making the ring of Nikki a series of islets.

As the pale light grew stronger they saw where the two settlements had been. The area was nearly unrecognizable. The channel could still be identified although it appeared much wider. The wharf was gone and so was the warehouse which had stood upon it. All of the coconut palms which had shaded the native village lay flat, like matches spilled from a box. Only the walls of the Catholic and Mormon churches stood out. There were no dwellings of any kind to be seen, and it took Pike some time to explain through Terry Mack that somehow he would arrange for their replacement. "If it's the last thing I ever do!" he added vehemently. "My government is spending millions to blow up another atoll. They're going to spend a few thousand and put yours back in shape!"

There was even less evidence that Pistol Two had ever existed.

"What the Atlas Construction Company created in seven days," Dr. Case said as he worked in the sand pit which served as an improvised aid station, "God must have had a lot of fun obliterating in maybe seven minutes."

The outlines of the airstrip were still apparent although the whole design shimmered with water. The crisscross of the streets was also distinguishable even though the pattern was frequently interrupted by lakes. There were dun-colored square patches where the buildings had stood, but nothing remained of the structures except scattered heaps of broken lumber.

"We think we have something in Zeus," Dr. Keim said, pulling on his nose, which was very sore and red from contact with the sand. He stared moodily at the devastation and said, "I feel sick . . . and puny."

Shortly after sunrise an airplane appeared. Skimming low over the still-turbulent ocean it circled Pistol Two first and then turned toward the hill. It banked once around the hill, then descended to fly past the happily waving people. They could clearly see the U.S. Navy markings along the fuselage. On the second pass along the hillside a series of parachutes vomited from the plane's door. The people ran toward them and the plane continued on its course. Before the chutes collapsed on the sand it was already a faintly humming insect against the gray northern sky.

Attached to the parachutes were more rations than had ever been contained in the combined stores of Yip Kee and Fat Sue. While the people of Pistol Two engaged themselves in opening the crates and passing out cigarettes and chocolate bars, which met with the most demand, the natives lost all restraint as they fingered the nylon chutes. Led by Huahenga, the ladies of Nikki ignored the stores and were soon parading before each other in hastily fashioned gowns of yellow and white.

They screamed with delight at its marvelous texture.

Sgt. Doolan brought Pike a letter which had been attached to one of the packages. Pike sat down in the sand and rubbed the stubble of his beard for several moments before he opened the envelope, though his name was prominently lettered across its face. He was looking at the gun hanging from Doolan's belt as he walked away, and he wondered if Doolan would suspect anything if he asked to borrow it for a little while. Now in the gray morning the promises which he had made to the natives seemed hollow and the leadership which he had tried to display appeared, on looking back, to be the vain strutting and hollering of a petty tyrant lost in his own catastrophe. That it had not been a disaster, he thought, looking across the lagoon at the north side of Nikki, where only a few specks of solid matter protruded above the water, was very little less than a miracle. He, General Zebulon Pike, U.S.A.-Ret. in accordance with the inscription on the envelope, had been, as that fellow Smith predicted, very nearly a murderer; and a mass murderer at that. "Thank God," he murmured as he slowly opened the envelope.

His eyes were almost too tired to read the letter and his brain took some time to absorb its numbered paragraphs and stilted phrasing. It began with a single word: Congratulations! Then it assumed a more normal tone.

1. You and your entire staff are commended for your foresight re the discovery and preparation for tropical Hurricane Lazy Ethel.

2. Upon the arrival rescue fleet you will report at your earliest convenience Tuamani to accept our personal congratulations and discuss immediate rehabilitation

station Pistol Two plus such other recommendations as you may have.

3. You will advise all personnel that Project Zeus will proceed on schedule. Any injured will receive appropriate disability compensation.

4. All personal effects lost or destroyed will be replaced at government expense.

5. Rescue fleet will arrive your station approximately 0900. They will anchor off present sight of Pistol Two and remain on station until reconstruction is completed. There are ample living accommodations for all personnel.

6. Atlas Construction Co. is providing crews and material for immediate rebuilding. Estimate seven days restoration of complete facilities.

For the Commission,
W. A. Keating

Pike refolded the letter and placed it in the envelope, trying not to soil it with his dirty fingers. He sighed and rubbed his eyes again. It was the first letter he had received in his entire career which began with a commendation.

He looked down the slope of the hill to where Doolan was standing near the parachutes, and he thought about his gun. That was one way and he was certain he was not afraid of it. In fact he could not remember ever having been much afraid of anything as long as the danger was physical. It was paper which terrorized him and always had; mountains of paper and the millions of words upon it had stifled his whole career.

There was a harder way than Doolan's gun, he thought, pressing the envelope into his shirt pocket. He would take this paper and read the first part of it to Sue-Anne. Because it was true that drunk or sober, he loved Sue-Anne. And then he would tell her the truth. Eventually he would take the paper to Tuamani and read the first part again. Aloud. And tell them the truth. Then he would see. . . .

By night most of the ocean had receded from Nikki atoll.

On the next day two freighters anchored just outside the narrow channel which led into the lagoon. In the morning the Atlas Construction people unloaded enough equipment so that the work could proceed. A new wharf was completed before darkness, and moving cautiously, the freighter became a temporary part of the land. Then again there was night.

On the second day the cargo booms worked with monotonous regularity, depositing all manner of gear upon the new wharf. Yet to all of this the natives of Nikki paid little attention. For they were chiefly concerned with the construction of a bridge which, before night had returned again, completely spanned the channel. They crossed the bridge freely and brought to their village such materials for building as they had never seen before.

On the third day the heavy earth-moving equipment roared and snorted and screeched in the hot sun. Guiding the equipment, the men from the freighter sweated and swore and tore and shoved at the confusion of coconut palms and debris. Among other things they caught up a pair of patent-leather pumps.

On the fourth day the airstrip was made serviceable

and the first airplane arrived. Those who unloaded it were amazed to find that a large portion of its cargo consisted of flashlight batteries. There were also a number of metal filing cases. And a flute.

On the fifth day . . .